Alisa Kwitney

Also by
Alisa Kwitney

THE DOMINANT BLONDE

Does She or Doesn't She?

Alisa Kwitney

AVON BOOKS

An Imprint of HarperCollins*Publishers*

HarperCollins books may be purchased for education, business, or sales promotional use. For information please write: Special Markets Department, HarperCollins Publishers Inc., 10 East 53rd Street, New York, NY 10022.

FIRST EDITION

Designed by Elizabeth M. Glover

Library of Congress Cataloging-in-Publication Data

Kwitney, Alisa, 1964–
    Does she or doesn't she? / by Alisa Kwitney.
      p. cm.
    ISBN 0-06-051237-7
    I. Title.

PS3611.W58 D64 2003
813'.54—dc21   2002034548

03 04 05 06 07 JT/RRD 10 9 8 7 6 5 4

*This book is for Ziva,
my mother and muse.*

Acknowledgments

I would like to thank my husband, Mark, for unflagging support and enthusiasm and the odd bit of sterling advice; Stephanie Braxton, for taking me under her wing, teaching me all about soap operas and helping me get Delilah into the right kind of trouble; Lucia Macro, my editor, for exuberant listening and gentle guidance; Jane Chelius, my agent, for being Melanie when I go all Scarlett; Neil Gaiman, for oracular plot utterances just when I need them; and Matthew and Elinor, for being the best under-age publicity team a mother ever had.

Friday, November 30
8:30 A.M.

"I'm going to take my hand off your mouth if you promise not to scream. Do you understand?"

I nod my head, which bangs into the man's chin. He grunts in a low and manly fashion. I can't see him clearly, because we are both lying on the floor of my closet. Well, I am lying on the floor. He is lying on top of me, his hand braced to keep some of his weight off my chest, but there is nothing he can do about our lower halves, which are sandwiched together like peanut butter and jelly.

Something is digging into my thigh, but I can't tell if it's animal, vegetable or mineral.

"Excuse me, but I think your wrench is . . ."

"Shh." The man puts his hand back over my mouth, a callused hand, I note, though whether from building birdcages or burying dead bodies I can only guess. Then I hear it, too. A kind of shuffle-thump, shuffle-thump. Somebody is dragging something just outside this closet. My heart kicks into a faster rhythm. I feel the tension of the man's long muscles all along my lower body. He has a quality of trained alertness, of coiled energy held in check. Like a Labrador about to seize a bird, I think, and suddenly realize that *this thought holds insight as to the identity of the man with his hand on my mouth.*

Labrador, retrieving, *the ability to hold something large in your teeth without biting down . . . Something wet drips onto my hand and at first I think it is water from the broken pipe, but then I see that the liquid is dark, and draining from the man's shoulder.*

"You're bleeding."

"And you're talking." His voice is low and rough and suggests all manner of pleasurable punishments.

"Ford? Is that you?" I see his eyes glint with something—exasperation? Affection? And then his mouth comes down to cover mine and my mind goes blank. . . .

"Mommy. Mommmy. Mom!"

Hold that last thought. "What is it, Sadie?"

"You're making me peanut butter and jelly and I had that yesterday!"

I'll admit that school lunches are the sort of thing I prepare on automatic pilot, thereby freeing the rest of my mental faculties to wander where they will. Still, I thought I'd given her cheese. "I thought I gave you cheese."

Behind my daughter's purple spectacles, I see her eyes glint with something—exasperation? Amusement? Then she folds her arms together. "No, I asked you for cheese. You gave me peanut butter and jelly."

I look at the time. Eight forty. "Sorry, sweetheart. It's so late already, do you think you could just . . ."

My husband wanders into the kitchen, tying his long hair back in a ponytail. That and the tiny gold hoop in his left ear are all that remain of a long-ago rebellious bohemian phase. Well, the ponytail, the earring, and me. "She's going to be late again," he comments, then wanders out with his habitual air of dissatisfaction.

I think of Turgenev's reference to middle age as that "vague, crepuscular time, the time of regrets that resemble hopes, of hopes that resemble regrets." I know better than to quote old Russian writers out loud, however. What is charming in a twenty-three-year-old who doesn't wear underwear and keeps vodka in her East Village fridge is less so in a thirty-five-year-old who keeps forgetting to buy the right brand of oat bran.

I go into the bedroom to get dressed and find my husband trying on a black cowboy hat. It conceals his receding hairline in a manner both attractive and sinister.

"What do you think?"

"Both attractive and sinister." I rummage in the laundry basket, which is filled with clean clothing I have not put away yet. At least I think it's clean.

"If you'd fold the clothes right away, it wouldn't take you half an hour to find a pair of underwear, and Sadie wouldn't get a stomachache because she needs another late pass."

I stop rummaging. "I'm taking Sadie today? I thought you said you were taking her."

My husband removes his hat and narrows his eyes. "I said I *couldn't* take her, Del. I have a big meeting today."

"Okay, no problem, I'll just throw on a long coat over my pj's." But my long coat, as it turns out, is at the dry cleaners. Dressed in a pea coat that only covers me down to my pajama-clad knees, I head for the door. "Sadie, we're ready now."

"Mom, did you put my lunch in my backpack?"

"Of course I did." Not. I slip it in while she's not looking. We find Jason holding the elevator for us.

"Hurry up," he says.

I touch Jason's shoulder. "It'll be better when Hilda gets back from vacation."

"You don't need a housekeeper. You need a schedule."

"Jason, there's no way I can keep house, volunteer at Sadie's school and work freelance without some outside help."

"Sure you can. You just need to plan ahead. Sadie's too old for a nanny, anyway, aren't you, punkin?" He ruffles Sadie's hair, which she detests.

"I like Hilda."

"Well, we can talk about this later."

We stand together silently, as the ancient elevator door shudders to a close. I imagine this as a scene from a movie: Probably something Swedish or German, black-and-white, the kind of film where the child begins to imagine a huge, invisible dragon of parental tension blowing brimstone. Atonal piano chords on the soundtrack.

I clear my throat. "So what are you doing today, Jason?"

"Big meeting today with this cowboy-hat company. They're looking to do a line of feminine hygiene products."

Sadly enough, even though I know Jason and his crew are manipulating me mercilessly, I can imagine myself buying something like that. Sanitary pads scented like sage and heather, new mountain-range tampons, designed for those long trips away from home.

Before Jason can say anything else about his new client, the slowest elevator in Manhattan stops and someone else gets on. It's Mrs. Kornislav, our new downstairs neighbor.

"Good morning, Mrs. Kornislav."

"Good morning. I have a leak. In my bedroom." For a woman who only moved into the building three weeks ago, she sure complains like a veteran.

"Really?" I try not to look at Mrs. Kornislav's wig too closely. Like many observant Jewish women, Mrs. Kornislav covers her natural hair with a wig. But Mrs. Kornislav's wig resembles a Dolly Parton extravaganza, which is not so common. Especially among septuagenarians.

"My ceiling is getting ruined. Are you letting your bathtubs overflow? Tell the child she must not splash in the bath. Young lady! You must not splash in the bath! My ceiling has a leak."

Sadie tries to disappear behind me.

"There's a leak in the pipes in our closet. We have the new handyman dealing with it." I say this with perfect matter-of-factness, as if speaking of some faceless stranger with dirt-encrusted fingernails and protuberant buttocks.

Mrs. Kornislav grunts at me. "You mean that short, fat guy with the moustache? He doesn't know how to handle a real plumbing problem!"

"Not Enrique. This guy's not a member of the regular building staff. He's someone new the managing agent hired to deal with bigger problems." The agent, a man with a cheery Irish face and a rumpled brown suit, had explained that out of all the apartments above, below and to either side of us, our walls held the secret nexus of faulty valves and rusting pipes, the tangled heart of the building's water supply. The agent couldn't explain exactly why apartment 7C should be our building's own plumbing Bermuda Triangle; he implied that the reasons were buried along with some long-dead engineer who designed the system back when it was the height of modern sanitarian fashion to put white tile in your bathroom and have a tub with feet.

There is a pause as Mrs. Kornislav adjusts her expression from affronted to suspicious. "So this isn't just some idiot who's going to rupture the wrong pipe and leak toxic fumes into my apartment?"

"We feel pretty sure he won't."

"And how long did you say this plumber's been working?"
"Since Monday."

He arrived the day after the long Thanksgiving weekend, when I was still bilious from the traditional surfeit of turkey and family tensions.

Expecting a squat, hirsute sort, I'd answered the door wearing my wet hair in a towel turban and the fluffy pink terrycloth bathrobe I'd originally bought for my mother.

I was confronted by a lean, muscular man resting one hand on my doorframe as if he owned it. I suddenly found I had far too much saliva in my mouth. "Ms. Levine? I'm here to fix the leak in your bedroom closet."

He said "fix the leak" as if it were a private joke between the two of us, with a sardonic lift of his slanted eyebrows. He smiled as if he knew every dirty thought I'd ever had. And he had hair and eyes as dark as the inside of a kiss.

"Excuse me?" I was holding my bathrobe closed at the neck as if it might fly apart of its own accord.

"I'm Ford, the new plumber."

"Oh. Oh! Why don't you come in?" I was still trying to figure out why he was the first man to make it past the double barricades of wifely indifference and maternal distraction and zap me in the ovaries with unsubstantiated desire. How to handle this? I tried to look a little less stupefied. He shifted his weight, hitching up his tool belt as if he were a gunslinger.

"You scared of dogs?" Fixated as I was on the man, it took me a moment to realize that he was referring to the black Labrador slouched against his calf.

"Only the ones bred to bite down really hard on your arm."

"I had to bring Fardles. He doesn't break the skin, but he likes to chew on your fingers." The dog thumped its tail at me and whined ingratiatingly.

"Fardles as in 'Who would fardles bear?' You must be a big *Hamlet* fan."

"Actually, he was already called that when I got him from the pound."

The dog, really an adolescent puppy, had that deceptively lazy Labrador look. I kneeled down to pet him, not thinking about the fact that I wasn't wearing any underwear till Fardles reminded me by sticking his nose between my thighs. I stood up so quickly that I nearly lost my balance. I didn't think I'd actually flashed anything, but then I'm the only person in the Western world too slow to catch the telling detail of Sharon Stone's famous leg crossing scene.

"So," I said, trying for a nonchalant, your-dog-is-not-a-giant-phallic-metaphor tone, "why did you say you had to bring him today?"

"He ate a poinsettia plant. I have to watch to make sure he doesn't go into convulsions."

"Oh, that's terrible."

"He's always sticking his nose where it doesn't belong."

For a moment, we just stared at each other, me blushing so hard I thought I might burst a blood vessel.

"Well," I said, "guess I better show you that leak."

Ford gave me a Cary Grant kind of expression—poker face from the cheekbones down, richly bemused from the eyebrows up. "Guess you'd better."

The things we didn't say to each other have occupied most of my waking moments since. And a few of my unconscious ones, as well.

*   *   *

Back in the elevator, I seem to have missed a few beats of conversation. Mrs. Kornislav is interrogating Jason about something to do with decorative moulding. "And this plumber—he has approval from the coop board?"

"They're the ones who hired him." Jason turns back to me. "By the way, Del, remind him about replastering the peeling section of wall after he's done. And tell him he's not bringing that dog of his again, is he? Because I don't want it in the apartment."

"It was just that one time, Jason, because Fardles had eaten a poisonous houseplant."

"Well, I don't want it dying in *my* house."

I remove myself from the conversation by kneeling down to check that Sadie's fake dalmation fur coat is zippered. Last week she had followed the gangling black puppy everywhere to make sure he didn't go into convulsions. It was the first time she hadn't been frightened of such a large animal.

We all get out at the lobby. Jason kisses Sadie and then strides off into the cold, pale November day, trench coat flapping. I get Jason's kisses secondhand from Sadie these days, or not at all.

I return to an empty apartment and a strong smell of sour fish. Fifteen minutes of futile investigation later, I give up searching for the source of the odor and sit down at my computer.

I am so behind deadline for my *Secrets* script that I find it almost impossible to begin. I glance down at the outline: Blackjack tells Ruby that he knows she stole the incriminating videotape, setting the stage for Ruby's big showdown with Skylar. How to fill five pages with this?

BLACKJACK: I think you know why I asked you to
    meet me here, Ruby.
RUBY: (Changing the mood) I don't even think *you*
    know why you really asked me here.

I would be more motivated to write if I knew that they
were really going to use my dialogue. The problem with
being on a trial contract is, I never know when they're going
to hand me an assignment and I never know if they have
someone else working on the same script. It's a little like
being in the National Guard: You must always be ready to
drop everything and assume active duty. Which means you
have to watch the show every day and read all the current
scripts, to be prepared for serendipity to strike. If it strikes
hard enough, you can achieve vaunted head-writer status,
make a bundle, and work steadily until your teeth fall out.

What did you do all day, honey? Watched soap operas.
And are you being paid for this, sweetheart? Well, not yet,
but soon, and possibly for the rest of my life. Suffice it to say
that Jason wants me to go back to my previous gig, proof-
reading.

BLACKJACK: Ruby, the only reason I'm here is to
    make sure Skylar doesn't get hurt. And make no
    mistake—I will do everything within my power to
    protect her.
RUBY: And that's really why you wanted to meet me
    here at the club, alone, after hours? Come on, Black-
    jack. Why not be honest—with yourself, if not with
    me.

Five more months of this and then I get to find out
whether or not they put me on a real contract or drop me.

*   *   *

After two hours of trading innuendo-laden ripostes with
myself, I take a break and discover that there is a moldy
tuna-fish sandwich in the breadbox. Mystery solved.

I have just finished throwing out the garbage when I
glance at the clock: Shit, shit, shit, two minutes to three and
I haven't shopped for dinner, or even gotten dressed. This is
bad. Dropping off your child in pajamas is not unheard of at
P.S. 98. But picking her up in them is something else entirely.

Despite my prayer for a speedy descent, the elevator
stops on the fifth floor and Caroline Moore gets on. Caroline is petite and fine-boned and was born with perfect skin
of the shade I have long tried to achieve for myself, first by
tanning myself leathery, then by streaking myself orange
with instant bronzers. Although she looks like a soap-opera
actress, Caroline is actually a practicing psychotherapist.

"Late start today, Del?" She is wearing her hair in a new,
elegant short style that showcases the swanlike quality of
her neck. Her coat looks like a gift from a tsar.

"It's my third late start, actually." I find myself hunching
like a gangly teenager in her presence.

Caroline makes a sympathetic noise.

"It's so hard to keep track of the time when you're working at home. My husband doesn't believe I'm even working, because to his mind, work is something which takes
place in an office."

Caroline laughs as if she, too, has encountered this problem with her husband, who looks like a Latin pop star but
is actually an architect.

"Jason actually suggested I keep a time chart to account
for every single hour of—" The elevator doors open, and
Caroline gives me a smile of such melting empathy that for a

moment, I believe we are about to become the kind of friends who drink coffee in each other's kitchen, comfortable enough to confide in each other in extreme close-ups that reveal every nuance of lip tremble and tear-welling emotion.

Then she says, "I'm afraid I have to run," and there is something in her tone that lets me know she thinks I need therapy, and should quit trying to use her time without paying for it.

I find my daughter huddled against the redbrick wall. It is like looking at my own childhood self in pain; she has the same lanky limbs, the same dejected slouch. The teacher is busy keeping one of the boys from hitting his head against a fence. The minute Sadie sees me she breaks into hysterical tears. I lead her home and try to make sense of what she tells me between convulsions. Someone is having a birthday party. Everyone has been invited, all the girls in Ms. De La Pena's second grade, except for Sadie. Serena, Sadie's best friend, is going.

"But doesn't Ms. De La Pena have a rule about not inviting only some of the students?"

Sadie hiccups and shakes. This is the kind of rejection that gets remembered on deathbeds. How can I cure this?

"I know. We'll see one of your other friends."

Sadie stares at me, owl-eyed.

I pick up the phone, try the number of my upstairs neighbor.

"Hello?"

"Hi, Kathy? It's me, Delilah."

"Delilah, hi! Oh, gosh, I owe you a phone call, don't I?"

"I think I did call a few weeks ago. . . ."

"And you called again a few days ago, didn't you? I'm so

sorry! Everything's been in such a state these days. We're renovating the apartment and I'm going through the whole application process for Tamlyn's preschool—you know how grueling a process that is. . . ."

"No, not really, we just decided to send Sadie to the nursery around the corner." There is a moment of silence as Kathy tries to think of something nonjudgmental to say.

"And you're probably the sane one! When I think of all the stress I put myself through trying to find just the right school for Tam . . ." Kathy gives a little laugh. "Not that there is just one right school, of course."

Because all children are gifted and challenged in some way or other, and no one school is right for everyone. Except no one currently living in New York City actually believes this.

I take that back. I shouldn't include the outer boroughs. But in Manhattan, there are three unquestionably right schools, just as there are three right restaurants. These are the places for the yoga-toned, opera-literate, Hegel-quoting, chess-playing, trilingual, independent thinkers who set high goals for themselves. And have families with twenty thousand a year to spare. There are also two top-drawer public schools harder to get into than the Special Forces, and six decent private runners-up, for the long-limbed, glossy and poised competitors who couldn't play the flute or piano, or flubbed one important interview question. The rest of us, the great unwashed horde, eat and educate our children at places no one has ever heard of.

My daughter goes to P.S. 98 because, as my husband never ceases to remind me, I missed the November deadline for preschool applications back when she was two. What can I say? I was a new mother, still in the blissful fog of long stroller walks to the library and afternoons in the playground watching Sadie dissolve Cheerios in her mouth. How was I to know that if you don't get your child into the right twos program, it's all over, because you have to take IQ tests to get into kindergarten (the Stanford-Binet test for the top public schools, the Educational Records Bureau test for private), and if your child is of a slightly nervous disposition and, say, chews her hair and blinks when talking to strangers, you are not likely to get a stellar score. Of course, there's also the little matter of parental performance. The top-drawer schools insist upon a personal interview with the parents as well as the child, and have questionnaires with essay and extra-credit sections: Please explain which major educational innovators shaped your child-rearing philosophy, and how you have adapted this theoretical base into practice.

My ability to quote Horace Mann aside, we wouldn't stand a chance.

According to Jason, this is beside the point. I committed the original sin of not applying for preschool a full fifteen months in advance, and must therefore crawl on my belly for all eternity.

"All the other mothers seemed to figure it out, and some of them actually have jobs. Now we have to hope that some family will move to Westchester before it's too late."

But even if a space opens up, it will probably go to some other child, as Sadie—a child so bright she could probably teach freshman English—has not become more poised now that she is in the second grade. On the contrary, there are days when she will not speak to any adult, a behavior I find slightly charming and magical, like something out of a Roald Dahl book. During these periods of extreme reticence, her friend Serena translates for her. Her best and only friend Serena. Who has just been poached.

Which brings me back to my conversation with my upstairs neighbor, who has been telling me something about her older daughter's French or Piano or Philosophy lessons.

"Of course, I don't push Fleur, she requests that the music lessons be conducted in French. . . ."

"Listen, Kathy, the reason I called. Would Fleur like to have a playdate with Sadie next week?"

Pause. "Well, let me think. She has ballet on Mondays, piano on Tuesdays, Wednesday is her standing playdate with Bronwyn, you know they've been like sisters ever since preschool. . . . Thursdays we used to have ceramics, but now we like to keep them free for homework and impromptu cultural outings. And Fridays we leave early for our house in Connecticut. Hmm. Perhaps next Thursday the girls could go to the Met together to see the Impressionist exhibit?"

"I was thinking more like, maybe Fleur and Sadie could meet up for an hour or so after school today. You see, there's this birthday party that one of the girls in Sadie's class is having, and she wasn't invited . . . and her best friend *was* invited. . . ."

"Oh."

"And our girls did seem to have such a nice time at the building's holiday party."

"They did? Ingrid never mentioned it."

"Your nanny seemed a little busy." Flirting with all the husbands.

"It's just that today is piano, and Fleur still needs to do her social studies homework. . . . Her school is studying the effect of architecture on work performance, and Fleur needs to finish her model of Grand Central Station by tomorrow."

I turn to look at my daughter's little tearstained face. Her glasses have become all fogged up. "That's all right," I say. "Another time."

I hang up the phone. "Never mind, Sadie. Why don't we do something together? Just the two of us? Ice skating. Want to go to Rockefeller Center? Or how about a pet store? We could go pet some puppies and kittens. No, that's depressing, they all look at you like they expect you to get them out of prison. How about adopting a kitten? Daddy would get used to it."

"Mom." My daughter is trembling now, biting her lip, standing with her arms held rigidly at her sides.

"Baby, what is it? What can I do?"

Sadie extends one hand and shows me the envelope as if it is the bloody head of someone I've decapitated. "Tell me what this is."

The envelope is addressed to Sadie Levine, 320 West End Avenue, apt 7C. It contains an invitation to Chieko Kim's birthday party today. "Oh, my God, Sadie, where did you find this?"

My daughter's thin-lipped rage looks almost exactly like my father's. "On your desk. Under three other envelopes."

"Oh, Sadie, that's horrible. I'm so sorry. I wasn't expecting any cards from anyone and I thought those were all the spam envelopes—you know how all the department stores send cards these days, to trick you into thinking you're being specially invited to a sale. . . ."

"Mommy, I wanted to go. So badly." I stroke Sadie's baby-fine hair and she jerks away, once, then accepts it.

"So let's go."

"But they don't think we're coming. I won't get a goody bag."

I kneel down in front of my daughter. A small muscle is spasming near her left eye, making it twitch. I touch it with my thumb. "Sadie, there's always one goody bag extra. Just in case. So. Do you want to go?"

Tears still streaming down her face, Sadie nods.

Years from now, Sadie will sit on the therapist's couch: It was then I realized that my mother wasn't in control of her life, let alone of mine. *That's why I don't really keep in touch with her now.*

Like those movie stars who won't talk about their mothers in interviews. Suddenly, I can imagine Sadie on the cover of *People* magazine, hair dyed strawberry blonde, wise, wide eyes no longer hidden by glasses. Sadie Levine stars in *Mother's Helper,* a heartwarming film about a daughter's special gift to her mother, yet has not invited her own mother to her impending nuptials.

"Mommy? Can you button this up?"

I fasten the tiny pearl buttons on Sadie's lavender sweater, which is trimmed with purple fur at collar and hem. Her taste in clothes is the only part of her that is loud.

"Mom, there's a stain on your shirt."

I glance down. It looks like blood. I'm one of those people who get nosebleeds when upset—probably because I fell off a bunk bed when I was ten, thereby breaking my already beaky nose. "Don't worry. Nobody will be looking at my shirt, Sadie."

My daughter hesitates. True, she is thinking, *No one notices mothers, yet what if I am embarrassed by Mom's unkempt hair, bloodstained shirt, ancient slacks?*

I find some lip gloss in my bag and apply it. "Okay, now, how do I look?"

Sadie considers. "Fluff the hair."

I finger comb my extremely unfluffy hair, which is the same fine texture as Sadie's. "Good now?"

Sadie smiles. "Good." She runs up to hug me and we leave the apartment together.

I come back for my coat while Sadie holds the elevator.

Still Monday, November 30 (but feels like it should be another day already) 5:30 P.M.

Ford pulls back from the kiss.

"I'm sorry," he says. "I shouldn't have done that." He stares down, half blindly, at the woman in his arms.

"No," she agrees. "You shouldn't." But she isn't moving away, he can't help but notice, and there is a suggestion of a smile in her voice. She is different in the dark, more certain of herself.

What would she be like in bed? He tries to imagine her naked, with her angular, long-limbed body. Elegant and awkward, he thinks, like a young, ethnic Katharine Hepburn. Could he bed a young Katharine Hepburn?

"Ford." He looks down at her face in the shadows and knows that what he sees is surrender. Everything in him stills for a moment, tightens, begins to pulse. He bends his head to claim her lips again, then stops.

"No," he says. "You're married." A man who doesn't seem to appreciate what he's got, but still, Ford has his personal code. You don't go poaching another man's woman, not when the sacred words have been said, and especially not when there's a child involved.

"Not really."

Ford lifts Delilah's head so that he can see her eyes more clearly. "You want to explain that?"
"He's dead."

No, not dead. Can't kill Jason, even in a fantasy. *He's disappeared.* No, then I'm a faithless bitch for cheating on him when he might be in danger. *He's leaving me.* Which makes me appear pathetic. *I don't think he's who he says he is.* Yes, that works. *A double agent. We were never legally married.* Poor Sadie, can I do this to her? Yes, it's my fantasy, it won't really affect her . . . but how can I consummate my fantasy if my daughter is left with a strange imposter for a father?

This is a very long pause, and Ford begins to suspect there is something Delilah isn't telling him. "Del. You know you can trust me, don't you?"
Delilah looks up, eyes awash in tears, to the man who is lying atop her so intimately it feels as if they have already made love. "I know," she whispers fiercely.
But what isn't she telling him about her husband?

These are the things I don't tell my husband:

1. I never actually completed my thesis on *Dialogue as Poetry: Talking Tough in the Films of Howard Hawks.*

2. When I was 18, I spent the money my parents gave me for a nose job on a debauched holiday in Amsterdam.

3. What I am thinking

These are the things my husband doesn't tell me:

1. Why he hasn't slept with me for the past three years

2. The exact location of his office at R. B. International

3. What he is thinking

When I say Jason hasn't slept with me for the past three years, I mean, of course, that he hasn't made love to me. We sleep together all the time. And I'm exaggerating about the three years: We did have sex once last June, when Sadie was over at Jason's parents' house for the weekend. And there may have been a time or two before that. But the poetic truth of it still stands: It's been three years since Jason demonstrated any real enthusiasm for the marital act.

It is commonly accepted that if a man loses all interest in you sexually, this means he's having an affair, but I don't think that's the case with Jason. First of all, he is neither more nor less irritable with me, and if he were passionately combining fluids with someone else, I would expect some change in mood.

Secondly, he has always been something of a boy scout. Even when I first met him and he was overflowing with the kind of expansive flirtatiousness that encompassed me, the waitress, the couple sitting in front of us at the movie theater and the elderly taxi driver, Jason had a base level of unshakably bourgeois morality. Cheating is wrong, stealing is wrong, spraying cologne on semi-clean clothes so you can get away with one more day of wear is wrong, wrong, wrong.

But my last and most convincing reason for believing my husband is not having an affair is this: Jason seems to have lost his antennae for sex. When we're watching a movie and it's clear that the hero and heroine are bickering because they are about to fall into bed together, Jason says, "I must've missed something. What are they arguing about?" If we're at a cocktail party (rare event) and some twenty-two-year-old model saunters by, Jason does not track the passage of her firm, young flesh with his eyes. He does not notice when men flirt with me (a rarer event), even if the man in question is someone I used to date before Jason and I were married. ("That was Diego? God, Del, what were you thinking? The man only has one eyebrow, to go with the one opinion he kept repeating.")

He doesn't even notice my fascination with Ford. I'd like to think my thoughts don't show on my face, but still, if Jason were having increasingly elaborate daydreams about, say, Hilda the housekeeper, I think I would suspect something.

Luckily, Hilda is sturdy and matronly. Unlike Ford of the pantherlike walk and slow and knowing grin.

Not that I go around flirting with Ford, or he with me. I pretend not to notice him, and Ford pretends not to notice me noticing. It's a very intense relationship, and I can only take small doses of it before I have to retreat to my study. Sometimes he calls me in, though, and I get to see him lying flat on his back on my closet floor like a gladiator chained for some decadent Roman lady's delectation. "Turn on the cold, will you? Damn, that's not holding." When he tightens a bolt, his biceps fill me with an almost maternal desire. I wish to hold them, stroke them, rub them with lotion.

I might offer him a drink from time to time—lemonade, a soda? He tends to accept with a thanks-ma'am innocence that is just this side of irony. Mind you, it's hard to tell what's irony in that dry, deliberate voice. I get the feeling most people probably miss the joke. And maybe that's not all they miss about Ford.

There's a definite hint there of something tigerishly restless and hungry behind the lazy grin and the assumed air of nonchalance. Or maybe I just think he's all that because of the exotica factor—those broad, high cheekbones, that golden tone to his skin, and, when his thick, dark hair isn't obscuring half his face, there's something about his eyes that suggests a hint of Genghis Khan lurking somewhere behind all that niceness.

Yes, I mean his eyes have a slightly almond shape, but I also mean there's a touch of the barbarian there. I think Ford is capable of getting the job done, even if it means getting messy. Even if it means getting hurt.

Yet Jason does not seem to think there is the slightest possibility of my being attracted to the Fordly attributes being displayed almost daily in our bedroom.

So I do not think Jason is having an affair. I think if he were he would suspect me of having one, too. We tend not to think that other people are capable of things we wouldn't do ourselves.

But then why doesn't Jason invite me to his office? It might be as simple as Jason's explanation that R. B. International has a corporate climate of slightly paranoid secrecy. Kleat Madigan, the chief executive, is ex-military, but nobody seems to know what branch of the armed services Kleat belonged to (although there are rumors that he knows how to kill a man using only his two index fingers). Which may explain why Kleat (who actually looks a bit like Brando) carries such *Apocalypse Now* weight with his colleagues: Who wants to argue with a guy who's used to gutting the opposition? Not me—I met the guy at a business dinner last year and couldn't decide whether he was checking me out in a guy-way or figuring out the quickest way to kill me during the soup course if I turned out to be a threat. I became so nervous I forced myself to laugh at two entirely offensive jokes, one of which pertained to "right-hand men" and seemed to be a veiled reference to Jason and, if I'm not imagining things, masturbation. Jason told me that this was just Kleat's army-style humor, but I was hugely relieved when the evening ended and I was no longer within range of the man's killing fingers.

Perhaps this is why my husband seems perennially tense these days: Jason, as one of R. B.'s chief patent attorneys, is closer than most to the company's secrets.

Although why one more lemon scent or banana flavor should be such a big secret is beyond me. I mean, when you go around smelling your detergent or face cream or room freshener or margarine, do you really ever jump and think, Aha! This truly is new and improved! As far as I can see, R. B.'s team of top chemists are all wasting their time. My lipsticks are no tastier now than they were in the eighties. My yogurts are no fruitier. And my shampoo is no more fragrant, despite advertisements suggesting a direct, pheremonal impact on the primitive reptilian centers of our brains.

As for what Jason's thinking, I have my suspicions. I was a poet, after all (published in the *Atlantic* and the *Utne Reader*, briefly under consideration for a position in Bard College's English department) and much of poetry is really about letting yourself know what you know, about making intuitive connections.

What Jason is Thinking: A Poem

Here I am again. Nothing for
Dinner. What can she have been doing all day,
My wife
That she cannot take ten minutes to shop
For meat. Delilah! Why is last week's empty milk carton
Still in the refrigerator? Why is there an untidiness
   of paper
All over the living-room floor. Ouch!
That was a tack.
Doesn't she know how deadly
These forces of chaos can be?

Hmm. I'll have to work on that. Maybe I should tighten the whole composition, make it something more formal, like a sonnet or villanelle?

"Delilah!"

Oh, Christ, it's seven o'clock all ready. After the sugar-fueled pandemonium of Chieko's birthday party, coming back to our apartment was so peaceful that I kind of went into a fugue state, cutting up onions. (The term "pandemonium" originally referred to the abode of all demons, and let me say that a second-grade make-your-own-pizza party does resemble the capital city of Hell.)

Jason comes in looking like one cranky cowboy. "What is going on in the living room? It looks like someone was having one helluva fight with your printer. And you've put papers all over my desk, which means I have no place to put my stuff."

"Sorry. I was just getting started on dinner and I forgot to put my script away. I'll do it in a second."

Jason removes his hat, rubs his forehead. He's an attractive man, really, even better now than when I married him. Age has roughened up that boyish, Wheaties-eating, blue-eyed face. "And were you doing something with pushpins? Because I just picked these up from the floor." He holds out three red plastic pushpins in the palm of his hand.

This was the result of my reading "A Professional Organizer's Top Ten Tips." Following Tip #6, I'd tried numbering my soap opera scenes and then tacking them onto a big sheet of corkboard, but had gotten confused and wound up having Skylar collapsing hysterically onto Blackjack *before* the villainous Ruby had done anything even vaguely threatening.

I tend to do experimental without intending to.

"Del? Maybe you could clean them up before someone steps on them?"

As if on cue, from across the house, we hear a muffled cry. "Mom! I just stepped on something sharp!"

Jason gives me what my mother always calls The Look. "So, Del. What's for dinner?"

I open my mouth and then realize I have forgotten to defrost the chicken. "Eggs."

"Eggs? Scrambled eggs? An omelet? Eggs over easy?"

"Um, whichever, I could also do poached if . . ."

"No. Stop. I wouldn't dream of interfering with this dinner you've got planned out. I'll just let you surprise me." Jason walks away, then stops just before leaving the kitchen.

"Del? You know how you keep asking to visit my office? Well, R. B. is having a big holiday office party. At first it was going to be employees only, but I kept arguing that my wife was never going to let me hear the end of it if I went without her. So, as a result, all the spouses are invited. Two weeks from today. Mark it on the calendar so you don't forget and decide to cook a big dinner that night." Then he smiles at me, to show he is just joking. The smile actually manages to reach his eyes.

Oh, great, another fun-filled evening with Kleat "I've killed men for less" Madigan. Well, at least it'll be an excuse to get dressed up, wear some jewelry, pluck the bristle I've just discovered on my chin.

"Jason? I'm sorry about tonight. I was going to do a chicken stir-fry, but then there was this birthday party that Sadie had and what with one thing and the other . . ."

At this precise moment Sadie limps into the kitchen. "Mommy forgot to give me my party invite," she announces. "We still owe Chieko a present. I think I got a splinter in the living room."

"Let Daddy wash his hands, then I'll see what's what."

Jason gives Sadie his hand and she hobbles off with him. "Mommy also said we might get a kitten from the pound. For Christmas."

Jason looks pained. "Sadie, we're Jewish." Which reminds me, I forgot to light the Shabbat candles at sundown. I rummage in the cupboard and discover a wax frog and a Santa Fe Sensuality candle in the shape of a mushroom. At least I think it's a mushroom.

"So we could get a kitten for Chanukah, then. Okay, Daddy? Daddy? Daddy, stop looking at Mommy while I'm talking to you!"

I look up and meet Jason's eyes. It doesn't take a lot of poetic insight to figure out what he is thinking.

Monday, December 3
5:55 A.M.

It was a dark and stormy night and the tigers were restlessly pacing in their cages, their fur crackling with electricity. The wind was building from the east, whipping across the dry August grass and filling the air with the promise of rain. The big cats wanted their evening meat, but today was payday at the circus, and their feckless keeper had imbibed his weekly salary and was now passed out in his trailer, atop the fat lady.

"Poor babies." Delilah Lombardy knew better than to approach the tigers too closely in their present mood, but the animals' futile roars of hunger disturbed her in a way she could not explain. "I wish I had something to feed you."

"You'd better be careful, lady, or you might wind up feeding them something you hadn't planned on."

Delilah whirled around and saw the dark figure of a man silhouetted against a corner of the big top. "Oh!" She took a step back. "I didn't realize . . . I didn't know anyone was still around."

"Stop acting so jumpy. I'm not going to bite you." The man stepped out of the shadows and as he shrugged out of his overcoat she realized he was wearing a thin, white acrobat's costume, which revealed every ripple of his long, muscled athlete's body. He seemed to fairly hum with energy; Delilah half expected him to leap atop the tiger's cage.

"When you're done staring, you can take the coat. Thought you might need it."

"I . . . thank you, but I was just about to leave, I . . ."

"No, you weren't." The acrobat settled his coat around her shoulders, and for a moment his warm hands rested on the sharp blades of her shoulders. "That better?"

"Yes, I . . . you didn't have to . . . I saw you in the show earlier. You were wonderful."

"I didn't do the triple."

"I didn't notice."

"Did you notice we don't have a girl flier? My sister got pregnant."

"Oh."

"Need to have a girl up there for the act." The acrobat shook out a cigarette. "Want one?"

"I don't smoke, thanks."

The acrobat watched Delilah through slitted eyes as he lit his own cigarette and she wondered what he saw that seemed to hold his interest. She was not an attractive woman, she knew that from thirty-five years of painful experience. Her older sister, Tamara, had been the family beauty, and had married the town solicitor, while Delilah stood awkwardly by, accepting, with a tight-lipped smile, the townspeople's assurances that she would be next. Too book-smart, that was her father's assessment; her mother said it was nobody's fault that the right man just hadn't come around yet.

"You the town schoolmarm?"

"I . . . how did you know? Oh, don't answer that. I suppose I look the part, all right."

The acrobat exhaled a plume of smoke, but behind the veil of gray Delilah thought she saw a look of bemusement cross his face.

He had very gentle eyes for such a hard face. "You dress like a schoolmarm."

Delilah reached up to touch the small pearl buttons of her blouse. "Do I?"

"Here." He stuck his cigarette in the corner of his mouth and before she could think to stop him his hands were at her throat, unbuttoning her shirt down to the point where she squealed in alarm. Then he pulled the starched fabric apart, his thumbs brushing her collarbones. "Now you look a little less proper."

"I think I know how to unbutton my shirt on my own, thank you. If I wanted to."

The acrobat grinned. "You just didn't know you wanted to. And I don't notice you buttoning yourself back up, either. Say, what's your name, sister?"

Delilah flashed the acrobat a severe look as she redid the lowest three buttons. "Delilah. Delilah Lombardy."

"Ford Markhov of the flying Markhovs. So how did the town schoolmarm get the name of one of the biggest hussies in the good book?"

"My mother was circus."

Ford braced an arm against a pole. "What kind of circus?"

Delilah gazed out over the trailers to the big top. "You'll need to take it down before the storm hits."

"You're not answering my question."

"She handled the horses."

"So she knew some tricks. She teach you anything?" Ford was close enough for Delilah to see the imperfections of his skin—the tiny scar high on his cheek, the rougher one low on his jaw. His eyes were so dark she could read nothing in their expression—the eyes of an alien being, from some distant barbaric land of fast horses and fierce justice. "She taught me. I practiced. When I was younger."

"You say that like you're some old lady, Delilah." His rough hand came up to caress her face like the lick of a cat's tongue.

"I am old. I'm thirty fi-"

"Shhh. Numbers lie. How old do you feel, Delilah?"

"I feel—" But now his hand was cupping her chin, bringing her lips up to his. His other hand supporting the back of her head, Ford devoured her with his kiss, his lean, warrior-athlete's body pressing down against her slender curves until she gasped and arched against him. He tasted of whiskey and cigarettes, and Delilah knew that she should be afraid, because she could feel the leashed strength of him in the fine tremors that raced down his heavily muscled arms.

"Christ, woman, you don't kiss like a spinster." Ford traced the line of Delilah's cheek with his finger, and for a moment the look on his face was neither mocking nor sexual, but disarmingly, hauntingly, open.

"What do I kiss like?" Her voice was throaty, provocative, barely recognizable.

"Like a woman in love." This time, when he bent to claim her lips, she met him halfway, her hands tangled in the unruly silk of his thick, dark hair. So engrossed were the two in their discovery of each other that at first, they did not even register the shrill summons of the alarm.

Delilah wrenched away from Ford, her heart pounding. "What is it?"

Ford turned to the sound, his hands still gripping her arms, suddenly comprehending what the bell meant: The worst calamity that could befall a circus. "I think the big top's on fire!"

"Am I calling at a bad time?"

I glance at the clock. Six A.M. "No, Mom. I had to get up to get Sadie ready for school." My mother no longer sleeps, as far as I can tell, and seems to have retained only a dim sense of the hours that other people like to spend unconscious.

"I was just trying you early because you're always busy when I try you later in the day. But if you're tired, I can call back."

Jason groans and rolls over in bed. "Hang on, let me take the phone into the other room, Mom."

In the kitchen I pour milk into the coffeemaker. "So what's going on?"

"I need to ask you a question."

I pour the milk out of the coffeemaker and into the sink. "What, you couldn't reach Tamara?" My mother tends to ask my older sister for advice, as my older sister tends to give the kind of advice my mother wants to hear. Buy the diamond bracelet, it's a keepsake, yes, I think that shade of beige is nice, no, you don't have to invite cousin Gila's niece to stay for more than two nights, even if she is backpacking through the States and short on money.

"Del, what are you doing? Washing the dishes? I can't hear myself think."

"I'm making coffee."

"Can't you do that later?"

"Mom, I require coffee to talk. Sensibly, that is."

"I'll wait." And she does, maintaining a bruised silence until I finish measuring and pouring. "Ready," I say as the coffee begins to brew.

"It's too late," she says in an injured voice. If I didn't know that my mother's Botoxed brow has been physically incapable of frowning since the late nineties, I would have imagined her scowling like Sadie.

"Why is it too late?" The clock says 6:10.

"Your father is awake."

Aha, I think. Secrets from my father and Tamara. "Take the phone into another room, then."

"Too obvious." More loudly, my mother says, "So, Del, remember how I told you about how my friend Dahlia had a rash on her chest, the one her daughter told her was from not wearing cotton brassieres? Well, guess what it really was?"

"Leprosy?"

"Lyme disease! If Dahlia had waited just one week more, the doctors said, she would have become paralyzed on half her face. Permanently!" My mother sounds oddly triumphant. "This is what you get when you don't worry about symptoms, Delilah."

Hoping caffeine will help me through this conversation, I yank the coffee pot out before it is ready and scald my hand on the liquid still dripping through.

". . . so then Lois was thinking about going to Israel, but what with everything that's going on, she decided it's safer not to fly. I suggested Miami Beach, but she told me that they have these wild parties there now, models and druggies and God-knows-what floating around in the pool . . ."

As my mother goes on about how hard it is to find a decent replacement for Israel these days, I sip my coffee and look for something exciting to do for Sadie's lunch. Hummus? Croque monsieur? Thai noodles?

". . . then I suggested a cruise ship. By the way, why don't you and Jason take Sadie on a cruise ship? She has vacation now, right?"

"In ten days. But Jason and I were figuring we'd go somewhere over spring break this year, possibly out West and . . ."

"Okay, forget the small talk. Your father's in the shower. Del, I need to know something. How do you catch a yeast infection?"

I have to think for a moment. "Well, it's not a matter of catching, exactly. It's more a matter of the flora and fauna down there getting out of whack. Have you been on antibiotics lately?"

"Good Lord, Del, don't you know how to whisper?"

"There's no one. Have you?"

"No. So it's not . . . communicable?"

"No. It could be stress, a change in diet . . . but yeast infections are not caused by extracurricular activities. All you need now is to relax and take a trip to the drugstore."

"There's something else I have to ask you."

I hear a sound and look over my shoulder. Sadie is dramatically staggering into the kitchen, draped in her lavender quilt. "I don't feel at all well," she says in the mannered tones of a thirties American actress trained by a British speech coach.

"Sit down and have some juice, Sadie. Okay, Mom, go ahead."

"God, Delilah. You're hopeless. Now she knows it's me you're talking to!"

I hand Sadie a glass. "I am being very discreet."

"Now she knows you have to be discreet about something!"

"Mom, let's talk about yeast after I get Sadie to school."

"Now she knows we're talking about yeast!"

"Nana's baking some bread at her house, Sadie." I hand her the phone. "Where'd you leave your glasses?"

Sadie squints in concentration. "In the bedroom. I don't need them anymore. Hi, Nana."

I walk into Sadie's bedroom, where I discover all the Barbies arranged in the shape of a pentagram. In the center of the five-pointed star I see Sadie's lavender spectacles. On her bedside, I find a book called *A Practical Guide to Witchcraft*, open to a healing spell.

Jason lurches by on his way to the bathroom. "What a mess," he says, indicating the dolls. "You better tell Sadie to clean that up before Hilda gets back from vacation."

Hilda! I had completely forgotten that our housekeeper was due back from Antigua. This is wonderful! The house will be clean, food will be cooked, Sadie will be entertained and my script will be completed by deadline.

I might even be able to go to a yoga class and attempt to locate my toes.

I hum to myself as I pick up the Barbies. I hum while I strip the sheets from Sadie's bed, arrange her books and pick up puzzle pieces from the floor.

Ordinarily I am overwhelmed by the state of Sadie's room, which is really supposed to be a maid's room, and has very little room for all the murals and knickknacks and dolls and paint-your-own tea sets that Sadie has acquired from two pairs of doting grandparents.

But today I am focused. I am in that very clear, creative state where your hands are doing one thing and your mind is busy with something else altogether. I am straightening Sadie's room but I am also thinking about Spanish soap operas, and how I would love to infuse my *Secrets* scripts with some of that Latin intensity of feeling. Maybe if I plumbed some Greek myths for inspiration? Suddenly I remember reading something in the newspaper about a production of *Lysistrata*, which the lead actress felt was too obscene. Wouldn't that make a marvelous soap plot—all the women banding together and refusing to have sex with their husbands until the husbands agreed to . . . do something or other. Or maybe it should be the husbands! The husbands all refusing to make love to their wives, growing more and more obsessed with sex until something as innocuous as a laundry commercial—look how clean and white these panties are now—has them hot and sweaty.

I am mulling over the plot potential of repressed sexuality and putting away one of Sadie's model horses when

Jason appears in the doorway. He is gray-suited and glinty-eyed, his hair slightly glossy from washing. I notice that his widow's peak is beginning to resemble the bat signal.

"Del, what the hell are you doing? It's almost half past and I just walked in on Sadie—not at all ready, not even dressed—gabbing on the phone with your mother about bread."

I charge into the kitchen. "Can I say hello to Nana again, Sadie? Hi, Mom, we have to go." I start throwing things in Sadie's lunchbox. A yogurt. Olives. An éclair. "Sadie, go and get dressed right away. And don't forget your glasses."

"But I don't need them anymore!"

"Just go!" My coffee is now ice cold. Where did the time go? I am just closing Sadie's lunchbox when Jason walks back in.

"Did you do something with the papers I left on my desk?"

"What are you talking about?"

"I had a folder with important papers on my desk that I brought home on Friday. Now somebody's moved them."

"Did you ask Sadie?"

"Del, you were the last person in the living room. Do you remember moving any papers?"

I try to remember. "What kind of papers were they?"

Jason's face looks puffy with fatigue, which is strange, as he went to sleep before I did. "It was a report on the new Biosensual account. Don't you remember my mentioning it to you over the weekend?"

Actually, now that I'm thinking about it, I do recall Jason telling me he was working on a big project involving an ex-Soviet chemist who was concocting some incredible new aphrodisiac lotion or potion.

As personal care products go, I thought this one was pretty interesting, considering the current abysmal state of our love life.

Jason is rifling through his briefcase again. "Are you sure you didn't remove anything from here?"

"I know I took *my* papers off your desk on Friday night, which you told me to do. . . ."

"Let's check, shall we?" Jason takes me by the hand as if I were a recalcitrant schoolgirl and walks me into the living room. "What is that? That box in there?"

"Breakdowns and scripts from the past six months of my soap opera."

"And that box?"

"Um, backstory, character studies and blueprints of the sets."

"What are those three boxes on the dining-room table? Can you go through all of these and make sure you haven't taken my report by mistake?"

I lean over the table and start at random. "This is medical research and police procedural stuff. You know, for when a character is in the hospital or the police station? 'I'm afraid his score on the Glasgow coma scale wasn't good. If he doesn't come out of it in the next twenty-four hours, chances are he never will.' "

Jason points to a pile of books on the floor. "Christ, what a mess. I'm better off just going back to the office and printing everything out again." He takes a breath, which I mistake for a sigh of resignation, and then erupts. "This is a fucking war zone! How can you even work in here? I mean, look at that. What is it—the leaning tower of hardcovers?"

"I needed some information on castles. . . ."

"So why aren't they in a bookcase?"

"Well, I was reading that book you gave me last Valentine's Day—*A Professional Organizer's Top Ten Tips*—and tip number four was to designate one area of the house as your study, so I tried to place everything I needed in a vague semicircle around my desk."

Jason looks, for one fleeting moment, amused, before his expression hardens. "Throw that book out. It's obviously dangerous in the wrong hands. And what about that smelly box? The one that rattles?"

"Sadie and I were doing a candle-making project."

"If it's done, Del, get rid of it. How about the huge pile of photo albums and baby stuff?"

"Sadie and I were going to start a scrapbook. . . ."

Jason's hands close over my shoulders, as if he is about to frog-march me toward the firing squad. "Del, look around you. All around. What do you see?"

I see a living room with high, turn-of-the-century ceilings and pretty plaster mouldings painted apricot. I see walls festooned with children's paintings and stencils and my own collages. I see a ragged army of books spilling out from ancient 1950s hipster bookcases, the kind of wood and metal affairs you see in old Dean Martin films. I see a maze of boxes—some on handsome needlework-cushioned chairs, some on the floor, some stuffed under the low coffee table I hand-tiled myself to look like a Gaudi mosaic I saw in Barcelona when I was in college.

Maybe Sadie and I could do a mosaic! I haven't played with tile in . . . no, no, don't think about that now.

I see a retro moderne couch that doesn't quite match the Indian tasseled cushions or the faded kilim rug peeking out from the obstacle course of boxes and books.

"I see a room badly in need of Hilda," I say.

"I see a junkyard. No wonder we can never find anything. Every room in this house is filled with boxes, books, old magazines, broken toys and half a dozen failed crafts projects. There is so much crap hanging off of every surface that Sadie thinks everyone eats dinner on a tray on their lap. You don't need a housekeeper, Del. You need a removal service. Either you start throwing things out," Jason says, picking up his briefcase, "or I will."

He leaves and I glance up at the wall only to discover that, as in spy films and thrillers, our antique British railway clock's minute hand seems to be speeding up.

"Sadie!" I shout. "Are you ready?"

My child appears wearing nothing, aside from princess underwear and an expression of royal sulkiness. "You ruined my spell, Mom."

By the time we make it into the elevator we are both sulking. Naturally, my upstairs neighbor Kathy Wheatley is riding down, the very image of an affluent West Side bohemienne from the top of her pale, mascaraless eyelashes to the bottom of her ruinously expensive German walking shoes. Her hair, which is naturally blonde, is braided into a thick rope and tied off with a turquoise and leather doodad that probably cost a fortune at some crafts fair in Albuquerque. I am suddenly very aware of the fact that my own hair is unwashed and I am still wearing threadbare, gray cotton pajamas under a navy pea coat that appears to be encrusted with actual peas.

"Hi," Kathy says as if seeing me is just one huge, happy surprise. "Aren't you lucky your daughter's school starts late!" Of course *her* nanny hustled both her children out the door and off at the crack of dawn. I'm not exactly sure what Kathy does, but whatever it is, it seems to require that her children be absent for most of the day. I get the impression that she is one of the Scary Sisterhood: stay-at-home moms who used to be high-powered Wall Street brokers or research chemists but now channel all their underutilized intelligence and drive into organizing silent auctions for private schools that already charge twenty grand a head.

Her husband, who is vaguely potato-like in demeanor and has a beard, is a history professor at Columbia University.

Kathy is directing the laser beam of her attention at my daughter. "And what are you studying, Peanut? Fleur is learning about genetic code in her school's section on Living Things. Do you like science?"

Sadie, who has been a little freaked out by science ever since discovering that we all have skeletons, hides her face in my pea coat. I place my hand reassuringly on her soft hair, hoping her head hides the crusty bit near my buttons.

"Sorry about the other day," Kathy says to me. "We'll just have to get our big girls together sometime soon."

"Yes, we should." But we won't, of course. Fleur will have her Cordon Bleu cooking class or horseback riding lesson or, let's be honest here, a playdate with one of the Bleeker twins from the mysterious other side of the building, where the apartments are larger and the bathrooms inlaid with marble. Why aren't we friends with Kathy and her kids? She wears a coat that looks like it has been made out of Raggedy Ann wigs. Surely this means she and I share a sensibility, while the Bleeker twins don't even seem to have a mother, just a succession of thin, dark, doe-eyed caretakers from distant lands.

Yet I know that there is a subtle hierarchy to the society of this building, and I sense that Kathy feels I am beneath her in more ways than one.

The elevator stops at the fifth floor and Caroline Moore gets on, with her short, dark hair slicked back and her high cheekbones flushed with happiness. She is carrying a new accessory, a puppy whose adorable ugliness sets off her beauty to perfection. When Kathy asks, Caroline says she has named it Mitchell, presumably after the author of that book on passionate marriage.

For once I am too tired to say something inappropriate, but Sadie compensates by announcing that she would like a puppy like the plumber's black lab but that her father thinks it would be too much for her mother to handle.

Kathy, who has two golden retrievers and a dog walker, looks at me pityingly while Caroline murmurs that dogs are an awful lot of work, especially in the city.

"God, yes, they're just like little babies on wheels when they're this little," says Kathy.

"That will be good practice, then." Caroline looks down and smiles, and before I have even fully processed what she means, Kathy is congratulating her and telling her about the perils of artificial additives in food and drink.

"I belong to a group of mothers who are trying to get all the unnecessary chemicals out of basic food groups," says Kathy, and by the time we reach the lobby the two are talking animatedly about the possibility that additives are causing the prevalence of attention deficit disorder in children these days.

Well, at least now I know one reason why Kathy isn't inviting me over for tea. She's probably afraid I'll dose her with some genetically mutated raspberry flavor sample from Jason's company.

As we walk down West End Avenue, Sadie asks how old Caroline is. I say she is about my age and my daughter glances at me, startled.

"What's wrong, Sadie, did you think women our age couldn't still have babies?"

"No, Mommy, I just thought she looked younger than you."

* * *

When we arrive at Sadie's class, Ms. De La Pena hands me a note. I must speak with Mrs. Giordano, the principal, about my daughter's habitual tardiness. As I am still in my pajamas, I realize I will have to keep my coat on through the whole interview.

I sit on the bench with two surly fifth graders for five minutes before Mrs. Giordano ushers me into her office. She is so large that she seems like more than just one person. Her thickly made-up face has the precarious expression of a former misfit now in a position of authority. When she shakes my hand, her arm reminds me of a balloon animal, tied off at the wrist by a tiny, delicate ladies' gold watch.

"Mrs. Levine," she says in a friendly tone, and then launches into a little speech on the importance of neatness, preparedness and organization. It seems Sadie has already been absent fourteen times since school began in September, and has received five late passes.

"I can explain about that," I say. "Four of those days in October, Sadie was sick with strep and then she had a really nasty ear infection in November. The other times, I've been tutoring Sadie at home. I'm always careful to check in with the teacher so that I cover whatever's going on in class that day, and then we go on and do independent study. For example, when the second grade was reading about habitats, Sadie and I went on to study how the changes in the earth's environment during the Eocene resulted in the mass mammalian extinctions of that era. We did a diorama, which we brought into class the next day."

"So," says Mrs. Giordano, "was Sadie sick on that occasion?"

"Not sick. But it sometimes gets a little much for her, dealing with the social dynamics of that classroom." *Be-*

cause of all your undiagnosed behavioral problems, I do not add. "Of course, Ms. De La Pena does a great job, but with twenty-nine students, there's a limit to what you can accomplish." *Particularly as my child is more curious and insightful than the average.*

I smile at Mrs. Giordano. She smiles back.

"Mrs. Levine," she says, "while I applaud your intentions, I must explain that attendance in a public school classroom is, in fact, compulsory. Surely you understand that we cannot bend the rules for this child and not for that one?" Mrs. Giordano goes on about the greater good and the needs of the many. There is a mention, said in an off-the-cuff, this-doesn't-really-apply-to-you fashion, of a committee on educational neglect. More than fifteen absences and I may have to appear before a panel to defend my daughter's eligibility for promotion to third grade.

"But you know me," I stammer. "I'm not a neglectful parent. I volunteer with the first graders who are having trouble reading, I did that schoolwide poetry workshop last year and I've been subbing for the librarian all this month because she had morning sickness. . . ."

"I'm afraid this has nothing to do with what *I* think, Mrs. Levine. It's just a question of new rules and regulations." Mrs. Giordano braces her hands on the table before standing up, and as she escorts me out of her office I think about the unhappy child she must once have been. No one, clearly, had allowed her to stay home for the day to study what she wanted without the taunts and politics of the other children to distract her.

I walk home and realize that for the first time since my own childhood, I have surrendered to the system.

Should I teach Sadie at home? No, probably not. The only

thing worse than being held hostage by bureaucrats is being held hostage by your mother.

I hear Hilda putting things away when I arrive home. "Hello, Miss," she calls. I follow her voice into the kitchen.

"Hello, Hilda. How are you?" I have given up fighting the "Miss." It seems to represent something to Hilda; some standard I suspect I don't live up to.

"Just fine." Hilda knows everything about us, from the state of my underwear to the number of antacids in Jason's medicine cabinet. I know she has a teenage daughter back in Antigua, and the rest is all surmise.

"We missed you." This meant as an apology for the state of the apartment.

"Mmm-hmm." A woman of size and color, Hilda carries herself with more natural authority in her brocaded slippers than I will ever possess in Ferragamo heels. Not that I possess Ferragamo heels.

I should explain, and often do, that I am filled with complex feelings of guilt about my position as Hilda's employer in particular and also more generally about the status of minority women performing the vital tasks of baby and young child care in middle- and upper-middle-class white households.

Also, I think Hilda looks down on me, and I suspect she has reservations about the quality of my parenting skills. As a socialist, I would like to fire her so that we could pursue a friendship on more equal terms, but as a realist, I know my life would fall apart and Hilda would never deign to speak to me again.

"So," I say, "how was it seeing your family, Hilda?"

"Oh, my sister, she had the baby at the beginning of the

week and we had a feast. We had so much food and so many visitors I couldn't even believe it." Hilda puts a solitary breakfast plate into the sink and we both look at it. "Miss, you know there's a man in your bedroom?"

My heart lurches, as if the Ford of my fantasy had anything to do with everyday life. "That's the plumber. We have a leak in the pipes in the bedroom closet."

"That's what *he* says." As if we get points for having our stories straight. I am almost flattered that Hilda suspects me of having a sex life.

I hang my coat up in the hall closet and confront the fact that Ford is in my bedroom with all my clothes, and I am in the foyer still wearing my pajamas.

And they are not the kind of pajamas which make a man think of lazy Sunday afternoons in bed, having sex and croissants. They are the kind which make you think, gosh, her breasts are rather flat and lifeless. I was seduced into buying them because, in the catalogue, the gray cotton looked sort of shleppy sexy, possibly because the serpentine female modeling them had unbuttoned the top down to her pubic bone. I continued wearing them even after acknowledging their almost comic ugliness, on the grounds that it is less belittling to be ignored by your husband wearing nun-like apparel than to be rejected while wearing a red silk teddy.

Nightgown trivia: Margery Kempe, the eccentric medieval mystic, managed to conceive and bear her husband several children while wearing a hair shirt.

But who knows what attractions Margery possessed? I am one of those women who can look surprisingly pretty or unexpectedly plain, and it seems to depend more on hormones or lunar phases than it does on grooming and makeup. Of course, it always helps to have had great sex in the past day or two, and a bit of mascara. Neither of which applies in this case.

I check myself in the mirror. Verdict: Horrible. Well, fuck it. I can always change it in my fantasy later.

I walk in and he is standing next to the closet, an intensely physical presence in faded Levis and a black flannel shirt that suggests the width of his shoulders. He is sticking some kind of meter into the wall. It leaves two little marks, like a vampire.

"Hi, Ford." I walk past him, very casual. I am assuming this is his first name—it's the only one he's offered.

"Mmph." He is still looking at the meter. "Ms. Levine?"

"Yes?" Not looking at him, very casual, rummaging for clothes in my drawer.

"Sorry I came in before you. Hope you don't mind."

"It's the least of my problems." There is a weighted silence and I turn to see that Ford is now crouched on the floor facing me, his left eyebrow very slightly raised.

"Bad day at school," I explain.

He continues to look at me as he comes to his feet, his expression unreadable. Not much for grunts of assurance, Ford. Dress him in a loincloth and streak his face with ochre and he could be a noble savage; hand him a cravat and knee-high leather boots and he'd make a dandy highwayman; or put him in a burnoose and hang him off a galloping horse, and he could play the sheik with a dagger in his teeth.

I have been looking at him looking at me for at least one beat too long. We are verging on the awkward here. I avert my gaze and am surprised by the sight of my nipples, which are disconcertingly visible under the thin cotton of my pajama top. Swiftly, I pivot back to my clothes drawer. "Guess I'd better get some clothes on."

"That's a hell of a thing to say to a man when he's in your bedroom."

Hold on. Rewind. What was that? Ford is offering no clues, his head bent to recheck the meter. But that was innuendo. My internal editor footnotes the line as a one-liner, not a come-on. Quick, I think, say something to show you're not taking it the wrong way. "So," I say, walking over to my clothes drawers, "has the patch worked, or are we still leaking?"

"So far, so . . ." Behind me, I hear Ford do something that makes a slight puncturing sound. "Damn, that's not good."

"It's leaking?" Suddenly this is too much to bear. Everything is breaking down today. I hear the threat of moisture in my voice as well as the pipes.

" 'Fraid so. Hey, you're not going to cry, are you?" I shake my head and find that Ford is crouching on the floor near the closet, wary with concern. "I will fix it, you know."

"It's not that." I find myself sitting on the bed, swollen with unshed tears. I forget that I am unwashed and unsightly, because Ford is attending to me with the concentration of a lover or a therapist. I begin with the principal's thinly disguised warning and inch backward toward Jason's tantrum.

Finally, in silence, I look up and see that Ford's brow is furrowed. For him, this is an extreme emotional reaction.

"Is that like your husband? Getting mad like that?" It's a question that reveals a penetrating intelligence, no pun intended. Is it like Jason to become coldly furious at my bad housekeeping? I suppose it is. But has this always been like Jason, this simmering anger just beneath the surface, this feeling that I am the allergen provoking his ire?

A wave of embarrassment hits. Why have I been spilling my guts to Ford like this? What has happened to my sense of boundaries? What next—start discussing my sex life, or lack thereof?

I have to say something. "He's not usually so touchy." There. That doesn't sound so bad.

"So maybe there's something going on right now. At work. Making him tense." Ford shrugs his shoulders. "But what do I know? This is why I stay single—no one to nag me about the mess I make."

Ford ducks his head back into the closet, and in the last moment before his head disappears into the shadows, his eyes meet mine and he gives me a slightly embarrassed smile, as if it were he, and not me, who had gotten personal.

"Want coffee?"

"God, yes."

I try not to look at his scuffed hiking boots, or wonder what his feet look like naked. Better one of us should retain some mystery.

As long as I do not have to know what he's really thinking of me, he is the stuff dreams are made of.

Tuesday, December 4
9:30 P.M.

For a very long time, his thoughts were animal in their simplicity. He remained in his crypt, quiet, for as long as possible, expending as little energy as possible. Near dawn, the thirst cramped his stomach and he wished he'd bestirred himself to hunt earlier, while there was still time. Then the sun rose and he surrendered to unconsciousness.

The people came in daylight, when he slept his dreamless, abbreviated death. By the time the sun had set, only the lower mammals skittered between the tombstones, squirrels and voles and even the odd fox. They thought him dead, until he snatched them by the neck with preternatural speed.

And then she came, breaking all the rules of her kind, and of his.

She came by twilight, properly corseted and bustled and gloved but flowerless, without a prayer book or candle. She came without comforts and sat on the ground near one of the graves, not a new one, yet not an old one either. A stone some ten years standing, the body beneath moldered to the bone. Around her, the crickets and bullfrogs filled the night with the wild music of summer's end.

Through the musk of insect and amphibian life, and the deeper funk of animals in rut, he could still smell the fertile, female scent of her, the unmistakable fragrance of a woman of childbearing years. Ford dragged himself through the shadows until he was within six feet of her. He was still able to move silently, even in his diminished state, but he knew his face bore the marks of illness. Well-fed and rested, he might have appeared human, even handsome; at the moment, barely sated by the little creatures he caught, he resembled nothing so much as an ambulatory corpse.

Not that the woman was anything much. As a mortal, he might not have found her appealing. She was slender and had an even, wistful face, and her huge, almond-shaped eyes reminded him of a courtesan he'd once known in Bombay. Yet despite these attractions, and the fairly elegant cut of her cloak, she was somehow lacking in allure. He thought she was one of those women who required the sting of lust to be made beautiful; without the tangle of hair and the sheen of desire in her eyes she was pallid, wan, a little lifeless.

Now there was irony; that he, the truly lifeless one, should shimmer with the nervous energy of a prowling cat, while she should move with such listless torpor.

He wondered if he should feed on her. She seemed half dead already, and the desire to taste her was surprisingly strong in him, the strongest desire he had felt in a century.

"You do a lot of watching." She spoke without looking, but Ford knew she addressed him. "I know you're there. Speak to me."

"Why should I?" His voice came out hoarse with disuse.

"Because it is a novelty for you, and you are bored. Because you think to hunt me, and it is in the predator's nature to examine his prey." The woman lifted her eyes to the shadows, found him. "Because you are too frightened to come and bite me directly."

"I? Frightened? Lady, you mistake me." Ford stepped out of the darkness and let what he thought might be a smile steal over his mouth. "I am a corpse." Now she could run in horror. Whatever she imagined he was—and Bram Stoker's novel had been published this three years, leading many women to conjecture how pleasurable a vampire's kiss might be—she had not conjured the image of a ghoul to nuzzle her neck with yellowed fangs.

But once again, she surprised him.

"You are a vampire, half starved. If you drank deeply enough, you would look like a man."

"Do you think so?" Ford took a step closer.

"I do."

"If I resemble a man, are you not afraid that I might avail myself of your womanly attractions?" Ford stopped some six feet from the woman, wondering if the stench of the grave accompanied him.

"You are not a man, even if you should resemble one. I do not think I attract you in the manner of a woman to a man." Up close, she was really something rather fine. The pulse of fear at the base of her throat, the flush of hectic color now flooding her cheeks, worked to her advantage. "I think you want to drink me."

The words stirred him. Had his starved body contained sufficient blood, he knew he would have reacted rather more like a man than she might suspect possible. "And you, lady? Are you here to receive a fatal kiss?"

"I do not wish to die." Her eyes found his and he saw no shred of pretense there. "You do not wish to kill. That is why you are frightened of me."

"I am not frightened." Holding his gaze, the woman reached down, pulling the fichu from her neckline and baring her neck and a goodly swell of bosom.

Ah, Christ. It was that damn Dracula fixation again. It made Ford nostalgic for the previous century, when females were still acknowledged to possess legs and sexual feelings. A hundred years ago, this woman might have known better than to bare her flesh to a murderer. But in this country, under the widowed Queen Victoria, it was no longer permissible for respectable women to have carnal needs, or for husbands to fulfill them. The men entered their wives without touching them and learned to ejaculate in two or three quick and furtive thrusts.

No wonder this widow thought the prick of his fangs might afford her some darkling pleasure that the marriage bed had so clearly not.

"Lady, you want a man between your legs, not a fiend at your throat."

Her eyes went round with shock. "Sir! I know full well what it is that I need, and it is most certainly not . . . what you suggest!"

He leaped with preternatural speed and was upon her, grabbing her hands. "You are a woman of appetite. I can feel it." And he could feel his own dark hunger rising in him, closing off other thoughts. Where she had bared it, her flesh was as white as a child's.

"So bite me and link me to your senses." Her chest heaved with the passion of her words. "I do not want to die. I do not want to be made vampire. But I want to feel . . . The book said the victim is linked to the vampire with the feeding, but not doomed. Not right away."

"What?" He was only half conscious of what she was saying. She had freed her hands and was unbuttoning her blouse still further, revealing the long line of her throat and the creamy flesh of her upper breasts where they swelled over her corset. It had been a very long time since a woman had undressed for him for any purpose.

"It was a creature such as you who killed my husband and took my child. I want revenge. And with your powers, I can find the fiend who robbed my Sebastian of life."

He could not make sense of her words, and yet he knew that something she had said would haunt him later. Sebastian. He knew that name. But it was impossible to recall anything when the sound of her heart was pounding in his ears like a drum.

"You must leave . . . you must . . . before . . ."

The woman placed her hand at the back of his head, and her touch, so like a lover's, drew his lips downward, toward her heart. He traced a kiss over the downy softness of her skin, and then he glanced up and their eyes met.

"If you promise not to harm me, I am not afraid." She spoke crisply, as if addressing a servant, and he almost laughed with delight.

"Tell me your name, then."

"Delilah. Delilah Langford." Her lashes fluttered at the feel of his teeth on her flesh but he willed her to look back at him. He summoned the old power, so seldom used now that he fed off the lower animals, and compelled her with his gaze.

"Delilah, I will not willingly take your life or make you vampire. But I will feed off your blood, and I will steal your will from you, and for the space of time that your senses are linked to mine, you will feel that you love me beyond all measure of reason and restraint. I am compelling you now. Can you feel it?"

Slowly, she nodded. He shifted his position so that now, instead of kneeling over her, he was holding her in his arms, across his lap.

"You said you did not want a man between your thighs. But if I am sated with your blood, I will be a man and you will want me. It is an effect of the blood-link. Are you still willing?" But he knew what her answer would be. He held her gaze and her will, for she had roused the old hunger in him, and though he warned her, he did so for the most ungentlemanly of reasons: Because it aroused him to tell this very proper widow that soon she would be begging him to bury himself between her thighs.

"And if you are a man, and if I want you, will you take me?" Her voice sounded drugged, but it surprised him that she had enough sense left to ask anything at all. His arms tightened about her and he lowered his head to the valley between her breasts. She smelled of lavender milk and woman. When he exhaled, it sounded almost like a sigh.

"I will not be capable, Delilah. Not unless I take more blood than you would be willing to give. I am too weak now to play the man unless I were to drain you to the point of weakness."

"Weakness, or illness?"

He stared at her, surprised. "Weakness. Like a woman after childbirth."

"What was your name, vampire, when you were alive?"

"Ford. I was called Ford."

Her hand came up to trace the sharp outline of his cheekbone where it pressed against his pale skin. "Then that will be our bargain, Ford. You may drain me to the point of weakness, and take me, if that is your will. And in return, I ask that you bend your will to mine, and help me find the one of your kind who took my child."

His throat was clogged with something that felt like laughter, or possibly tears. She offered him the world in her spinsterish voice, and touched him as if he were a man she cared for, instead of the vicious monster he truly was. "How do you know that I am not the vampire who killed your son?"

"Because I saw him, Ford. He made me watch. And I have watched you. You do not hunt people, and so I have hunted— you." Her smile was something to behold. For a moment, he wished only to smile back at her, like some besotted youth out with his first girl. And then she shifted in his arms and he saw the pale tracery of her veins through the thin barrier of her translucent skin.

"Will it . . . will it hurt much?"

He knew from the sound of her voice that his fangs had extended to their greatest length. "No," he said. "And yes. But the pain will be mingled—with pleasure." He could see that she did not understand. And so he bent his head, and penetrated her flesh with one sharp stab as her hands gripped convulsively at his shoulders.

*   *   *

There is a scream of anguish from Sadie's bedroom. I have only just put her to bed, and it is an hour past her bedtime. Jason is still at work.

"What is it, Sadie?" I sound tired and cranky.

"My eye hurts, Mommy!" I lean over Sadie in her bed and inhale the just-washed fragrance of her skin. Then I look at her right eye, which is pink and oozing a yellowish fluid.

"Pinkeye. You'll have to stay home tomorrow and I'll take you to the doctor."

"But it hurts now!"

I put my hand on her forehead and stroke her hair back from her face. "Go to sleep and it'll feel better."

"I can't!" She begins to cry, and the angry, frightened sound reminds me of when she was a toddler. I ease myself into the bed and spoon myself around her, but even this comfort is not enough. She turns herself so that she is nestled into my neck and side, and her shaky breaths deepen and slow. Lulled by the unfamiliar sensation of someone in my arms, I fall asleep there and do not wake up until three thirty A.M.

I get up and walk into my own dark bedroom, where Jason is snoring lightly. My side of the bed is cold and I lie in it for an hour before finally falling asleep.

The next day I have conjunctivitis as well. My regular eye doctor is on vacation and I make an appointment with someone who is covering for him, a Dr. Freeman, who is all the way on the East Side in the sixties. After taking Sadie to the pediatrician, I hand her off to Hilda with a new Magic Tree House book and a Scooby Doo video, and remind them both that Ford will be coming around noon. Then I make my escape.

The East Side is a different world, a pretty, festive, bustling place where all the stunted sidewalk trees are strung with lights and all the store windows gleam with handsome objects cunningly arranged. This is the New York of romantic comedies and classic tearjerkers, and everyone walks around a little self-consciously, as if they have wandered onto a stage set. Even the lampposts are festooned with happy green and red bows and if you don't watch where you're going, a tourist will body slam you to the street.

Dr. Freeman's office is in one of those grand old Manhattan buildings, with a high, arched ceiling gilded with decorative whorls and patterns and a dark marble floor. I ride up to the eleventh floor and try to locate 1104. The numbers are all written in a calligraphic style that makes them hard to read, and I open a door which I instantly surmise is not the door to Dr. Freeman's office, as upscale opthalmologists do not generally display dildos in their waiting rooms.

And what a lot of dildos there are: pink ones, black ones, purple ones, smooth ones and strange bumpy ones which seem to have been molded from libidinous extraterrestrials. As I get my bearings, I take in the lavender-and-pink sign proclaiming that this is A Secret Place, the rack of videos with Georgia O'Keeffe–style vaginal flowers on the covers, jars of what appear to be lotion or oil, and a comprehensive selection of very comfortable-looking handcuffs.

A young man is standing by the counter, speaking with a lovely blonde saleswoman who looks like an elementary-school teacher from Iowa.

"And this one has an attachment that can stimulate the clitoris while the main shaft oscillates," she says. Then she looks at me. "Hi, come right in," she says. "I'll be with you in a minute."

I step obediently inside the shop. It is not like the other sex shops I have passed by in the village, where drag queens haggle and tourists titter over fake breasts and enormous harnesses. This shop reminds me of the expensive little boutiques where women go to find the perfect accessory. After a moment, I realize that, indeed, this is what this place is.

I find myself looking at one of the videos. *A Guide to Self Pleasure, for Women, by Women,*" it reads. Another offers advice on tantric sex. Moving along, I see what appears to be a real male penis. I poke it in the testicle, and it feels alarmingly like the skin of one of Sadie's realistic baby dolls.

"Now this one hits the G-spot," the saleswoman was saying. "Does your girlfriend like a strong touch or a light one? Because there are three settings—here, hold out your hand."

I try to imagine Jason coming into a shop like this to buy me an oscillating vibrator.

I try to imagine Jason coming into a shop like this to buy *another* woman an oscillating vibrator.

I try to imagine Jason coming into a shop like this for any reason at all, including mistaking it for an opthalmologist's office.

Nothing. Not even a mental snapshot.

I try *not* to imagine Ford. Dressed in something black that molds to the shape of his muscular chest. Arms folded. Face impassive. Myself handcuffed to a table, looking up at him defiantly.

"You can't make me talk."

"Not with pain, perhaps," he says, drawing closer, his voice almost gentle, something akin to regret flickering in the darkness of his eyes. "But there are other ways of eliciting information from spies. . . ."

I jolt out of the fantasy, much as I used to wake abruptly in the middle of algebra. I check my watch: No time to be tortured. Onward to Dr. Freeman.

I am on my way out, really I am, when I notice a vibrator shaped like a Japanese woman with a squirrel on her stomach. For a moment, I cannot imagine what the squirrel is for. Then the saleswoman appears. With her swingy, shiny, cornsilk hair and dimpled smile, she reminds me of one of those old Clairol ads. Does She or Doesn't She? Only her hairdresser knows for sure. With that coy look over the shoulder that says, maybe I'm not so damn wholesome as I appear. I may color my hair. I may wear black latex. Hey, I may do gynecological tricks with Ping-Pong balls. But you'll never really know for sure, will you?

The saleswoman points to the object in my hand and beams at me as if I were a particularly bright first grader. "I see you've found one of my favorite items," she says, "Here, hold out your hand." I comply and she demonstrates how the squirrel's tail can flick, flick, flick while the Japanese lady moves her head in a slow circle.

"Wow," I say.

"Do you prefer the look of a penis? Because if you do, there's this one." The saleswoman holds out a hot pink penis-shaped object, which seems to contain tiny marbles. "Myself, I like this one, because the little balls move up and down, like this."

"Sheesh."

"Or were you looking for something different?" She looks at me. Silence is not an option, and I have lingered too long to say that I was really looking for the eye doctor.

"I don't really know. I'm kind of a—you know—do it yourselfer." Somehow admitting to this is not so embarrassing when the saleswoman herself seems so unabashed.

"Well, if you've a mind to try something different, this is the best in the store, in my personal opinion." The saleswoman selects a paler pink tube, less openly phallic, that boasts a small hummingbird near the base. When she turns the device on, the hummingbird moves its wings and dips its beak.

"Silicone," she adds, "safe to boil and it has a nice smell, too."

As the object rotates against my palm in five different speeds the doorbell jingles and I turn to see a woman come in. She is gray-haired and matronly, in a Burberry coat and beige silk scarf.

"Be with you in a moment, Margie," says the saleslady.

"Oh, is that the happy hummingbird? I like that one," the lady says, nodding at the vibrator. "Gives you lovely, fluttery orgasms. Not too harsh."

"Maybe you'd like some time on your own to decide?" The saleswoman looks at me as if I am one of the less emotionally developed first graders in the class.

I know that my cheeks are probably as red as my eye, and this annoys me. Goddamn it, I used to be a bohemian! I smoked pot in college! I went skinny-dipping with boys!

"No," I say, looking the saleswoman right in the eye, "I've decided. I want this one."

"You won't be sorry," she informs me as she rings it up. One hundred and twenty dollars, but, as the matronly woman points out, quality means no loud buzzing sound, and that's worth its weight in gold.

"Let me know how it works for you," says the sales-woman as she wraps the vibrator like a present in purple tissue paper before slipping it into a plain white paper bag.

At Dr. Freeman's office, I cannot decide if the receptionist is looking at me strangely or not.

I return home to chaos. It seems that Jason got back early from work and tried to tell Hilda that she hadn't adequately cleaned something, which caused Hilda to threaten to quit, which launched Sadie into a plate-throwing, toy-stomping tantrum that demolished much of the house. There is a torn Harry Potter novel on top of the fish tank and a lot of doll hair all over the living room rug. At least I hope it's doll hair.

"And where the hell were you?" Jason demands as I struggle out of my coat. "You should have dealt with the Hilda situation weeks ago. You leave it to me and this is what happens. Well, deal with your own mess. I'm going out."

The Hilda situation? What Hilda situation? Hilda and I have an understanding: Like Burt Lancaster's savvy sergeant in *From Here to Eternity*, she's the one who's really running things.

"Mommy, Daddy tried to tell Hilda she's supposed to clean the floors! And toilets! He said we don't pay her to just push dust around and she said housekeeper didn't mean house cleaner and he said he didn't know there was a rule book and she said a lot of things really fast and then she gave me a hug and told me to be a good girl and walked out the door. And slammed it."

Sacrilege. Clean toilets? What was the man thinking! Everyone knows you have to hire one person to tidy and another to do serious cleaning. Our serious cleaner is a sinewy lady from Hungary with a complete list of her own requirements, including organic cleaning products and spelt-free bread. She does not, admittedly, clean very well, or maybe it's just that additive-free cleansers are not as strong as their chemically-laden counterparts. But as long as I remember to clean a bit after her, everything gets done very nicely.

But I would never, ever dream of asking Hilda to clean after the cleaner. Oh, lord, this is a diplomatic crisis. To put it to rights will require hours of feather-smoothing and possibly a raise. I take a moment to comfort Sadie and then begin sorting out the broken plates.

"We won't really lose Hilda, will we?" Sadie is sitting on the radiator, the only clear surface in the entire living room.

"I'll talk to Daddy."

Sadie runs into another room, and I lose myself in the seemingly endless process of righting cartons of crafts supplies, putting books back in bookcases, and sorting out what appears to be the entire contents of the linen closet, which Sadie has managed to throw over lampshades, paintings and the antique spinning wheel I bought in Virginia ten years ago.

When the living room is back to its usual state of controlled madness, I make my way into my bedroom.

"Look," Sadie is saying to Ford, "I found a present for me in Mommy's bag." Before I can scream no, no, please, no or fall into a convenient dead faint, Sadie has ripped open the wrapping paper, revealing the happy hummingbird in all its pink glory. She turns it on and it whirls and dips its beak, for all the world like some bizarre children's toy.

"I don't get it," Sadie says. "What's it for?"

Ford takes it from her. "I believe it may be a kind of cat toy."

"But we don't have a cat!"

"Maybe it's a present for someone who does."

"Oh." Sadie looks sulky. "Don't I get something?" Then she perks up. "Maybe it's for your puppy! Maybe it's a dog toy!"

Ford kneels down to look Sadie in the eye. "I don't think so, Sade. You see, dogs don't need fancy things to play with. They're more straightforward than cats—all it takes is a ball or two to make them happy." His sardonic gaze cuts to me and I'd like to tell him a thing or two about the undifferentiated enthusiasm of dogs, the lousy bastard, but Sadie is already turning to me, beaming. "Mom! Is this because . . . is this for . . . are we getting a cat?"

"Well, that's what we're going to talk to your dad about, but just let's go and put on some television right now, okay, sweetheart?" I take her hand and start pulling her away.

I avoid saying good-bye to Ford. I am contemplating an impromptu trip abroad to someplace where everyone is genial and drinks a lot and doesn't ask personal questions.

Thursday, December 6
10-ish

Linley's wife walked into the bedroom with a lightness of step that spoke of a background in dance, or the martial arts; she rolled the weight of her stride all along the sole of her foot, unlike the husband and child, who thumped heavily from room to room. Ford continued checking the closet wall for moisture. It would not serve his purposes to appear overly interested in any member of the family, least of all the loveless lady of the house.

"Hello, Ford." She still had a faint American accent, which made her sound a little bit Hollywood bad girl to his ears. Her husband sounded like he'd gotten his accent from the BBC, so he had to have started out somewhere working class, and their little girl had achieved something of an upper-middle-class clip from her school before she'd been shipped off to the countryside. But the lady herself was still from New Yawk and would have drunk cawfee, if there was any left to be had this side of the Atlantic.

That accent must have been something of a disadvantage for a woman living in London these days. The British public's impatience was turning to irritation: Would those damn Yanks never pull themselves out of their endless, mindless, gum-chewing, Coke swilling, hey-honey-let's-take-the-automobile-for-a-spin *holiday and join the bloody war effort before Jerry bombed his way into Buckingham Palace?*

Ford walked over to his tool kit, careful to favor his left leg as he bent to retrieve a hammer. Wouldn't do for the all-too observant Mrs. Linley to catch her 4F handyman moving like a fit and able potential soldier, lest the lady start to question his story more closely. With nothing better to occupy her intelligence, she might even start looking at him closely enough to notice what no one else had: That his darkly exotic features were Eurasian, not Welsh. Ford sometimes wondered if his superiors knew that to the Japanese, he was as suspect as he was to them. Perhaps they would trust him more if they knew that to his mother's people, he looked like a foreigner. As it was, Ford knew that if it hadn't been for his rare ability with languages, and his ability to pass as a non-Asian, he would never have been allowed to work this assignment. But while there were plenty of folks at HQ who spoke German, understanding Japanese as well was a far less common talent.

Ford was just beginning to secure the board he'd pried up back into position when he heard the abrupt feminine sniff and exhalation that means the same thing in every culture, whether it be English or American or Japanese. Tears. Swell, just what he needed.

"Mrs. Linley? I'm just finishing up here."

"Don't worry—you're the least of my problems."

Suddenly Ford longed for a cigarette with all the passion of love forsworn. When the bored housewife starts to confide in you, brother, you're in trouble.

Of course, he could turn it into useful trouble. Before he could stop himself, he moved closer to where she sat on the corner of her bed, crouching down so he was literally at her feet.

"You want to talk about it?"

She kept her face covered with her hands for a moment, then looked up. "Bad day at the hospital," she said at last.

"You don't have to go back there."

She looked at him sharply. "Don't I? What else should I do, then, to fill the empty days?"

Ford felt his heart trip into a faster rhythm. Christ, was she coming on to him? She didn't look like she was trying to seduce him. She looked like she was angry, or about to cry, or both; and she looked starkly beautiful in the way women can do in their thirties, when the underlying bone structure of cheeks and jaw is at its cleanest.

"You miss your daughter."

She did laugh at that, a quick, startled gasp of a laugh, and then she put her head down so that her forehead was resting on her knees. She was wearing trousers, as so many women had started to do these days. He was surprised to realize that he missed the sight of her calves in stockings. "God," she said, "I didn't think it would take so little to make my life feel— meaningless." Delilah lifted her head and met his eyes. "And, yes, I know that everyone around me is going through the same thing and not falling to pieces. But for me, without Sadie around—there's nothing, really. And maybe for all those other people—those other women—" Her voice caught, and she drew a breath.

"Shhh, it's all right." He didn't want her to continue. Suddenly he was aware of the emptiness of the old house, and of their isolation. Outside these walls, there was a row of other semidetached Victorians identical to this one, and within them other people were beginning to prepare their evening meals. But here, in this house, there was a growing sense of imminence as the late-afternoon light gilded the dust motes dancing on the invisible currents between them.

There had been something between them from the beginning, Ford realized. He had ignored it because his mandate had been clear: He was meant to be a fly on the wall, a silent and unobtru-

sive observer of the Linley household. He was not meant to be-come involved with the precocious little Linley girl, or to get him-self entangled with the all-too-perceptive wife. Even if it might seem like a route to gaining information about the husband's true loyalties, it was considered too risky.

But what if the situation were forced upon him? For reasons that Ford chose not to examine too closely, a rush of excitement flooded his veins, leaving him dry-mouthed and light-headed.

"You're not what you seem, are you, Ford?"

Her question caught him by surprise and for a moment, as he looked into her pale blue eyes, so surprising against the darkness of her eyelashes and brows, he thought she knew everything.

"What were you, before the war?"

"A carpenter."

"No, you weren't. What were you, Ford? A thief? I don't mind."

He was sweating now, but he managed to keep a mask of com-posure on his face. "Why do you think I might have been a bur-glar, Mrs. Linley?"

She reached down and touched his face then, the lightest of touches, but his nerves transmitted the sensation straight to his groin. "Because of your face. Your eyes. Wary, watchful, careful face. Hooded eyes. The eyes of a criminal. Or a cop. Are you a cop, Ford?"

"I can't be a police officer, Mrs. Linley. My leg." Rising un-steadily to his feet, Ford massaged his left thigh as though it were cramping.

"Ah, yes, your leg." She was smiling into his eyes now, teas-ing him. And then, to his shock, her hand was on his thigh. "Does it hurt you much?"

"Just when I stay too long in one position." Her eyes said she wasn't buying it. What was going on here? How had she found him out? His heart was racing now, and yet his fear was mixed with an almost painful excitement. He was so hard that if she moved her hand a fraction of an inch to the left he felt he might explode.

"My husband doesn't pay you enough to make it worth your while to work here, Ford. And that board you keep fixing and then prising loose again—it can't really be taking up this much of your time. So tell me why you're really here." The flirtatiousness had left her face and her voice. Her hand was still on his thigh, massaging him, and it was becoming abundantly clear that what he was feeling was not pain. Ford knew that whatever he came up with, it had to be now and it had to be good.

"I love you. I'm obsessed with you. Here!" Ford grabbed her slender wrist and yanked her up against him so she could feel his straining erection through the wool of his trousers. *"This is what you do to me, Delilah. I know you want me, too. I feel it—that fool of a husband of yours doesn't matter, he neglects you, and I—mmmmph!"* Suddenly her mouth was plastered to his as she kissed him with such unexpected fierceness that Ford fell backward on the bed. Her arms twined around his neck as he reached around and pressed the firm roundness of her buttocks, making her moan.

"Delilah," he whispered, then kissed her with everything he had, entering her mouth with his tongue, moving his hands up to tangle in her silky hair.

"Wait," she gasped, but he knew he couldn't afford to stop touching her and let her start thinking again. He nipped at her neck and then looked her straight in the eyes, letting his fear show, and behind that fear, the fierceness of his desire for her.

"Let me inside you, Delilah Linley." He kept his voice a whisper. *"Let me share your secrets."*

"This isn't real," she said. *"You're hiding something."*

"Yes," he said, *"I'm hiding something. And this is meant to distract you. But that's also just an excuse, because I've been wanting you for weeks and it could cost my life to have you."* Ford no longer knew what he was saying. He only knew that his primary objective was to seduce, and that once he'd possessed her, she would be on his side, because she was lonely and empty and

loyal and if he truly became her lover, she would fight for him.
And he also knew that he was aching for her because somehow she
had managed to see past his disguise.

"Let me inside you," he said again, and their eyes met.

"So she was worried about a yeast infection? God, what is our mother, sixteen all of a sudden?"

I am feeling too guilty about confiding Mom's secret to roll my eyes back at Tamara. I only told her because there has been an uncomfortable flatness between us all day. My sister has come into the city to help me shop for a dress to wear to Jason's Christmas party next week.

I try to think of a way to change the subject away from our mother. Tamara is wearing a navy suit with a logo I don't recognize and a fur coat. I am wearing black jeans, a black turtleneck and my long olive green Russian Army coat, which I have finally remembered to get back from the cleaner's.

"Nice fur," I say. "And at least standard poodles aren't on anybody's endangered list."

"Actually, it's shearling lamb. And unless your shoes and bag are plastic, you might want to consider your next sarcastic remark more carefully. Are you on antidepressants right now, Delilah?"

Isn't everybody? These days the only women I know who aren't taking mood stabilizers are pregnant, nursing, or in the first six weeks of a new relationship. "Why do you ask?"

"You seem a little on edge."

Trying to turn the conversation back to her, I ask Tam if she is seeing anybody new. Her answer takes half an hour and depresses us both, so I start to joke with her about my Ford fantasies.

The next thing I know it is big-sister time and Tamara is giving me a lecture on marital danger signs and asking if I know where all our bank accounts are kept.

I say something along the lines of, I'm pretty sure Jason's not really a Nazi sympathizer and Ford's not with the Secret Service, so an affair is definitely out.

Tamara still appears unconvinced.

In movies and sitcoms, sisters are either bitter rivals or best friends, but Tamara and I are neither. We have phases of feeling close and phases of feeling wildly out of sync, and most of the time we bop around somewhere in the middle.

Right now, somewhere in the middle is the women's department of Bloomingdale's, and my sister and I are walking around a display of lavishly sequined ball gowns clearly designed for somebody else's life and not for the hot buffet at R. B. International. It is still early enough in the season that the almost subliminal susurrus of piped-in Christmas music is still effective. I want to buy gay apparel, drink things reminiscent of milk and blood, wear lipstick the color of poisonous berries. I want to frolic through the darkest night before the winter solstice, goddamn it.

Even though I am Jewish, I feel I have the right to enjoy Christmas, as I consider it to be basically a pagan holiday. After all, most of the fun stuff has been borrowed from the Druids—the mistletoe, the holly, the Yule log, the human sacrifice.

I once had a nun lecture me on the relative meanings of Christmas and Easter for an hour and a half at a cocktail party before I had a chance to explain that the last item was just meant as a little joke.

"How's this?" Tamara holds up something long and blue that reminds me of what Julie the cruise director used to wear on the Love Boat.

I shake my head. Tamara, who was born with a perfectly straight nose and is only three years older and fifteen pounds heavier than I am, has a penchant for the matronly. At twenty-nine, she began to dress in the kind of stiffly preppy clothing that suggests golf has replaced sex as the exercise of choice. Now fast approaching forty and still unmarried, Tamara lives ten minutes from our parents in one of those huge New Jersey condominiums, complete with health club, pool and a permanent reservoir of semi-successful bachelors. I assume that she is still hoping to meet Mr. Right, Esquire, to join the practice of Levine and Levine, Teaneck's premier father-and-daughter law firm, although secretly I think my sister would do better with a bald, muscled, grinning Mr. Clean type.

Now what do you think those ad execs were thinking way back when, to have this sexy piratical weight-lifter type with an earring in his ear, for God's sake, appearing to bored housewives as the patron saint of clean floors? It almost sounds like the premise for a porn film. Want to polish the floors, dearie? Let me show you how powerful clean can be. . . .

"How about something short, Del?"

I look at the cocktail waitress's outfit that Tamara is offering for my approval and shake my head, no, no, a thousand times no.

"Well, what *do* you want? And please, no more Morticia Addams black with the droopy sleeves. I still remember you at your Bat Mitzvah. . . ."

"Oh, God, not this again . . ."

"Daddy nearly had a heart attack when he saw you in that skirt and those boots with the stiletto heels. . . ."

I used to wear stiletto heels? *Tamara* used to wear stiletto heels. Heels that weren't even in fashion in the early eighties, I might add.

" . . . and then when Great Aunt Shirley was toasting you, you had to start quoting that crazy poet who stuck her head in the oven—"

"Sylvia Plath. Listen, I never asked for Mom and Dad to rent out that hotel ballroom. . . ."

"All I'm saying is, time to outgrow the tortured-artist routine. You're getting too old for it, anyway. Black makes you look sallow."

These are the things you wish someone would have told you back before you bought an entire wardrobe of black turtlenecks. "Gee, thanks, Tam. I'm so glad I decided to invite you along."

My sister sighs and makes a face that reminds me forcibly of our mother. "Don't turn this into an argument. Let's start over. What kind of thing were you hoping to find?"

"I was thinking sloppy sexy. Vaguely nineteen thirties droopy and silky, like something Katharine Hepburn would have worn in her debutante phase."

"You're talking nightgown, Delilah. Try again."

"Something Emma Thompson might have worn in *Sense and Sensibility.*"

"I'll say it again—nightgown. You can't go in some flimsy *schmatta*, Del. Your breasts need some support."

This is the real reason I asked my sister to help me shop. Painful honesty. In the spirit of filial truthfulness, I let slip that I think her current hairstyle—a flip—is frightening rather than charmingly retro. My sister, who can be really charming, touches her bangs and says, "Are we talking too Marlo Thomas in *That Girl?*"

"We're talking scary Betty Crocker hair."

I tousle her into a looser look and we resume shopping with the equation of power balanced more easily between us.

We settle on a black, tight-sleeved, empire-waisted dress that dips down low in the front. Even my sister agrees it is a flattering choice, but insists I buy a choker of dark red beads and matching earrings to add color, because, she says, I never wear enough blusher.

We have enough time left to retreat to a Starbucks for a hit of caffeine.

"So," says Tamara over her tall decaffeinated cappuccino with skim milk, "what does he look like, this plumber of yours?"

I sip my espresso and try to think of a description she might understand. "He's boy-next-door exotic."

"So sort of a hunky Boy Scout?"

"No, he's more, I don't know, archly bemused. I think he's part Asian. Part something."

"Is he short? Sort of quiet and polite? I don't really find Japanese men attractive."

I suddenly wish I had a cigarette, even though I haven't smoked one in ten years. "You forgot the buck teeth and glasses."

"Oh, here it comes. Little Miss Politically Correct . . ."

"All right, try this. He's banked fires, all simmering passion barely held in check. Remember those books you used to read, where all the men were sort of emotionally constipated until the right woman came along?"

My sister considers this. "I suppose I can see it. Sort of Dean Cain, or more Keanu Reeves?"

"Less boyish."

"Benjamin Bratt?"

"Not so elegant."

"I don't see it."

Tamara and I have played casting couch since we were fifteen. The criteria: Who would play your current inamorado onscreen? In my life, I have had one Simon LeBon of Duran Duran, one Antonio Banderas, two Gary Sinises, three Aidan Quinns, one Eric Roberts before he got scary, one Ralph Fiennes sans accent, one Bruce Willis avec hair, a Jeff Goldblum who dumped me without warning and a Denzel. Well, one of the Sinises was really more Eric Stoltz. I came close to having a Burt Lancaster but he was just a little too old, sort of Burt in late-sixties Swimmer Mode rather than robust pirate Burt, so I passed. And Jason always confounded me, being a bizarre mixture of James Taylor, Donny Osmond and William Hurt.

But Ford, oddly enough, seems to be defying description altogether.

Tamara reapplies her lipstick. "And he's not short?"

I close my eyes for a moment. "No, he's not short."

Suddenly we are looking at each other and we are both laughing. "Oh, all right then," Tamara says. "Go for it."

I stop laughing. I think I may even stop breathing for a moment. "What?"

"You heard me. Look, you're asking what I think about the idea of you cheating on Jason with this guy. You think I'm going to get all huffy and offended and say, No, no, no getting your pipes cleaned by the hired help. Then you get to say that I'm naïve and that a little judicious cheating is what makes most marriages work in the long term."

I lean forward, elbows on the table. "So let me get this straight. You're saying I *should* betray my husband?"

"Betray's a big word. I'm not saying you should leave Jason for the handyman. That's betrayal. I'm saying there's really not that big a difference between spending your afternoons mentally shacked up with Mr. Bedroom Eyes and doing the deed for real."

"I can't believe you're saying this. . . ."

"As long as you're safe about it, and as long as you keep it in the harmless diversion category, whom does it really hurt?"

I stare at Tamara's plumply pretty face. "You're seeing a married man, aren't you? That's what this is really about. You want me to cheat, because then you won't lose the moral high ground."

"Oh, please! Like you even have a moral high ground! It was flooded under during the first Bush administration."

"I may not have been a nun when Jason met me—"

"You were *shtupping* three guys at once!"

"But I never cheated on anyone. Everyone knew what the score was. I didn't keep secrets, Tam."

We sit there for a moment, unsure what to say to each other next. It's not quite out and out war, but battle lines are being drawn. And then I check my watch, to make sure I'm absolutely, positively not going to be late picking Sadie up from school.

Tamara, always keen to take offense, notices my gesture. "Running away so soon?"

"I have to get Sadie from school."

"Why can't Hilda do it?"

"She quit because Jason tried to tell her what to do. And now he says we don't need her, she's too expensive."

My sister is round-eyed with surprise. "She's too expensive? But your husband once said that if it weren't for Hilda, he'd have to buy another apartment, because there wouldn't be room for any of his stuff in all your mess."

"What do you do, memorize his speeches?"

"No, he just repeats them all the time."

"Well, Tam, I guess money's getting a little tight, and Jason felt . . ."

"Wait a minute." Tamara slams her peach-tinted and beringed hands down on the table, making our drinks slop a little. "Delilah, the man pulls down six figures. Okay, so the big pre-war apartment costs a bundle. But Sadie goes to public school. You hardly spend a lot on home decoration, and this is the first time you've bought new clothes in over a year. So what exactly is this big money problem?"

Income, taxes, and budget considerations have always been more or less Jason's concern. I may be a feminist, but I am a feminist who stinks at math. "I'm not exactly sure," I say carefully. "I think Jason's bonus was smaller this year. . . ."

Tamara is looking at me as if I'm singing "Stand by Your Man." "Listen, you know how it is. Everyone always has their own idea of where to scrimp and where to save. One person thinks a cab ride is a ridiculous luxury, another person thinks it's a basic necessity. So Jason thinks some of my necessities are luxuries. Like Hilda."

Tamara thumps her hands down on the table again. "Look, you've always been a bit of a space cadet, it's part of your charm, and Lord knows Mom and Dad have always babied you. . . ."

"Keep on topic, please."

"But really, Delilah, you can't just delegate all the grown-up stuff to your husband. What did Jason earn last year, without bonus? Is his job in danger? Have you two had some big medical expense I don't know about?"

"I, uh, I'm not exactly . . ." I am beginning to feel like Porky Pig, hemming and hawing. "No."

"So why is there not enough money all of a sudden? Is there somewhere the money's going that he's not telling you about—to a mistress, to a drug habit, to a secret Run-Away-From-Home fund? What's Jason hiding from *you*, Sis?"

And then I understand that Tamara is still worried that my daydreams about Ford are symptoms of some deep-rooted marital malignancy. I want to tell her that she is mistaken—my fantasies are not the first cracks presaging an earthquake. But she is single, and she looks to marriage as the beginning of a companionable journey with frequent stops for sex, conversation and the occasional concert or Broadway show. And all that is true—for a year, or five, or until you have children.

How can I explain that after a while, you may find yourself in the parallel-universe stage of marriage, where his world and yours barely intersect? Oh, once in a while you meet in the middle of the bed for sex or conversation, and there may even be the occasional concert or Broadway show, but in general, you are like England and America—two nations divided by one language, because a word that means one thing on this side of the divide may mean something else entirely on the other.

All my married friends seem to be living this stage out in one form or another. It doesn't mean everything's about to fall apart.

"Listen," I say. "Remember how you were laughing at Mom's flipping out about a little yeast infection? Well, *they're* not exactly on the same page, and we don't think Dad's having a big secret affair."

Tamara shrugs her shoulders and gives me a rueful smile. "So maybe Mom is. One thing I've learned from practicing law: If your client is acting suspicious, it means he's probably hiding something."

Jason arrives home late, in a wonderful mood. He swings Sadie up and around and then asks her to keep him company while he changes out of his suit. I can hear them from the other room:

> JASON: So who did you play with in school today?
> SADIE: Serena. Who did you play with at work?
> JASON: Irina. Isn't that funny? Their names sound almost the same.
> SADIE: Is she pretty?
> JASON: Nah, she's built like a tank and has a face a little like a bulldog's.
> SADIE: (Screams with laughter.)
> JASON: Now, you won't go repeating that, will you, Princess?

They curl up together on our bed for Sadie's nighttime story. I can't remember my parents reading to me after the first grade, but I am glad Sadie still enjoys it. Tonight it's *Puss in Boots*, with the crafty feline calling his poor master the Marquis of Carabas.

"I want a cat, Daddy," Sadie says, and yawns hugely. Jason's bright blue eyes meet mine, and there is a kind of twinkle of rueful humor in them that I recognize. Ah, yes, that's the you I thought you were when I married you.

"Well, I don't know, Sadie. You know how Mommy hates cats. . . ."

Sadie sits upright as if electrocuted. "She doesn't hate cats!"

"She doesn't? Are you sure?"

"You don't hate cats, do you, Mommy? You like animals!"

I smile at Jason and he smiles back. It's almost like sex: Wordless communication, the promise of pleasure. Except it's Sadie's pleasure we're anticipating.

"Daddy, if Mommy likes cats and you like cats, then can we have a cat? A kitten with stripes? Daddy? Answer me right now! Stop smiling and talk to me, please please please?"

"Just no big hairy monsters, please," says Jason, and then we both pounce on him with glee, tickling and laughing and rolling around.

And then Sadie yells something about calling Serena and barrels out of the room, leaving her parents tumbled together on the bed.

It is nearly eleven when Sadie finally falls asleep at the foot of our bed. Jason carries her into her own room and then returns.

"Move over," he says. I scoot a few inches over onto my side and then he sighs. "No, no, this way." I move toward him until we are cuddled together, his arm around me, my head pillowed on his shoulder. Well, hello, what's going on here?

"Want to watch CNN?" I ask.

"Mmm," he says.

"Should I turn off the light? Are you ready to sleep?"

"Mmm."

"What's brought on this sudden change of mood, Jason? I swear, one minute you're a stressed-out grump, and the next you're—"

"Massaging your back."

So I lie there, silently trying to figure out what's going on, with me as well as with him. I keep imagining my questions in bold print, like the oversimplified discussion topics in the back of a women's issue novel: Why do you think Delilah isn't simply pleased that her husband is turning to her again? What do you think has caused Jason's sudden renewal of interest?

"Delilah. You're so tense you're vibrating. Stop trying to analyze everything and just go with the flow." His hand moves in slow circles on my back, but all I can think is, there had to be some precipitating event. What am I missing?

"Relax, Del." He turns me over in his arms and starts to kiss me in earnest, but we are out of the habit of intimacy and for some strange reason, I feel like I used to feel when I was thirteen: That there is a basic level of weirdness in opening your mouth to somebody else's tongue. Without the mindless impulse of passion to guide us, we fumble for remembered rhythms.

"Is that good? Does that feel good?"

Actually, no. Which you would know if you were listening to my body language.

"Are you close?"

I thought I'd broken him of this irritating habit. We're not negotiating a contract, Jason. You have to pay attention to the nonverbal cues. But once the question has been posed, I am faced with the age-old female dilemma—supply a neat couplet of gasp-gasp to complete the coupling, or go for the more honest, ambiguous, open-ended terminus? I suck in a breath to reply and Jason thinks he has his answer. Afterward I excuse myself to go to the bathroom and wash off, because the last thing I need are stains on the sheets.

The last of the bohemians bites the dust.

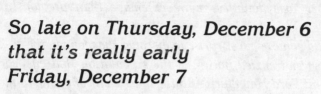

So late on Thursday, December 6 that it's really early Friday, December 7

It was one thing to have been caught doing something illegal; that was excusable, for Viscount Ford Hawthorne-Blythe was a member of an elite class allowed the occasional vice, so long as it was done on the quiet. But to have demonstrated cowardice—that was quite another matter, for while polite society might forgive a gentleman for participating in a duel, it would grant no such pardon to one who was known to have fled the field of honor. As to the veracity of the report that he had turned on his heel and run from his opponent, Ford would make no reply.

"You see the evidence of the wound," he would say, proffering his injured right leg, which still appeared muscular beneath expertly fitted buff trousers, "and the doctor's report verifying the direction of the bullet as anterior. So what else needs to be said?"

Yet the very event that had ruined his standing among the pillars of society served to enhance his stature elsewhere. Lean and handsome despite his injury, Ford developed something of a reputation among the Prince of Wales's fast set. He was just outcast enough to appeal to Bertie, who enjoyed the younger man's caustic wit and irreverent asides. Ford's limp may have kept him from dancing, but it did not diminish his attractiveness among the

sparkling ladies who warmed beds other than their husbands'.
The subject of Ford's disinclination for these ladies was much dis-
cussed, and it was finally agreed upon by all that the poor vis-
count's injury was doubtless more extensive than previously
imagined.

So it should come as no surprise to discover the wonder, the ag-
itation, the sheer frenzied nature of the speculation that ensued
when Viscount Ford Hawthorne-Blythe married a commoner and
an American, the brassy, auburn-haired heiress to a vast mercan-
tile fortune. What could have possessed the sardonic Ford to
marry so very far beneath him? Without the added incentive of
producing an heir, even the lure of the American's millions
seemed insufficient to account for the union.

In truth, the lady herself was wondering what had induced her
husband to offer for her, for here she was on her wedding night,
lying in the great medieval bed where countless generations of
Hawthorne-Blythes had been conceived, and her new bridegroom
was nowhere to be seen. Tall and gangly, Delilah Lewinson knew
that most of the men her father had paraded before her were attracted more to her dowry than to personal attributes. Could it be
that the Viscount had changed his mind about making her his wife
in fact as well as form?

"Hello, Delilah."

Startled, Delilah turned to see the man she had married lurch-
ing unsteadily across the Aubusson carpet. In the flickering can-
dlelight, she could see that his brow was beaded with perspiration
and his normally dusky skin tone was tinged with pallor.

"My lord? Are you unwell?"

Ford's eyes sharpened with a glint of humor. "I am not foxed,
my dear, if that is your concern."

"It is not." Delilah was very aware of her unbound breasts, her
naked legs beneath the thin, embroidered white cotton nightgown
that had been her mother's parting gift.

"Calm yourself, lady, you look nearly as undone as I do, and I haven't dealt you an injury, yet." Ford's mouth twisted into a wry grin, and Delilah blushed to think of the intimate injury he meant to inflict on her virgin flesh. Then he came closer, and Delilah could see the lines of tension around his mouth.

"You're in pain."

"All that standing around, promising to honor you with my body. Don't suppose virgin brides are allowed to stand up and give their lusty husbands a hand, now?"

This Delilah knew how to do. Her older brother, Lionel, had been felled by a wasting sickness, and she had grown quite used to helping bear his weight. As she slipped her hand around her new husband's waist, he turned to her, and for a moment they each felt the pressure of the other's body, the warmth of the contact, and stilled. For a moment, eyes as black as ebony met eyes as blue as a Colorado sky, and then Delilah looked away.

"Come," she said, "don't be afraid to put your weight on me. I'm quite a strapping girl, as all the English ladies keep reminding me."

But Ford remained as he was, his lean frame pressed against the voluptuous swell of her breast. "I didn't choose you for your money, you know," he said, his voice hoarse. "I picked you because your father had worked with his hands. Because people told me—it was reported—you were unrefined."

Delilah's eyes were round as she whispered, "You . . . liked that I was not . . . delicate, as ladies of rank should be?"

Ford's arm tightened around her, surprising her with its strength. "I am crippled, my flesh marred by ugly scars that might offend a more delicate lady's sensibility. And there is more. . . . My right leg is weakened. For a woman to be with me, she must be . . . clever in country matters."

Country matters. Delilah knew that term, and all it implied; farmboys plundering milkmaids up against the haystacks, lusty *wenches who would think nothing of tossing up their skirts for a likely lad.*

"I assure you, I am pure, sir," she said.

"Pure as in untouched, or pure as in too milk-fed to enjoy a man's touch?" She did not see his smile; she could hardly bear to meet his eyes while talking of such subjects.

"Let me help you to the bed," she said.

"Meaning, you know your duty. But I was once thought to be a man who could bring a woman pleasure."

Now Delilah did look at her husband, her cheeks red with embarrassment. "Will you come to bed or not, sir?"

"Delilah." His hand contracted around her waist, and something about that simple contact with his warm, callused fingers quickened her heartbeat. "There are things I can never tell you. About this wound that afflicts me. About where I may be forced to ride in the darksome hours of the night, on an errand that I would not have you mistake for amorous wanderings."

She opened her mouth to speak, and Ford pressed his finger against her lips, causing her to give a small, involuntary shiver.

"But I wish you to know that I chose you because I wished—I hoped—that with your open, frank nature, with your strength, you might be a true wife to me." Ford's sudden laugh was harsh in the quiet room. "Yet now I regret my action, for I cannot help but think that a nature as dark as my own will compromise the virtue of one so innocent."

"I hardly think standing here like this compromises my virtue."

Ford's laugh was softer, throatier this time as he brought his other arm around to bring her flush against him. "Then you might be very surprised, my little American." His arousal nudged bluntly at the thin fabric covering the juncture of her thighs, drawing a startled gasp from Delilah's lips. "Can you help me, I wonder, my wife? Can you help me be a man again? The vi-

cious ladies of Bertie's court think I am . . . ruined. And I was too much a coward to try my luck at proving them wrong."

"You don't feel ruined to me, sir," she said, a smile playing about her full lips.

I stop fantasizing abruptly when I realize that a sudden change in sexual behavior is one of the classic warning signs that the other spouse may be taking a little detour from the marital highway. It occurs to me that no one describes a woman as being "built like a tank, with a face like a bulldog" unless she is actually extremely attractive. It is the kind of hyperbole that guilty husbands employ. Add the mention of a mysterious Irina to the sudden lift in Jason's mood, and his miraculous surge of interest in my familiar person, and what does it spell?

I think I had better have a look through our financial records.

Jason Green
Visa Platinum Select
Statement Date 12/08/02

11/02	Asia Gardens	New Jersey	$40.52
11/03	American Cowboy	New York	$100.59
11/03	Zaftigue	New York	$600.00
11/06	Liquors	New York	$120.39
11/06	The Russian Tea Room	New York	$300.50
11/18	The Day and Night Inn	New Jersey	$284.00

In addition, there are two canceled checks, both made out to Caroline Moore, resident psychotherapist and Halle Berry look-alike.

Asia Gardens I understand: That's a business lunch. American Cowboy is the hat to impress the Stetson clients.

Liquors is our standard order of gin and Chardonnay. But which client warranted a trip to the Russian Tea Room? And why is Jason writing checks to Caroline?

Last but certainly not least on my list of questions: I am not aware of Jason having spent any nights away last month, so he must have rented a room at the Day and Night Inn—during the daytime?

I check October's statement and there are four more checks made out to Caroline Moore, although no record of any motels.

There is no mention of anyone named Irina. Maybe she is a prostitute.

If Jason is seeing a prostitute, I could have caught something.

No, no, I am turning into my mother, Our Lady of Perpetual Fretting.

What on earth could Jason be paying Caroline Moore for? One thing's for certain: It's not therapy. Jason once said that he would only go in for analysis if he found a psychiatrist he felt was smarter than he is. And he doesn't believe in psychologists, let alone psychotherapists—he calls them "human trainers." Plus, he hates having anyone in the building knowing our business.

It is two in the morning. Now it is two thirty. It is three. I cannot read or watch TV or even think clearly about what this means or what I will do if there is something going on. All I can do is sit here and feel scared. For someone who has lusted a lot in her mind, I am finding it very hard to accept that Jason might have been unfaithful.

It is four in the morning and I think I may have a yeast infection, either caused by the sudden resumption of marital relations or by stress, or both.

On the bright side, I have managed to finish my script. I

wonder if the actress who plays Goody Two-shoes Skylar will mind that I gave her a little psychotic episode during her scene with that bitch, Ruby.

It is six thirty now and I think I was imagining things. Sadie is awake and watching The Cartoon Network with Jason, who is still in a very good mood. He wants to know if I would like to go to Florida with Sadie in February. Suddenly, we do not appear to be having money problems.

Could Jason have had some other reason for getting rid of Hilda?

When I first met Jason, he was very impressed by my lack of interest in his money. This was the end of the eighties, a decade when everyone was fascinated by money, to the extent that movies were actually made about the exciting climb up the corporate ladder.

Of course, there were also movies made about the solid, conservative young man who falls from the neat, corporate, wing-tipped New York to the underworld of some bohemian woman who dwells in dangerous thrift-shop decadence on Avenue A.

I think that one of those movies must have been playing in Jason's head when we met at my cousin Benjamin's bar mitzvah in Teaneck, New Jersey. He was there, ostensibly, because he was friends with Benjamin's older brother, David. But to paraphrase Jane Austen, it is a truth universally acknowledged that a single man in possession of a good fortune does not attend the bar mitzvah of a non-relative, unless he is in want of a wife.

Among all the permed and shoulder-padded women,

cheekbones boldly painted warrior red, I must have looked like one of the wait staff in a little black dress with a white collar, black tights and Mary Janes. I was doing my impression of downtown folkie doing an impression of conservative, and if you leaned close enough to me, you could smell the moth balls (the dress was circa 1942).

"Couldn't you at least have done something about your hair," my sister hissed. I believe I must have been the only flathead woman in the synagogue.

"It's a look," I hissed back. "Now shut up so I can listen to Benny whine his way through the blessings."

I heard a snort of laughter and turned to see this really attractive guy. He had the kind of shaggy hair that even corporate men wore back then, and a faint shadow of fashionable stubble, and his eyes were clever and amazingly blue.

"You're sarcastic. I like that in a woman."

"I'm sardonic," I said. "Sarcasm is easy. As Oscar Wilde always said," I added. As I have mentioned, quoting is more attractive in the young, who are otherwise supposed to know nothing.

Jason, as I recall, looked suitably intimidated. "So," he said after a pause, "what is it you do?"

Because I was bored, both with the endless ritual of early adolescent Jewish manhood and with the question of my occupation (graduate student, at the time), I stepped close enough to Jason to give him a good whiff of mothballs, and whispered in his ear, "Unspeakable acts, if you play your cards right."

I didn't find out that he was in law school until much later that night, when we were naked on my lumpy futon. I thought it didn't really matter, because this was, after all, nothing but a one-night stand. A nice, friendly one-night stand, the kind where no one gets hurt because it's not that he doesn't like you, it's just that he's got to get back to finals at Harvard, and it's not that you don't like him, it's just that you are an artist, consumed by your art, and by your forty-five close and intimate college and post-grad friends.

And then Dad had his heart attack and everything changed. Seduced by my early air of indifference, Jason kept driving from Harvard to spend time with me, at my parents' Teaneck home, at the East Village apartment I shared with four friends, at the hospital. By the time it was clear Dad wasn't going to die, Jason and I were a couple. The joke at the time was that Jason was taking the familiar female role of the one eager to get married, and I was acting like a man, reluctant to surrender my freedom.

Of all the things I feared, I never worried that Jason would cheat on me. I always figured that if anyone had an affair, it would be me, stifled by a life of conformity.

Suddenly I wonder what's become of my old roommates. They came to my wedding. I didn't exactly turn into Princess Diana afterward, too busy with royal engagements to see her old proletariat pals. So why did we lose touch?

Go back ten years and I would have sworn that my brief affair with Mr. Harvard Law School would end, and that what would endure would be the circle of friends who knew the most embarrassingly intimate details of my life (such as the panic attack from a particularly strong bong hit, which sent me to the emergency room of Mt. Sinai, complaining of chest pains). I mean, those were the people I thought were my soul mates, the ones who could make sangria out of 7UP and Bordeaux and write politically incorrect bad poetry that made me laugh so hard I lost bladder control.

Okay, maybe that was because of the sangria, but the point is, did I really realize that I was trading Leah and Carlos and Devon and Zohar for the Ikea-commercial illusion of one bosom companion amidst the ready-to-assemble maple-finish furniture?

Jason has taken Sadie to school. I am rechecking that credit-card bill. A–hah. I knew I missed something. Zaftigue. What is a Zaftigue, and why is it worth $500?

ZAFTIGUE: Hello, Zaftigue.

ME: Hello. Um, I'm calling because, because . . . could you please tell me what kind of establishment this is?

ZAFTIGUE: Certainly. This is a boutique for the fuller-figured woman.

ME: Ah. By fuller figured, do you mean . . . I'm usually a size eight, but I'm fairly tall. Would you have anything that might, you know, fit me?

ZAFTIGUE: I'm afraid not. You sound as if you are tall and slim. We cater to tall women and petite women who are . . . more generously proportioned.

ME: Thank you.

ZAFTIGUE: Have a nice day.

ME: Wait! One more question. Do you have . . . Do you carry big, muumuu kind of dresses? Or do you have—I don't know how to put this . . . party dresses? Lingerie?

ZAFTIGUE: We carry a full line of designer clothing. Our dresses and slacks are very pretty, and yes, we have some very nice lacy brassiere-and-panty sets. But as I said, our sizing would be too . . .

ME: It's for a gift. I'm thinking of something for my sister. Bigger sister. Uh, do you have garter belts?

ZAFTIGUE: Absolutely.

ME: Honeymoon-type nightgowns?

ZAFTIGUE: Is your sister getting married?

ME: Do you have them?

ZAFTIGUE: Why don't you drop by and visit us? Or if
you live outside the city, we have a catalogue. . . .

I write down the store's address, thinking, *Jason's buying
$500 worth of clothes for a large woman.* The mysterious
Irina? Maybe she's a big, ripe peach of a woman, all rosy
Slavic cheeks and flaxen hair. A hefty East European Heidi
who can cook pierogi and give a back rub at the same
time.

Or maybe she has some other skill. Classical piano.
Watercolors. Rocket science. We all have that cannibalis-
tic desire to consume the possessor of some longed-for
attribute.

I write the script several different ways. Angry and accusa-
tory. Calm and almost objectively curious. Gentle and
pained. So, tell me, Jason, I say, playing the devious Ruby,
the long-suffering Skylar, the tightly controlled Blackjack,
what's going on?

But for some reason, Sadie has trouble falling asleep, and
Jason and I take turns lying down in her bed with her,
stroking her back. It is almost eleven when we sit down to
eat our dinner—reheated Chinese food.

Jason spears a dumpling with one chopstick and gestures
at the frog candle burning in the center of the table. "What
is that—more of Sadie's witchcraft?"

"We ran out of Shabbat candles. Listen, I need to talk to
you about something."

"Make it quick, I'm exhausted," he replies, shoveling in another bite of Moo Goo Gai Pan.

"I was going through our financial records . . ."

"Christ, if you have that much free time, clear out the damn boxes in the living room."

"Jason, I found some things that seem very curious to me. Why have you written checks to Caroline Moore? And there is a boutique called Zaftigue where I know *I* didn't buy anything. . . ."

Jason is looking at me with his mouth hanging open. There are dark shadows under his eyes, and he reminds me a little of Jack Nicholson, hearing the angry ghosts telling him that his wife's to blame for all his troubles. "What, Jason? Why are you looking at me like—"

"I just can't fucking believe this! You think I'm having an *affair*?"

Well, it's hardly unheard of. I mean, it's not as if I've just accused him of collecting Nazi memorabilia or wearing frilly underwear. "I'm not saying that. I'm just saying there are these bills that I don't understand. . . ."

"Caroline has been doing some career counseling with me, not that it's any of your business. And I bought my mother a dress for her birthday. But I do not, repeat, do not have the patience to sit here and have you accusing me of things I didn't do."

"I didn't accuse you!"

"If you want to look for what's wrong in our marriage, Delilah, I suggest you take a look at yourself. The problem's not with me. And now, if you will excuse me, I am exhausted from working my ass off to support you and our daughter, and I am going to finish my supper in the living room. Please do not follow."

I watch my husband stalk off with a tray of Chinese food,

thinking, career counseling? And why exactly is that none of my business?

But in general, I am relieved by Jason's reaction. I hadn't really expected to hear that Jason was having a wild fling with a large Russian woman, or that he was paying the stunning, intellectual and newly pregnant Caroline Moore for unprofessional favors, but still, you never know. And if he were having an affair, I'd have to decide whether or not to leave him. I'd have to choose between accepting that my conservative husband was the one in the marriage who had the wild passion going on, or else wind up spending every other weekend alone while Sadie slept over with Daddy and Daddy's new girlfriend Bambi.

Every ordinary, mother-daughter tussle over brushing teeth or doing homework would become loaded with emotional baggage. I would never feel free to just yell or get angry if Sadie talked back, because then Sadie might say that she hated me and wanted to go live with Daddy.

And even if I did manage to meet someone else myself, no new man, no matter how wonderful, would ever love Sadie the way Jason does. If I ever married again, I would be replacing the daily presence of a beloved father with that of a stranger who had never seen my daughter's first, toothless smile or urged her across the carpet to take her first steps.

No, I do not really want to learn that Jason is cheating. I do not want an excuse to leave—I want an excuse to stay. When we wake up in the morning, I lean over to kiss him quietly on the cheek.

"Maybe I should ask you if *you're* seeing someone," he says.

"Jason, I'm sorry if I offended you, but you've been so concerned about the money lately, and then when I saw all those charges on the card—I just wanted to know what was going on."

"Nothing's going on, Del, except in your imagination." Just what the wolf must have said to Little Red when she commented on how big the old nose was getting. What if Jason is lying through his sharp lawyer's teeth?

Jason kisses me back, also on the cheek. But it is a tepid sort of comfort, and like reheated Chinese food, it does not completely satisfy.

Saturday, December 8
9 A.M.

Lieutenant Ford Burns, known to his men as "the Wolf," paused as he heard the rustle of an enemy solder moving somewhere on the rocks overhead. Damn. This was too soon; Ford couldn't risk a shot alerting the other guerrillas above the rise. His own men weren't in position yet. He would have to deal with this silently.

Stilling his body as he had been taught by his Mongol grandfather, Ford waited until the guerrilla was a mere arm's breadth away before pouncing, his knife slicing across the man's throat before there was a chance for his opponent to turn his gasp into a scream.

Hands red with blood, Ford felt for a moment that he was looking down on himself from a great height. It was a form of depersonalization, the army psychologist had said. Back when he was regular army.

These days, there were no psychologists, no pictures in the paper, and certainly no hero's welcome when he returned from the frigid borderlands where Genghis Khan had once sent his hordes to go forth and conquer in more forgiving climates.

Suddenly, Ford heard the whisper of a footfall, and whirled to see the broad, grinning face of Vladimir, the Mongol hunter who had led Omega Force to the terrorist outpost.

"You know, Wolf, in the fur hat, you look like one of us," whispered Vladimir in his faintly accented Russian.

"Maybe I do," Ford replied in the same language, "but I'm freezing my ass off just like an American."

Vladimir laughed silently, revealing a gold tooth. "That's because you follow American rules—no vodka, no women." Vladimir's dark eyes glittered with mirth above the high cheekbones that proclaimed his Asiatic ancestry. "You keep your head warm, but you don't tend to your balls."

The truth was, Ford and Vladimir could have been distantly related. Ford's grandfather was Mongol, although his grandmother was Russian. She had emigrated from Ukraine to a tiny town on the border between the former Soviet Union and China, an area the Soviets had designated an autonomous Jewish homeland before World War II turned it into an autonomous Jewish graveyard.

Ford had spent his first nine years with his grandparents in the small, hilly city of Khabarovsk while his mother worked at the local school and tried to find a man to replace the husband she had lost to the army. And then one day his mother announced she had discovered her Jewish roots, and was emigrating with little Feodor to Israel.

They'd made it as far as Brighton Beach in Brooklyn, New York.

And now Feodor was back, not thirty miles from Khabarovsk. But as part of Omega Force, he didn't exist, so there was no point looking up his boyhood friends. Or trying to find a grandfather who was almost certainly dead.

"It's long enough. I think they are asleep," said the guide.

"No," said Ford. "Something's wrong."

"You hear something?" Vladimir looked puzzled. His ability as *a hunter was renowned from the dangerous back alleys of Vladivostok to the frozen tundra of Yakutia: If something larger than a worm was on the move in the Russian Far East, he knew about it.*

"No, but I was expecting that when this guy didn't return, that there'd be some kind of a reaction—"

At that precise moment, the still Siberian evening exploded. Flinging himself down next to Vladimir, Ford rolled until he was farther from the blast. "Shit, shit, shit." Where were his men? His vision still blurry from the flash of light, Ford could hear shouts— in Russian, in Mongol—and smell the acrid odor of burnt metal and charred flesh.

Pulling back into the cover of the dense pines that marked the forest's edge, Ford squinted, trying to clear his eyes. If he couldn't see, he couldn't shoot, but he damn well could get shot at. Shit. Ford moved cautiously through the trees. Those were his men down there, and . . .

His foot connected with something solid, and Ford whirled, his finger ready to squeeze the trigger of his gun. But even through the starbursts of light, Ford could see the posture of fear, not aggression: hands covering the head, eyes white with fear.

Though he couldn't see well enough to make out if this was prisoner or terrorist, he did know a bullet through the head would be his safest option. But that was mercenary-think, and whatever else he had become, he wasn't that. He was a black operative, but not that black.

"Who are you?" he barked in Russian.

"Don't hurt me," *the figure responded, still huddled at his feet. A woman. Good God. With an American accent, no less.*

Possibilities raced through Ford's head. A hostage. A student. A fucking reporter. A whore. Could she be a spy? "Don't move," *he said, holding his gun at a midway point between her head and the battle still raging beyond the treeline in bursts of light and sound.*

Shit, he should be there, but now that his eyesight was improving all he could see were dead bodies littered like disjointed dolls on the half-frozen ground. And then Ford heard it: the high whine of an aircraft, flying low overhead. Great, the cavalry, but what they were going to drop wasn't going to differentiate between friend and foe. As the sound built to an ear-splitting roar, he made up his mind: He was 99 percent certain his men were dead. A better man would check to be sure, but he wasn't here to play John Wayne. Retreat or become hamburger meat—those were the choices.

"Come on, lady, we've got to get the fuck out of here!" He grabbed the woman by the hood of her coat as if she were a cat and hauled her up. He was off and running without looking to see if she was following him or not.

"Wait!" She was running badly, he could hear her behind him: her feet falling too heavily, her breath coming in panicky gasps.

"Run!" He didn't slow down. She wasn't his goddamn sister and he wasn't about to offer her a hand only to have it blown off when the bomb dropped.

"There're caves," she said, panting, "to your right."

"Shut up," he said, because he already knew, and because the woman could barely run when she wasn't talking. When they were within three yards of the caves Ford slowed just enough to grab her hand and haul her alongside. The opening was nearly invisible, just a crack almost six feet up, but the woman clearly knew what she was about. She scrambled up the sheer, rocky face, sending a small shower of pebbles down on Ford.

"Hurry the fuck up," he said, and placed his broad hand on her heavily winter-jacketed rear, shoving her through the aperture and then launching himself after her. He landed on top of her—he heard the distinct "oof" she gave as he pressed the air out

of her lungs with his weight—and then there was a flash of light and a clap of man-made thunder as the bomb dropped, the impact pushing him harder into the softness of her body, his face crushing into hers.

And then—this was the seriously weird part—he was kissing her, his body moving against hers, this woman whose features he had yet to see clearly, who might be old or young, beautiful or ugly, good or evil. He was as hard as iron, pressing against her, trying to feel her through all the layers of clothing, and she was grabbing at him, at his backside, her mouth opening in a gasp of pleasure.

Ford grabbed her face in his half-mittened hands and kissed her again, his teeth grinding against hers, his tongue so deep in her that he felt the throb of his erection, as if he could fuck her with a kiss, as if he could swallow her soul.

Now where the hell had that come from? Just as Ford was beginning to question the wisdom of following his dick's adrenalized sense of direction—as in, men get stabbed for screwing first and asking questions later—the woman said something that instantly froze his lust.

"Feodor." She raised herself up, trying to pull her hands free. "Wait." She spoke in English, but for a moment his confusion was such that he thought she had spoken Russian.

Nobody knew that name. Nobody alive. Feodor Buryat, who rode a horse as if it were an extension of his body, who drank fermented mare's milk and knew the honeycomb caves called the Proschalnaya Peschera like the back of his hand, had died at the age of nine and a half. He was Ford Burns, a lieutenant in the United States Army, an expert in martial arts, munitions, and sabotage, a member of the fabled Omega Force.

"Who are you?" His voice was hoarse as he pulled her hood back, his hands hovering near her throat. It would be nice to know how badly he was compromised in his mission before he killed her.

"One of you. So you'd better not strangle me, Lieutenant, unless you want to explain to Colonel Bleekmann why you snuffed a CIA operative."

"Strangling still seems like a pretty good option to me. What the hell did you just call me, and for the second time, who the fucking hell are you, lady?"

She sat up, her head just clearing the low ceiling of the cave, pulled her jacket completely away from her body, revealing a slender, feminine shape in a tight-fitting black turtleneck. Her face wasn't bad, either—a little bruised around the left eye, but she was pretty, in a refined, slightly stick-up-the-ass way. Hard to believe Ms. CIA with the haughty brown eyes and the stubborn little chin could have been grinding her pelvis against his hard-on not two minutes ago.

"I'm Delilah Lee, on assignment to find a suspected U.S. citizen among the terrorists. . . ."

"Name sounds like a goddamn stripper's." He knew he looked mean and part of him was sorry that he might be scaring her. A larger part was just frightened and bruised and shaking with adrenaline let-down.

"I was taken by the militia when they started raping the local women," Delilah said sharply. "When they removed my veil, they could see I wasn't one of the villagers, so they decided to torture me a little to find out more."

"Oh, Jesus." Ford moved back. "I didn't realize . . . I mean, did they . . . Were you . . ."

"I was tied up for about six hours waiting for their leader. They were just about to get started when your men arrived. So the answer is no, they didn't. But it did make it kind of hard to go for a quick sprint."

"I'm sorry." Ford raked his hair away from his face.

"What for?"

"For nearly . . . for, uh, kissing you like that . . ." he could feel *his ears burning with embarrassment. Way to go, pal. Nearly force yourself on a CIA operative who had come within minutes of being beaten and raped by the enemy.*

"Feodor, I was kissing you the same way." It took Ford a moment to assimilate the words, along with the frank, almost earnest expression on her face. When he did, all the blood rushed from his face straight down to his groin.

"Why . . . why . . . why the fuck do you keep calling me Feodor?"

She leaned closer to him, a maddening little smile on her lips. "You're cute when you're flustered. I called you Feodor because it's your real name, isn't it? I saw it in your file."

"You . . . saw my file?" *Damn, she was licking her lip with nervousness. Why was he responding like this? His men were dead, he was in shit up to his armpits, this was not the time to start bumping bellies with a spook.*

Suddenly there was the distant crackle of rifle fire. "That's the guerrillas' guns," she said. "Do you still know your way through these caves?"

She was right; the ammo was definitely small grade, and that meant their guys. "I'm not sure. We're not exactly equipped for spelunking."

"Well, Feodor . . ."

"Ford."

She arched an eyebrow. "I think we're intimate enough for me to use your real name."

"It's not my real name. No one calls me Feodor." *There was another report of gunfire, this time closer.* "Shit. Never mind. Listen, lady, you just follow me, all right?"

"No problem." He pulled out his flashlight and began to crawl through the tunnel that led to the network of caves he recalled from boyhood, and heard her moving behind him. Her breathing was labored.

"You in pain?"

"No."

"My butt making you wild?"

A half-choked laugh. "No."

"So stop panting."

They crawled on, the uneven stone walls getting tighter and darker. Her breathing grew sharp, as she drew the damp, still cave air in quickly through her nose, then tried to let it out slowly through her mouth.

"What are you, in labor? Slow your breathing down, Delilah."

She made a shaky, gasping sound. "C—can't."

"You're fucking claustrophobic?"

"A l—little."

"I can't turn around in here, you know. The cave opens up some if you can hold out."

Her reply was to take three fast breaths, one right after the other.

"Take a deep breath."

"Can't."

"Grab hold of me. Grab my belt." He could feel her hands scrabbling to reach around his waist, her head coming to rest just above his rear. "Okay. Good. Now just try to synchronize your breathing with mine. Can you do that?"

She nodded, and he could feel her against his ass, which made him go hard as a fucking pole. Very appropriate, you dumb bastard, he told himself. She's in a panic, so don't go thinking this is some weird new form of foreplay.

"All right, Spooky Girl, here we go." He moved slowly, letting her move along with him, inch by knee-grinding inch across the jagged floor of the cave. "I can see the larger chamber up ahead. You okay back there?"

"I have my face up your backside. How okay can I be?" Her voice was still shaky, but at least she was making jokes.

"Well, I'm not complaining." He heard her snort of laughter, and then he descended into the lower level of the cave, where the ceiling opened up and other tunnels connected. "Here, let me help you down." He lifted her under her armpits, and lowered her gently to her feet, hoping that the increased headroom would do the trick, and that being smack-dab in the deepest part of the cave system wasn't going to do her head in.

"Thank you." She quickly unzipped her coat and stood with her hands on her thighs, bent over, like a runner having just finished a marathon.

"Better now?"

She looked up at him, and he could see that, yes, she was better, but no, she wasn't all right.

"Feodor?"

"What?"

"Kiss me again."

"What did you . . ."

"Oh, wasn't that clear enough? Your file said you spoke five languages fluently. Okay, let me translate into military lingo. I am sixty fucking feet deep inside a fucking cave, and I fucking well want to be fucking distracted!"

"Fucking A," said Ford, catching her in his arms and bringing his mouth down on hers so hard their teeth clicked. Her head dropped back as he grabbed her around the delicious roundness of her hips, holding her hard against him while he gritted his teeth against the sudden rush of pleasure. Slow down, he thought, or you'll lose it completely.

"You are so soft," he whispered. She gasped as his callused hands slipped underneath her turtleneck, tracing the undersides of her breasts and then brushing his thumbs lightly over her nipples until she made a sound halfway between a laugh and a sob.

"Shhh," he said, moving his mouth to the side of her neck, inhaling the scent of her, his arms braced against the cave wall as *the deep tremble of desire quaked through him. She pulled back and looked into his face, and he knew from her expression that what she found there surprised her—not the mindless glaze of desire, but something very like anguish in his eyes.*

"What's wrong?"

His reply was to kiss her again, deeper and more desperately, and this time his hands came up to cup her face. Her hands began to push against his chest, a gentle pressure, the faint beginning of a "no."

"Don't be scared," he murmured into her hair, and then he kissed her again, his tongue in her mouth, and he moved his hips against her and shuddered, but kept his hands gentle in her hair.

"It's this place, isn't it? It means something to you. It means something . . . to Feodor."

This time, when he looked at her with his dark hunter's eyes, he wondered if she could see the shadow of the lost boy in him, left in a cave in a frozen land, trapped now in a man who knew how to kill with a flick of his wrist.

"Hey," he said roughly, "if you want to go inventing sob stories, go right ahead. Whatever it takes to get me inside your pants, baby." He thrust against her, deliberately crude, but the expression on her face didn't change.

"What happened to you here, Feodor?"

"I am not that name!" The echo of his shout bounced off the walls around them: that name, that name, that name.

I roll into Jason's side of the bed, hoping for some pre-Sadie Saturday morning affection, but my husband looks at me as if I were a cat walking on his fish dinner and tells me that he has to catch up on paperwork, best to get an early start.

I decide to take Sadie to a Disney children's movie. As always, there are the foolish and amusing animal helpers, a spunky yet feminine heroine, and the lurking threat of death that moves imperturbably through all the bright and pretty forests and castles, until it is vanquished with a marriage.

"Why are you crying, Mommy?" Sadie's hand is plump and moistly comforting in mine.

Because I want it all. A princess nightgown and a pretty house on Main Street, U.S.A., roller coaster excitement in a nice, controlled environment, everything clean and tidy and neat, with fireworks at night. I want a Disney marriage. I will go home and clean out the boxes in the living room. I will get a Palm Pilot and record everything I need to remember.

Oh, wait, I have a Palm Pilot. Well, now I will find it and actually use it. I will reinvent myself as the spunky, conquering heroine.

I decide to surprise Jason by organizing the living room. Halfway through the boxes. There is a bit of a mess in the living room—the storm before the quiet. And inside every box there are the agonizing reminders of fantasies past. The fantasy of me as rebellious teen. The fantasy of me as bohemian poet. The fantasy of me as glowing bride, as pregnant Earth Mother, as Ivory Soap ponytailed Mommy Supreme.

"Look at this, Mom!" Sadie holds out a picture of herself as a baby, plump and grinning, with Jason and myself gazing down at her, awestruck, at the beginning of the great parental adventure.

"Hello, girls, I'm done with my work—Christ, what happened here?" Jason looks at me as if I have murdered someone and am playing with the entrails.

"We're cleaning up," I say.

"Jesus, I hope so. Well, don't let me stop you."

Maybe instead of Disney heroine I should go for villain-ess. Wear puppy skins. Poison virgins. Wrap up husbands in my scary tentacles and crush the living breath from their lungs.

Monday, December 10
11 A.M.

Delilah woke to find her husband of six days with his head pillowed on his arm, watching her.

"What? Was I snoring? Grunting? Drooling?"

"No. Your eyelids were fluttering." He touched one, lightly, with his finger. "I was just wondering what you were dreaming." He moved so that he was lying over her, his arms braced on either side of her face. She was riveted by the sight of his bare chest, flat and muscular and all but hairless. "Tell me all your secrets, woman."

"Mmm, maybe I could just brush my teeth first. . . ." Delilah tried to slide out of Ford's embrace, but he flung one strong thigh across both her legs, preventing escape.

"Not a chance, sweetheart. We have a condition here." He pressed his hard body more firmly against her, and her eyes widened.

"Hmm, that does feel serious. . . . Maybe if I could just face the other way . . ."

"Hang on, let me do the test for morning breath." His eyes were heavy-lidded, unreadable.

"I did it already, and let me tell you, I failed miserab . . ." His *sudden, fierce, unabashed kiss caught her by surprise, and she was just beginning to tangle her hands in his hair when he surprised her again by pulling back.*

"So how's the breath?"

His eyes were warm with humor. "I don't know about yours," *he said, softly. "But you keep taking mine away."*

Here are the reasons why *Secrets* will not be using the script I sent them:

1. The character of Skylar was not written in a manner consistent with her previous behavior to date.

2. I used the wrong formatting and my script was two lines over for each page, which would have resulted in the show running for five extra minutes.

3. I am an inferior writer with minimal ability to create believable dramatic tension and a surprisingly clumsy handle on dialogue, given my academic background in film and poetry.

The first two items were explained by Anne Erlanger, the head writer, the last implied. I think they are considering whether or not to cancel my trial contract. I am going to take a look at Sadie's *Practical Guide to Witchcraft*, still conveniently hidden in her underwear drawer.

Wait—I just discovered an additional letter, and from the producer, no less. Seems that in addition to screwing up the page layout, I also managed to print out my script on the back of some of Jason's R. B. International paperwork. Well, this last stroke of slatternly disorganization turned out to be serendipitous, because the soap people read Jason's report and mistook it for long story notes. So at least they don't think I'm completely incompetent. No wait—it's better than that—

Oh, my God. They love it. And they want it . . . tomorrow?

Here it is, verbatim:

Delilah,

At first I thought you'd started giving us scripts with writing on both sides of the page (you do have your share of formatting glitches), but as I read through the B-side of your copy, I realized I was looking at your long story notes.

Quite frankly, Anne Erlanger handed me the script because she had done so much editing on it that she was on the verge of canceling your trial contract.

And then I saw your ideas for future stories and I was blown away. Your problem is that you're not a script writer; you're a storyteller.

I love everything you've got here—the scientifically viable aphrodisiac that may prove dangerous in the wrong hands, the hint of black market involvement, the morally ambiguous ex-Soviet scientist Irina Skulnikovna (great name!) with her record of truly spectacular failures, including (this had us all in stitches) the spermicidal cream that turned the male organ blue for an undetermined period of time. I can't tell you how clever you were in combining the dramatic and comic elements in your faux report (and what a cunning way to present the material!).

I particularly liked the suggestion that the company might be under FBI or CIA surveillance (very hot right now), as well as the paranoid ex-military head of the company.

Delilah, this couldn't come at a better time for us. The big

Blackjack/Skylar romantic storyline, which has been build-ing for over six months and is supposed to end in next week's special earthquake event, is going to have to be post-poned because of an unforeseen medical crisis (Scott Derwin won't be able to talk without lisping and drooling for at least another two weeks, and the fans won't stand for us bringing in another actor to play Blackjack now).

In addition, the network has been less than thrilled with our ratings and has been questioning whether or not we have enough "high-concept" stuff happening. I think your idea is just what we need to bring into the story meeting to-morrow at ten.

Could you work up a document ASAP? I know this is short notice, but Anne and I would really like to have some-thing to show the network execs. So go for it, Delilah—be just as sexy, dramatic and funny as you were in your notes, and I see a real future for you with Secrets.

Nigel Broadbelt, Producer

I wonder if this means I will have to admit to Jason that I am responsible for those disappearing papers? Or that he is responsible for the salvation of my writing career? Oh, my God, I have less than twenty-four hours to produce a document outlining plot arcs for fifteen characters. And that's assuming no sleep.

Tuesday, December 11
3 A.M.

No fantasies—entire erotic imagination sublimated into Secrets *plots.*

No sooner did I tell Ford about my amazing stroke of luck then he went M.I.A., claiming to need a new valve and setting off across town to some fixtures shop on the East Side. He never returned, which was good for my concentration, though no doubt portends poorly for the closet, which looks half disemboweled.

Jason also has been out of contact, purportedly in back-to-back meetings. I've taken advantage of his absence and managed to convince Hilda to come back for a $20-a-week raise.

I feel justified in doing this because of all the work I've been doing. I've just mined a day and a night's worth of erotic, paranoid and hypochondriacal fantasies and incorporated them with Jason's report on the challenges facing the launch of the Biosensual product. The result: one incredible kick-ass document with six months' worth of heady plot projection.

Blackjack has now been kidnapped, Ruby's a rogue agent, and Skylar's an innocent victim who gets dosed with high levels of aphrodisiac. All in all, it's sort of a nice, safe, sexy bio-terror scenario. I have a feeling this is it, the career-making moment when your private obsessions take off on a collision course with the zeitgeist and the personal becomes cultural phenomenon.

Or I might just offend everyone in three time zones.

Maybe taking a glance at Sadie's witchcraft book before the meeting today might not be such a bad idea.

From *The Practical Guide to Witchcraft*

To Insure Good Fortune:

Take cold cream and mix with rosewater, a little red wine and the heart of a living mole. Preserve in a jar for seven days. Then put it in a gold silk bag with three sage leaves and carry it with you always. You will have your heart's desire.

To Insure Marital Harmony:

Gather sticks, three for the woman and three and a half for the man, and tie them separately. With the woman's sticks, put a sprig of vervain and ten strands of her hair. With a man's, put a bit of St. John's Wort and seven drops of his blood. Tie the two bundles together with a red silk thread and keep in a safe place.

To Make a Transvection (Flying) Ointment:

Capture two live toads and render them in a black cauldron. Boil until the bones are clean and then use a mortar to crush the bones into a powder. Add four drops of saliva, five drops of blood and the milk of a nursing mother to form a paste, and then apply to your naked thighs when the moon is full.

I am really going to have to speak to Sadie about this book.

Tuesday, December 11
3 P.M.

No fantasies—entire higher brain function given over to thoughts of my brilliant career.

Well, it may have been a mistake to take a double dose of my anti-anxiety medication before the meeting with the network execs; while I do feel I projected an admirable (and professional) aura of calm competence, I am having some difficulty recalling all the details of the event.

I do remember being surprised that the producer, Nigel Broadbelt, was so very short. He has a sort of terrier-bark laugh that I found extremely disconcerting in the meeting, especially as he kept laughing after I said things in all seriousness. Such as, Could we use the aphrodisiac storyline to flirt with the idea of some same-sex attractions?

After that, Anne Erlanger began interrupting me every time I tried to open my mouth. I was slightly irritated by this and so it took me a few beats to comprehend what she meant when she told me the staggering news: I am now part of the breakdown team, an associate head writer, and they are dumping the old storyline and going with my Biosensual plot next week!!!

I am in the grip of the kind of euphoria I used to feel in the first heady days of a love affair. I feel clever. I feel desirable. I feel as if I am in some heightened metabolic state where I am burning extra calories just by thinking hard.

I just decided to call Jason to tell him the news but he was so irritable at being interrupted at work that I think I'll tell Tamara first instead.

Tamara, irritatingly enough, is not at home, so I am calling my mother.

My mother is not home. My father says she is at the doctor's for some kind of women's troubles. Trust my mother to spend $100 to hear she has a yeast infection.

Ford is back in my closet but still no time for fantasies. I must go and daydream on paper.

Break time. I am finding the current *Secrets* storyline very convoluted. Went on line to check out the *Secrets* website and spent an hour checking out the Hot Rumors bulletin board to see if my new plotline was being mentioned. Nothing. Then wasted some time thinking about all the famous literary writers who wrote screenplays—Faulkner, Hemingway, Hammet, Chandler, and my personal favorite, Graham Greene. Read a bit of *The End of the Affair* for inspiration. Now I feel that I deserve a little break. After all, I'm not going to feel very creative just sitting at my desk hour after hour, now am I?

Oh shit. Oh shit. Oh shit. Since Ford is still trapped in the Bermuda triangle of my bedroom closet pipes, I am in the guest bathroom, finishing a very interesting article in *Soap Opera Addict* magazine (one of the major competitors in our time slot is bringing back a big name from the eighties). Unfortunately, I seem to have gotten my period a couple of days early. Why do these things happen to me? All my sanitary supplies are in the other bathroom.

The problem here is that I do not want Ford to know the precise timing of my bodily functions.

I remember the day Jason saw me walk into the bathroom with a tampon; we had been sleeping together for a few weeks and in typical boho fashion, I'd just grabbed one and said, "Got to plug a leak." Jason had looked at me with thinly disguised horror for a full day afterward.

I think if he had his way, I would abstain from touching him for the duration, before immersing myself in a ritual bath to be purified for his marital touch. At first I thought this might be a purely Jewish reaction, given all the biblical injunctions about menstruation, but Irish Catholic friends have told me of similar experiences.

I do not know exactly what ethnicity Ford is (although I'm pretty sure he's neither Jewish nor Irish), but he could be Native American, and I've heard they're as bad as my people, with a tradition of separate huts instead of separate beds.

For the first time since he arrived, I wish Ford gone. I want my privacy back, goddamn it. How long does it take to fix a leak? What is he, the world's slowest plumber?

Aha! I have it!

Dressed again, I walk casually into my bedroom. Ford is bare-chested, sweating and flat on his back. Even the window, opened to the chill December air, cannot fight the heat steaming from the radiator ducts.

I'd turn it off, but then, of course, Ford might put his shirt back on.

"Excuse me." I rummage through the big plastic bag filled with detritus from my closet and retrieve a hideous black handbag, bought because I thought I needed something ergonomic and practical and discarded because I am not ready to turn into my mother.

"Need something?" Ford sticks his head out, hair disheveled, face flushed and boyish. "'Cause if you need to use this bathroom, I could always leave. . . ."

"No, no, I found what I need."

Since I never empty out any of my handbags, I find a strange assortment of items inside: Dusty pacifier, health club I.D., strange purple lipstick, and the phone number of someone named Helvetica scrawled on a napkin with the words $10 an hour.

No tampon.

I mutter, "Wrong lipstick," and head for the bathroom cabinet, where I find three different bottles of Tylenol, five unused tubes of foundation in various fleshy shades, and a rubber-tipped thingamajig which I suddenly remember that the dentist told me to use on my gums without fail if I don't want to spend a fortune fixing my teeth.

I also find a rubber spider, a prescription for eye drops, a matted hairbrush and a damp $20 bill.

No tampon.

I stick the $20 in the back pocket of my black jeans and prepare to brave the cold for a quick trip to the drugstore.

"Hey. Delilah."

I turn and find Ford standing right in front of me. Thick layers of muscle pad his shoulders and chest. He has almost no body hair. I bring my gaze up to meet his; his eyes are darkly amused.

"Thought you might need this." He presses something into my palm, but I can't see what; both his hands are cupping mine. "I found it in the closet and thought it just might be the last of its tribe."

For a moment, I can't breathe. His fingers give mine a little squeeze, and I know this is one man who would never want separate huts. He is comfortable with women's bodies, with all our complicated and arcane plumbing.

"Ford—just one question. How did you know?"

"You were vibing a little cranky."

"Experience from a score of cranky girlfriends?"

Ford smiles in a way that lets me know I have just given too much away. I want to hit myself in the head. Why not just announce that I lust for him in my heart and am jealous at the thought of the other women he has had?

"I never knew there was a special group name for girlfriends before," he murmurs. "A gaggle of geese, a murder of crows . . . a score of girlfriends. Yeah, it fits."

I walk away, amused and slightly irritated, only to find that Ford has taken up residence in my imagination again.

Friday, December 14
4 P.M.

It was the end of summer, and life was stepping up its pace, fruit ripening in a matter of hours on the vine, cornstalks launching themselves at the skies. The evenings were filled with the discordant melodies of bullfrogs and bullfinches, and the chirrup of ten thousand crickets winding down their lives.

It was a bittersweet time, and Delilah Lewis found herself walking farther and farther from her settlement, straying to the outskirts between the last log house and the sentry station where John Fairchild stood watch.

She was engaged to John after harvest time; surely he would unbend himself enough to grant her a kiss were she to surprise him this evening?

Her stiff skirts heavy around her ankles, Delilah moved purposefully toward the treeline. She stopped for a moment to wipe a damp tendril of auburn hair away from her forehead with the back of her arm, and that was when the heard it; the distant, almost playful sound of popping gunfire. And then she heard the shouts.

The Indians had planned their raid with military expertise for the end of the day, when most of the settlement's menfolk were still working the fields or exhausted from the day's labor.

Delilah's first, mad impulse was to run toward the melee; the higher-pitched shrieks of women and children were rising over the other sounds of battle: the pounding of horse's hooves, the crash and clatter of weapons.

Instead, Delilah turned and raced to the sentry's tower, shouting John's name at the top of her lungs. What she found there strangled the breath in her throat; an Indian brave, his face streaked with paint, jumping from the tower with a tomahawk in one hand.

There was blood on the weapon's flat blade.

"You whoreson bastard!" Gentle John, her betrothed, had been her friend since childhood—a timid boy with a weak constitution, no match for her in size and energy. The years had given him more height than strength; the joke of the settlement was that Delilah had the strength of two women, and John that of half a man, so they were well suited.

The Crow brave said something liquid and incomprehensible in his own tongue; Delilah thought that he might even have been amused. And that was why she grabbed the little slingshot she had carried over her shoulder since girlhood, to catch the odd rabbit for supper, and shot off a stone at him with the speed and accuracy of long practice.

For a moment, the Indian just looked at her in stunned surprise, a red spot blossoming on his forehead; and then he fell, seemingly lifeless, to the ground fifteen feet from where she stood.

A sane woman would have run. But Delilah ran up to the brave and put her hand on his throat, feeling for a pulse. It was there, and for a moment, Delilah just sat, her hand on the stranger's strong, bronzed throat, looking at the remarkably handsome face of her enemy. She was responsible for his life now; she could take the weapon from his hand and kill him while he lay here, helpless, and avenge her kin and neighbors. Yet could she bare to slice that smooth, sun-darkened skin? She stared down at the leanly muscled chest, aware of the shallow rise and fall of his breathing, and found her gaze traveling lower, to the breechclout slung over his narrow hips. Her own breath caught; she felt a treacherous pooling of heat between her legs. How could she feel this wanton desire to touch this savage, murdering heathen?

And then, as suddenly as a hawk swooping down to seize its prey, the brave's hand darted out and captured her own, yanking her down over his body so that they were eye to eye.

"Do not move, Fire Hair," he snarled, and Delilah swallowed hard as she realized that the Indian's other hand was between them, holding the blade of his tomahawk against her throat.

The brave rolled, and now he was atop her, his eyes dark with fury. "You have killed Snow Wolf's woman when she was big with child, and you have killed the buffalo so that Snow Wolf's mother and small brother had no food in the cold winter. But this is not your day to kill, Fire Hair. This is my day."

"You filthy coward!" Delilah writhed in her captor's grip, straining to break her wrists free of his grip, but his fingers merely tightened, as did the press of his rock-hard thighs over her hips. "I could have killed you while you lay there, you pig! But you were helpless and I am not a murderer." Tears leaked from her eyes, but they were tears of rage, not fear.

"Were you coming to meet your man?" The Indian's tone turned taunting. "He was not so brave as you."

"No," Delilah said, suddenly quieting. "He was not." Their gazes met, and something passed between them; and then, her enemy's weapon still at her throat, a strange sort of tremor passed through Delilah, a shiver that widened her eyes and his. Through the fabric of her skirts, Delilah felt the press of something blunt and hard between her thighs, and Delilah remembered that for some men, battle lust became a carnal desire.

"What is this?" Snow Wolf's voice was a hoarse whisper. "Are you casting a spell on me?" His gaze lowered to her mouth. "I did not think so before, but maybe I will take you as a man takes a woman before I end your life."

"You owe me a life," Delilah said, her voice low. "I spared yours."

"You did not," said the Indian, looking mildly surprised. "I was lying for you like a cat lies in wait for a mouse. I owe you nothing."

For the first time, Delilah felt afraid. "No," she said. He reached under her skirts, and suddenly his hand was between her thighs, parting the sensitive flesh there with a surprisingly sure touch, and Delilah felt a rush of panic mingle with a shameful, mad desire she did not understand to part her thighs. "No," she said again, louder this time, and found his neck near her face. Without thinking she seized hold of his throat with her teeth.

"Aieeee!" The Indian reared back, but strangely enough, Delilah could see a light, almost of amusement, flickering in his expression. "Sharp teeth for such a little mouse. And yet you are wet below. I could feel you. Do you want Snow Wolf in the manner of a woman for a man?"

"No!" Delilah swung her arm free to slap him, but Snow Wolf caught her wrist easily.

"Our bodies do not seem to know we are enemies, Fire Hair," he said.

"Get off me!"

His lean hips moved against hers and to her eternal shame, Delilah felt herself pushing back against him. "I could slide inside you and you would not stop me," he taunted. "I could make you wrap your legs around me and ride me like a mustang."

"I hate you," snarled Delilah, but the Indian only looked bemused.

"I hate you, too," he said, "but I think I am going to take you home with me."

*   *   *

"Mommy! You're supposed to be helping me with my Native American dwellings project!"

I would like to state here that the above fantasy bears absolutely no relationship to my political, social or historical beliefs and that as a feminist and an ardent supporter of Native American rights, I take a firm stand against rape and against the depiction of Native American males as being more primitive or savage and hence more virile than their Caucasian counterparts. The long, complex and tragic history of Native Americans in this country has been overlooked in favor of a sensationalized, overly simplistic Hollywood revisionism.

But every once in a while I have had the odd, uncontrollable, historically inaccurate fantasy.

Sadie and I are sitting in Rainbow Nails, the little Korean-owned manicure shop around the corner from our home. Outside the glass window with its neon sign, the sky is heavy and gray and feels like midnight even though it is only four in the afternoon.

I am in serious beauty-preparation mode for Jason's office Christmas party tonight, having already had my hair layered into one of those casual, messy porcupine cuts. Unfortunately, removing the outer, artichoke-like layers of my hair revealed the inner layer of emergent gray, and Paris, my hairdresser, told me that color was no longer a luxury but a necessity.

"You are far too young," he said, "to look old." How could I disagree? Strangely enough, looking young involved the application of a color I cannot remember ever possessing in my youth—a sort of glisteny reddish bronze that would look great as a pair of patent leather boots.

I can't argue with the results, though. Now, instead of looking like a lesbian Bloomsbury poetess of the 1920s, I look as if I might actually contemplate carnal congress with a man in this century. In the same spirit of redefining myself as a desirable woman, I had a nice lady wax the layer of abominable winter hair from my legs, which now look like battery chickens in a state of post-plucked shock.

Since I was in the neighborhood, I also went back to Bloomingdale's and bought new eye shadow, blush, undereye concealer, lipstick and something hugely expensive in a small tube that seems to do nothing but must be worn underneath all other makeup to insure that all other makeup does not trickle, lavalike, into the fissures around my mouth and eyes. All this is according to the very young lady in the white lab coat, and her makeup artist, Jerome. Jerome then pressed my hand to his chest as if he were about to declare his love for me and advised me to have a manicure.

So now Sadie and I are having our nails painted. I love Sadie's hands—each knuckle is a dimple in the flesh. I wish I could just sit here and be Fun, Youthful Mom with Nice Hair and Nails (a popular soap-opera archetype). Fun Mom wears pretty dresses and is spontaneous in a very organized manner, appearing with full picnic hamper whenever Sweet Child is in need of some extra chicken salad comfort. Sweet Child requires a great deal of coddling between the ages of five and eight, because that is when she is most susceptible to Rapid Aging Syndrome, the malady that afflicts soap children the minute they lose their front teeth. One day Sweet Child goes off to visit Grandma and the next she reappears as a nubile and exceptionally well-groomed adolescent, ripe with sexuality and plot potential.

Deep down, I know I am not Fun Mom, but when other people are listening, I try to fake it. Like now, for instance. I am going to invoke Fun Mom voice to have Serious Mom talk.

"Sadie, you know that witchcraft book you've been reading?" My voice is too fake-casual, and three women whip their heads around. Witchcraft! Child of the devil! I lower my voice. "Where'd it come from, Sade?"

"The library?"

"It's not a library book."

"Grandma?"

"Grandma, as in Grandma Levine? Or Nana?"

"Nana. I think." Her brows are furrowed, and I am aware that she is trying to think of the answer that will please me best. I can see how easily children can be led as witnesses.

"It's not that I'm upset or anything, but there are some things in that book . . . I mean, I don't want you to try something that requires the beating heart of a small rodent. . . ."

Sadie fixes me with a look of utter condescension. "Of course not, Mom, you're not supposed to really use a heart! It's just a, you know, sort of thing that stands for something else."

"You mean a metaphor?" (*The things they teach second-graders these days.*)

"Ye-es." The word drawn out, as if she were speaking to a not particularly bright student.

I look at my nails, which are being shaped by a very young woman with rhinestone barrettes in her dark, glossy hair. "So you do know that this kind of magic doesn't really work, don't you, Sadie?"

A pause. Sadie watches her nails receive their first coat of pink glitter. "What kind of magic does work, Mommy?"

I think of metaphors for what I want to say. I think of

T. S. Eliot's clairvoyant with a bad cold: "Here is Bel-ladonna, the Lady of the Rocks, the lady of situations. Here is the man with three staves, and here the Wheel, And here is the one-eyed merchant. . . ." it ends with something about being careful to trust no one these days. I used to know "The Waste Land" by heart, beginning to end: "April is the cruelest month, breeding Lilacs out of the dead land, mix-ing memory and desire . . ." Oh, God, where has my poetry gone? I no longer write it. I no longer read it. I no longer try to conjure anything with words.

What can I say about magic to my adorably mousy daughter, regarding me now so seriously behind her pur-ple glasses? She is still young enough to believe that the sprinkle of colored acetone on her nails can confer glam-our. And glamour, of course, is the word people use to use to describe what fairies do: Deceive people with pretty illusions.

"What kind of magic works? The kind you can't control, Sadie." I am about to give an example—the magic of touching a wild animal, the magic of looking deeply into someone's eyes, the magic of moving through water at night—but Sadie looks back at the manicurist.

"Don't throw out my nail clippings! I want them all back for a spell!"

As usual, I take my hands out of the little hand-dryer things too soon and smudge a nail. While my manicurist scowls at me, I hear the bell over the door ring and look to see that Kathy Wheatley is walking in, looking flushed and almost pretty.

"I need an emergency pedicure," she tells the shop's owner, a middle-aged woman who never actually touches a foot herself. "I'll pay double if you do it, Lucy."

Lucy agrees with a big, fake smile. It's not until Kathy removes her wooly red coat and walks over to choose a nail polish that she spots me.

"Delilah!" Kathy gives me a bigger, brighter version of the smile Lucy gave her. "I didn't expect to see you here."

"Well, it's for a special occasion. . . ."

"And here's Sadie! Hi, Sadie! Let me see your nails!" Sadie holds them out as if expecting to be rapped on the knuckles with a ruler. "Oooh, glittery! Very nice!"

Any more blonde enthusiasm and I may have to start making nasty brunette comments. But do I still count as a brunette, with my auburn-bronzey rinse, or am I a sort of redhead-in-training? And what's Kathy doing having her toes done, anyway? It's December. No one will see her toes except her husband.

"Going somewhere for the winter break, Kathy?"

Kathy blinks her blonde eyelashes at me. "No, not this year. Why do you ask?"

"I was just wondering what the pedicure emergency was."

Suddenly Kathy blushes scarlet. "Oh! That! I just—you know, wanted to look nice."

And just like that, I realize that my wholesome upstairs neighbor must be having an affair. My father, Tamara, now Kathy. Is there anyone in the entire tristate area who isn't seeing more action than I am?

"Come on, Mommy," says Sadie, tugging my arm. "I want to show Hilda my nails."

Well, there's Hilda.

Hilda, who has agreed to baby-sit for the evening, is in the living room, admiring Sadie's nails. I am in the bedroom, listening to Van Morrison on the radio as I make up my face the way I used to: black eyeliner, black mascara, glossy lips. I tease my hair until it is full and spiky and wild around my face, and try on the black dress I bought with Tamara. I am a siren, I am a seductress, I am a woman to be reckoned with.

"What do you think?" I ask Hilda and Sadie. "Will I make Daddy drool?"

"Oh, yes, Daddy's gonna *love* that dress," says Hilda. As often happens with Hilda, there is a trace of something approaching sarcasm in her tone, but for the life of me I cannot figure what she is being sarcastic about. Maybe it's just her Island lilt that makes her sound that way.

"I just hope he doesn't think it's too expensive," I say, smoothing the fabric over my stomach.

"Mr. Levine knows it costs to look good, now. Don't you worry. Just go out and be gorgeous."

I smile at Hilda and she smiles back, and I think about shaking her shoulders until she coughs up whatever she thinks she knows about my husband. Whose last name is Green, not Levine; sometimes I think Hilda gets it wrong on purpose.

But maybe I'd sound a bit snotty, too, if I'd been working for the same boss for five years. You get to the point where you know where the bodies are buried. You get to the point of adolescent disdain for the figure in power. It is probably time for Hilda to break away and become independent, but like a clinging parent, I'm not ready to let her go.

I kiss Sadie and then go downstairs and stand in front of the building, trying to find a taxi to convince that I really, really do want to go all the way downtown. Even if the traffic is bad.

I have printed out Jason's instructions, but even so, the driver is as utterly confused as I am by the location of the R. B. International building. We speed down the West Side

Highway with some confidence until we pass the prostitutes walking with cinematic confidence through the meatpacking district.

"What street is it?" The driver has an accent two parts Spanish to one part Middle Eastern. He looks nothing like his license photo.

"It's one of those strange West Village streets that start out as one thing and turn into another."

The driver gives me a baleful look. "Lady, this isn't the Village."

"Well, it's villagey."

We drive around and around blocks that keep changing shape and turning back on themselves. It's like an Escher nightmare, with sidewalks going up and sideways and nowhere. Finally, in disgust, the driver drops me on the block where logic dictates the R. B. building must be. I walk up and down in my clattery high heels; nary a dogwalker or streetwalker to be seen to ask for assistance. My feet are already sore from the damn shoes and the third time I walk the block I head into an alley in the back of one building and discover it is really a courtyard. I have found it: Fortress R. B. International.

In a previous incarnation, I remember Jason telling me the building had been some kind of factory. Now the lobby stretches before me, vast and dark, like the first level of hell.

It takes me a full three minutes just to locate the doorman, who looks like a bald, tattooed Maori warrior in a gray uniform.

"R. B. International," I say.

His face expressionless, he stares at me for a full three seconds before attempting to call upstairs on his phone. "Your name?"

"Delilah Levine. I'm here for the Christmas party."

He repeats the information. "Lady," he says, in the same tone as the cab driver, "they say there's no party there tonight."

All right, I understand corporate secrecy, but this is getting ridiculous. I can feel my temper rise. "Get my husband on the line, please. Jason Green." I am cold and I am cranky and the arches of my feet want to lie down for the night.

My husband is not in his office. The Maori doorman waits for my next move, face impassive. "Try his secretary, Nola. Try anyone. There's supposed to be a party here tonight."

"Not that I heard of."

I am getting a sinking feeling in the pit of my stomach. "Could you try someone? Anyone else? I've come a long way." Reduced to pleading. The doorman dials a number.

"Mr. Madigan? There's a lady here says she's come for the office Christmas party. No, I don't think so." He looks at me. "You can go up. Seventh floor."

Now this was more like it. "Thanks," I say. The elevator does not have company names on many of the floors, which makes it feel sort of like a stage set of a building. R. B. The doors open on the seventh floor, where a sharp-featured receptionist sits behind a glass-and-steel desk, doing nothing with an air of efficient authority.

"Hi, I'm Jason Green's wife, here for the—"

"It's not tonight."

"It's not?" I stare at her, and she seems perfectly willing to just sit there and say nothing more. "But what—"

"Your husband's in a meeting. Mr. Madigan is coming out to see you."

"He is? But I don't understand. . . ."

But he is already striding toward me, Kleat Madigan, the chief executive officer of R. B. International, in crew cut and pinstripes. He looks like Marlon Brando somewhere between his handsome, ruthless prime and his sci-fi expansion into blobular old age. I can imagine him as the commanding army general he might have been, planning attacks, coordinating supplies, ordering young men to their untimely deaths.

"Kleat," I say cheerily, trying not to sound like the god-less, leftist pinko that I am. "You're working late."

"Delilah," he says, his smile not moving either his eyes or his forehead. "At R. B. International, we all work late. In battle and in business, you don't get ahead by doing just what the other guy does. You have to think ahead. You have to plan ahead. You have to work ahead."

"Sounds very heady," I say, and then instantly regret it.

"We seem to have a failure in communication here."

I get the exact feeling I used to get from the old Chiller Theatre credits, with the hand rising up out of a pool of blood. I say, "Sorry?"

"The party."

"I have it on my calendar that it's tonight. . . ."

"Too much work to do. We changed it to next Wednes-day." His flat, gray eyes move over me, assessing. "And you dressed up and everything. What a shame."

"Oh, that's all right." I am going to kill Jason.

"Well, we look forward to talking to you more next week."

I hate *we*-speakers. I fight the urge to tell him that all my multiple personalities and I are also looking forward to the occasion. "That'll be fun," I say.

"You'll have to tell me all about your kids," Madigan says, in an obvious attempt to appear human.

Well, mister, I can meet your friendly and raise you to borderline flirtatious. "Sure. And then maybe we can have a drink and you can tell me more about Jason's top-secret sex project." I give a little wink and nudge to show the scary man that I am, indeed, joking.

"What the hell are you talking about?"

Where did this guy learn his professional manners? "I just meant the Biosensual project." Christ, some people spend way too much time worrying about harassment suits. Just mention the word sex and they're sweating bullets. "I've actually taken the idea as a starting point for this soap opera plotline I'm writing. . . ."

"You can't do that!" He barks the words at me and something coldly foreboding sweeps down the back of my neck. I am now so very, very sorry that I started telling Jason's boss about my soap writing. I am also sorry I came out tonight, sorry I ever said I wanted to see Jason's office, and, truth be told, somewhat sorry I ever agreed to marry Jason when I should have just gotten pregnant with Sadie and then run off to raise Sadie in Santa Fe or Jackson Hole.

"Don't worry," I say as lightly as I can manage when my husband's big boss is slowly turning a mottled shade of wrathful. "I changed the names and details and everything. Instead of Biosensual, it's Love Potion Number 900, and instead of a woman ex-Soviet scientist, we have a deranged Yugoslavian guy sort of modeled after the Professor on *Gilligan's Island*. . . ."

"Shut up and listen. There is absolutely no way that I will allow you to use any material connected with a project in development here at R. B. International."

Suddenly I feel my cold fear turn into hot anger. Boss or no boss, nobody tells me to shut up unless the next words are "Your hair's on fire." "While I can understand your concern for the viability of your project," I say through gritted teeth, "there is no need for you to worry. I have changed all the pertinent facts and there is no way a rival manufacturer could make use of a plotline."

Kleat Madigan lowers his head like a bull. "And I'm telling you you are compromising our lead project on a goddamn soap opera! Most of our flavors and fragrances go into soaps sold by your main freakin' corporate sponsors!"

I wipe his excess saliva from my eye. "And I am telling you that your lawyers will be hard pressed to sue me for inappropriate inspiration. I am the only non-lawyer in an entire family of lawyers and I know what I'm saying here. A writer can use anything and everything as a starting point as long as there is not sufficient grounds to prove invasion of privacy, libel or plagiarism. And so neither you nor I have anything to worry about here." I take a deep breath, remember that this is, in fact, someone I should placate. " In fact, if you think about it, I might even provide you with some free advertising—once Bionsensual comes out, both the soap's audience and the corporate sponsors will probably get excited about doing a product tie-in. So we are both fine. Okay?"

A strange smile appears on Kleat Madigan's rare beef of a face. The kind of smile that comes from knowing that you are holding the right side of an axe. "I think you and Jason need to have a little talk, Mrs. Levine. Maybe he hasn't explained how I see this company. To me, we're a platoon. We have a clear chain of command, so that every man Jack knows where he stands. And we are all absolutely in this thing together. I don't cut a man loose just because he's floundering. But I don't hold with disloyalty, and I won't put up with betrayal."

"Mr. Madigan, I didn't enlist in your company, but I do support it. I assure you that I am not betraying you or my

husband by writing a storyline that is distantly inspired by
something Jason is working on over here."

We are both breathing hard. Madigan's smile has gone
from sharp to shrapnel. "Well, Mrs. Green . . ."

"Ms. Levine."

His cold eyes hold mine as the massive head dips in ac-
knowledgment. "Ms. Levine. It seems this is too much conversation for just one meeting. So I will just say I look
forward to our next meeting and you can show yourself
out."

"Thank you." I march out of the office building on a
drumbeat of adrenaline that quickly winds down to a nervous flutter, leaving me drained and shaky. There are no
taxicabs to be seen, but a black sedan drives by me twice,
probably trying to figure out whether or not I'm a well-
heeled prostitute.

By the time I find a subway station I am on the verge of
tears.

All the way home I think of arguments to have with Jason.
I think of arguing that if we didn't have this big office party
to attend, he should at least have come home for a traditional Friday-night dinner.

Okay, so ordering in Chinese the way we usually do is
more Woody Allen Jewish than Jewish traditional. But the
point is, family togetherness, right? Unfortunately, no matter how I phrase this little speech in my head, I know that
when it comes out of my lips I will sound like my mother. I
am not ready to be saying my mother's lines.

And I am also frightened that there is more to all this
than my getting ditzy and failing to remember a change in
plans. Because as forgetful as I am, I think I would have

written something as big as the new date for Jason's office Christmas party down on the calendar. Which means maybe, just maybe, it was Mr. Organized who forgot this time. And that isn't like Jason, unless there's something that's gotten him so preoccupied he can't think about the usual details.

I walk out of the subway station into the kind of apocalyptic atmosphere that portends a deluge. This sky isn't just threatening, it means business.

I put my head down and start walking quickly, my heels loud on the pavement. A man strides by, his umbrella held like a shield in front of him; I guess it must be raining already farther uptown.

The traffic light is red so I pause for a moment, but when I see that the black sedan coming up West End is still half a block away I start to cross the avenue. Suddenly, the sedan picks up speed, its headlights reflecting the sheen of puddles as it barrels toward me. I dart across, clickety-clacking on my heels, and am almost out of the sedan's way when it swerves out of its lane, causing another driver to honk and yell something.

For a moment, I freeze and just stare deerishly at the headlights, thinking, oh, shit, that car is closing in on me. It is a very long moment. I have time to grieve at leaving my child motherless, regret that I'd never finished my Ph.D. and wish I'd had one truly great love affair to flash before my eyes right about now.

And then someone snatches me back against a solid chest and we both fall to the ground and roll. The someone makes a *whumph* sound. The sedan skids to a stop, guns its engine and then takes off onto a side street.

"Jesus Christ," I say. If Jason were here I'm sure he would remind me that invoking someone else's deity is never appropriate, but somehow "Oy Gevalt" does not cover this situation. I am sitting on somebody in the middle of the street and a yellow taxi is hurtling past us as if we were a couple of tires that have fallen onto the road. The sky gives a loud rumble and I see a flash of lightning to the east.

"Hey," says my rescuer, "we've got to move before someone else runs us over." For a moment, I think I am having one of my fantasies again.

I look over my shoulder and it *is* Ford. He must have gotten caught in the rain earlier, because his dark hair is plastered back against his skull, and his leather jacket looks saturated. Stirring dull roots with spring rain, as Mr. Eliot put it, except this rain is cold and I am the only one feeling a burst of unwanted desire. I am ashamed of myself in my good dress coat and my ruined plans.

I notice Fardles, the black Labrador puppy, coiled around one of Ford's legs, and the dog launches into a little dance of cringing, tail-wagging ambivalence.

"Easy, boy," Ford tells his dog. "Delilah, I'm going to help you stand up, okay?"

"Thanks."

Ford takes my hand to help me up and then steadies me, his hands on my upper arms. "Are you all right?"

"As all right as you get when crazy people decide to kill you for jaywalking."

"You're not hurt? Can you walk?"

"I'm fine," I say, and then my right ankle wobbles and I stagger back into his chest. Ford keeps his arm around my shoulders as he guides me back to the sidewalk and then draws me into his leather jacket, his large hand cupping the back of my head.

"Shh, shh," he says, and right on cue, I start crying.

"Shit," I say. "Shit." My tailbone feels bruised and my

hands are filthy, so I hold them down at my sides, but still I am aware of him, the firm gentleness of his touch, the strength with which he is braced against my weight.

"Take deep breaths."

I sniff loudly, trying to compose myself. My nose is running and I swipe at it with the back of my hand. "I just can't believe that guy was going to run me over just because I jaywalked."

Ford extends his arms so he can peer into my face. "Your nose is bleeding." He tips my head back and dabs some piece of fabric under my nose.

"Bhut is dhat?" I can't see what is staunching the nosebleed without putting my chin down. Whatever it is, it feels scratchy.

"My glove."

"I dhink it's stopped."

I look down and touch the skin under my nose. Feels clear. Christ, I wish I hadn't blown my folks' nose-job money on that wild spring break in Amsterdam.

"You'll need to wash the rest of the blood off a bit better with some water," Ford says. "So is that what you think? That the driver was some right-of-way nut?" He sounds merely curious, as if this is the kind of conversation he's used to having with people.

"Well, what else? Unless it was some maniac out to take a life for *no* reason." This is New York, after all, where crazy people drop bricks on tourist's heads and shove young women into the path of express trains. Just a little brush up against the city's beastly underbelly. Wouldn't even make the evening news. A little shiver runs through my body and Ford pulls me back into his chest. His fingers move absently through my hair, against my scalp, hypnotizing me.

"Unless you have any enemies who might have a reason to want you dead."

Now I move my head so that I can get a look at Ford's expression. "I'm assuming this is your ironic face."

Ford's mouth twitches. "No, this is deadpan. What about your husband?"

"You mean, does he want me dead or does somebody want him dead? Yeah, the Russian mafia's probably after him," I say, and then mentally count to five as Ford furrows his brow in a considering way. "Okay. That was *my* ironic face. As in, no, my husband does not possess any scheming mistresses bent on running me over so they can make free with his fortune and body. Jason's boss may be deciding that he'd like me dead right about now, but this is moving a little fast, even for an ex-general. Now, not to insult you, but I am going to limp quietly back home for a nice, hot bath."

Ford looks at me, one side of his mouth lifting in a smile. "You've been thinking a lot about death plots?"

"I watch a lot of soap operas."

"You need to broaden your horizons. Ever watch cop shows? That new one on the CIA is really—"

"Listen, real life is scary enough, and when I want to confirm my suspicions about people's warped and ambiguous morality, I indulge in literature. Now, if you'll excuse me, I would like to go take a hot bath and watch a video of Burt Lancaster pretending to be a stupid truck driver."

"Wait." Ford's brow is furrowed again, his eyes searching my face. "You sure you want to just go back upstairs?"

"Somehow I'm not in the mood for dancing."

"But you're all dressed up." And there it is, in his eyes: A lightning flash of masculine approval, gone before I am sure it was really there. I am aware that my sexy, spiky hair is now flat on one side and suspect my mascara has probably run in dark streams down my cheeks.

"I look dressed up and washed out. Which I am. Anyway, I'd better be getting on with it. . . ." I make a sort of intending-to-leave gesture, but like most women, I wait for it to be reciprocated before I actually leave.

"Can I talk to you for a moment? Would you like—would you come for a drink with me?"

I stand there, stunned by the slight hesitation in his voice. Ford does not sound like his usual imperturbable self. He sounds like a man stumbling over an invitation to a woman, not a pal. A surge of electricity shoots through me. Do I want to talk to him in a smoky bar, with the adrenaline of my near-death experience still zinging through my veins? Maybe someone else will try to run me over on the way home and I can fall back into Ford's arms again.

Except I've fallen into my share of arms in the past, and found no great mystery there. So there's a gleam of something in Ford's hooded raptor gaze. So what? This is not my fantasy lover. This is a guy who probably spends all his free time in the gym and reads books with sports scores in the index. Even if this man I have fantasized about in a myriad of ways did look at me with interest for a fraction of a second, even if he had enough interest in me to last for the full fifteen minutes of disappointing intercourse with a stranger, so what? He has no illusions about me, no fantasy, no narrative. I am not the heroine of his story, and I have slept with enough men before I got married to know exactly what it feels like to act on this kind of impulse. Intimacy as a five-finger exercise. Practice sex.

Ford narrows his eyes and cocks his head to the side, picking up some frequency I don't realize I am transmitting. "What's wrong, Delilah?"

The sound of his voice saying my name stirs all the old fantasies: acrobat, warrior, vampire, thief; aristocrat, handy-man, Indian chief.

"I thought my husband's Christmas party was tonight." There. I've said it: My husband. Stand back and behold the sign of the cross!

"Ah. And it's not tonight?"

I shake my head. There is a clap of thunder.

Ford looks at me with his unreadable face. "I was actu-ally looking for you tonight. I needed to check how the closet was holding up in the rain."

"Check it tomorrow."

"Okay. So come have a drink with me instead."

I sigh and shake my head. "Listen, Ford . . ."

"Just a beer. I'll drop Fardles off at my place and then we can talk, and I'll walk you back here safe and sound." He puts his large, capable hand on my arm, and it makes a convincing argument.

I hadn't realized Ford lived around here. "I'm not sure I need a drink and I'm really not sure about wanting com-pany." The puppy gives a little whine, picking up the tension.

"And you're not sure about coming to my apartment." Ford takes a breath, then huffs it out. Almost a sigh. "It's not that kind of an invitation," he says, his hands jammed into his pockets.

"I know." It's just that I'm tired and something else, maybe worried about Jason's boss. Maybe worried about Jason. "I just don't really think I feel up to it."

Ford looks up, his expression rueful. "Why am I doing this wrong? What would a woman do differently?"

"Why? You're rehearsing to become a woman?"

"Women are just so good at the whole friendship thing. Knowing what to say. Knowing what not to say."

"You're doing all right."

"Then why are you turning me down?"

All right. So the object of my lustful fantasies wants to be my pal. I can handle that. It's rather sweet, really. He probably wants to ask my advice about some gorgeous twenty-three-year-old. After first making sure I'm not going to pass out from near-hit-and-run shock, of course.

"One drink," I say, because clearly this is the way the universe intends me to pay for my adulterous imaginings.

Ford's grin is like a flash of lightning. And then the rain begins in earnest.

The reality of Ford is strangely disappointing. We are sitting in the bar of Mucho Mexico, beneath the mural of the gypsy dancers and the oddly proportioned donkey.

Ford's building was old and somewhat derelict and smelled of rice and beans, reminding me of the places I used to live before marriage. We took Fardles up the stairs rather than the elevator, probably because the elevator made an odd, rattling sound as it moved up and down.

Ford's apartment had the anonymous, slightly forlorn look that all cheap, furnished places acquire over time. In the bathroom, where I discovered that my plumber wears boxer shorts and reads SF from the mid-sixties, I did what I could to make repairs, washing my face clean of streaked makeup and blood and slicking my hair back.

Still, I knew I was not looking my best, and I did not care.

We ran the four blocks to the restaurant, huddled together, Ford holding an umbrella with his left hand, his right hand dangling awkwardly between us. I was very aware of that hand, which seemed as if it should have gone around my waist or shoulders. I tried not to want it there.

And now we're sitting at the bar, safe from the marauding mariachi band but not from the plumes of secondhand smoke, and Ford is just a nice-looking guy in a slouchy black sweater, not a half-Mongol modern-day warrior with a tragic past. He drinks Dos Equis with lime and polishes off the tortilla chips as if he's forgotten to have dinner.

"Are you hungry, Ford? They have good guacamole, or we could order some real food. . . ."

"Nah. I love the spicy stuff, but it makes me, ah, doesn't agree with me."

"Go on, Ford, live a little. It's not like we have some romantic evening planned." I figure it's best to make this clear right off the bat, just in case. I raise my hand, summon the bartender, and order the cheese and jalapeno appetizer. When I turn back to Ford, his face is flushing deeply, and I'm not sure whether it's with embarrassment or an incipient stroke. There is literally a bright band of color across his cheeks and nose. I feel I must say something, in case he is about to keel over.

"Your face is turning really red. Are you okay, or would you rather go out for a minute?"

"I'm fine. It's an Asian thing." Ford taps the beer bottle. "Reaction to alcohol."

"So you're . . ."

"Half Chinese."

I think about what I know about Chinese culture. *In The Joy Luck Club,* there were a lot of old mothers playing mahjong and pushing marriage and food on their grown daughters. *In Crouching Tiger, Hidden Dragon,* there was a lot of leaping in the air and kicking things in slow motion. So I have a sort of confused impression of the Chinese as being sort of supernaturally fit Jewish people, albeit with more mystery.

"What's your other half?"

"Russian. My mother and father met here in an English class. Turned out that they were from towns that were within an hour's drive of each other."

Aha, so the Siberian fantasy wasn't completely off base. I wait, to see if he will continue. After a moment, not looking at me, he says, "My mom and grandmother raised me. Forty miles may not be too much to look at on a map, but it got to be a pretty fair distance across the kitchen table."

"Kitchen tables can be pretty dangerous places even without the international tension. So—how did a boy from two cultures get a name that doesn't belong to either?"

Ford turns back to me with a slightly crooked smile. "My father didn't figure much in the decision. My mother named me Ford Carter, after both presidents. Ford Carter Michaelovich. I changed it to Michaels in high school." There is something practiced in his delivery that let me know this is the version of his life he's prepared and polished for public consumption. Or maybe he's just comfortable with his past. I'd had him pegged for the quietly tormented loner type, but there's an ease about Ford I didn't expect.

"And you're in no contact with your father whatsoever?"

"He did come by when I graduated high school, just before I enlisted in the navy. He told me not to let my life be run by something hanging between my legs and then he took off. I guess he thought he owed me some parental advice."

"God, how very *Officer and a Gentleman*."

"Actually, I spent most of my time in a submarine with a lot of flatulent guys. Not a lot of hot townie girls to be had."

I imagine Ford in dogtags, hurtling himself over an obstacle course, all sweaty and determined. There's something incredibly sexy about enforced celibacy, and I know I am not the only woman who gets a little flushed when the ships dock at New York Harbor for Fleet Week. "Aw, c'mon. I bet you've had your share of hello, sailoring."

Ford just looks at me, one eyebrow raised.

"You're the only man I've ever met who can actually do that." I point to his left eyebrow, nearly touching it.

Ford grins. "I used to practice. It's my Mr. Spock look."

"You're too young to have a Mr. Spock look."

Ford raises one hand in a Vulcan salute, pointer and middle finger pointing right, ring finger and pinky pointing left. "Live long and prosper. I'm thirty-three, by the way."

So he's two years younger than I am. Not that it matters. "Are we talking minor fanboy here, or . . ."

"Conventions, pointy ear prosthetics, bedroom stuffed with memorabilia."

"Just the original *Star Trek*, or . . .?"

"Also *Star Wars*. But only the first trilogy."

"You don't look like the type."

"What type do I look like?"

"I'm not sure. I've been trying to place you. You know, as in who would play you in the movie of your life? But you elude easy definition."

"That's because the Asian thing is distracting you. The answer is obvious—John Cusack."

"You're right! You're absolutely right! Wow. Very good. And insightful."

"He's got that quality of being secure in his insecurity. The cool nerd thing."

"You aren't nerdy. And I don't see the insecurity at all. You seem perfectly comfortable talking about yourself."

Ford rests his chin on his fist, and I can't help but notice the generous swell of his bicep. "Maybe you're easy to talk to."

"I'm still having trouble picturing you as a science fiction nerd."

"Well, I started working out when I was fifteen. Before then, I was small and scrawny and asthmatic. Forget sports—I wasn't even allowed out of the house when the pollen index was too high, or if it was humid and smoggy, or if my mother thought it might conceivably *become* too humid or smoggy . . . so I lived half my life on alternate planets, fighting alien invaders and trying my luck with sexy extraterrestrials."

"And at fifteen you pulled a male Cinderella?"

Ford laughs, but stiltedly. "Yeah, well, my mom got sick, so there wasn't anyone watching me so closely. I started doing weights and switched to martial arts. So by the time I enlisted I was just short, but not so scrawny."

There is a silence in which I consider what to ask. "Did your mom get better?"

Ford's face looks like it has been carved out of stone. "No. But I'd rather not talk about that right now, if you don't mind."

"Okay." Another moment of silence, rockier than the first. "We could talk about your being short. You're not short. You're what, five foot ten?"

Ford smiles. "Five foot nine and a half."

"You seem taller."

"If we stand eye to eye, we're almost the same height."

For a moment, inadvertently, I think about what that might mean in a different, more intimate context. A current passes between us, the telepathy of attraction.

Uh-oh. Time, as Monty Python used to say, for something completely different.

"So," I say, "why don't you start with the bad news."

He looks completely mystified.

"You wanted to talk to me about the closet, remember? That can't be good."

"Well, it has to do with the leak. . . ."

I thank the powers that be when the nachos arrive, as jalapeno and cheese topping goes a long way toward alleviating boredom. And I am beginning to suspect Ford may be the crown prince of boring. For the next ten minutes, he goes into excruciating detail about the building's one-hundred-year-old hot water system, and the fact that my mid-level apartment was where the expansion coupling for the steam riser connects to the whatsit. The upshot seems to be that Ford needs to take out everything he has already done and start again from scratch. Ordinarily I would be feeling sort of pleased to have more of Ford, but somehow I know that whatever has been fueling my fantasies, it is not here. He is so very ordinary, sitting here beside me, and besides his raffishly handsome looks and general air of competence, there is nothing much there.

"You're sick of the disruption," Ford says. He is watching me carefully, as if I were a tricky valve.

"A bit," I say.

"Did you and Jason have another fight?"

This is what I get for not setting clear boundaries. "No, we did not."

"Then why isn't he home with you now?"

"He had to work late." But as soon as the words are out, they seem false. What about Irina, his new friend from work? What about the expensive plus-size clothing, the visits to Caroline Moore, the motel bill? What secrets has my husband neglected to tell me?

Ford's hand comes out and covers mine, and the shock of his warm, dry skin against my naked knuckles makes me take a deep, audible breath. "You know, Delilah, sometimes there's a stage of marriage where you both lead parallel lives. But that's not a place to remain indefinitely. Maybe the time has come to start looking carefully at what's really going on between you and Jason."

We sit, not looking at each other, my hand still underneath his. My frozen margarita has melted into a salty puddle, and I take a sip of it more out of duty than desire. "That's my line," I say. "About parallel lives."

"I know. I've read your poetry." Ford releases my hand to take a swig of his beer.

I turn to look at him. "You're kidding."

"After I started working at your place, one of the building guys—Enrique?—said you were a poet. He said you were published in some anthology of best young poets, so I decided to pick it up."

The poems in that collection date from the late eighties, when I was having a lot of sex and feeling very irritated with men. There is a lot of what writing instructors like to call telling detail in those poems. Now *I'm* blushing. "I thought it was out of print."

Ford's dark gaze meets mine. "It is."

And suddenly I see that I have been wrong in one respect. Ford does have a fantasy about me; it is written clearly on his features, like a scarlet mask of intoxication. I am the ordinary woman with the wicked past, the reformed harlot all the more seductive because I have renounced the gin and feathers and cigarettes for a life of domestic sobriety. Ford looks at me and sees the possibility of a secret life, and that is a very seductive thing.

"Well," I say deliberately, "that was all years ago. I lead a very dull existence now. And there's not much poetry in schlepping Sadie to school and back."

"Yeah, I got that from the poems," Ford says. "How dull you are inside."

And the funny thing is, I am reminded of nothing so much as the beginning with Jason: How he thought I was wild and bohemian and exciting, and wondered if he could tame me just enough to bring me home.

"I'm not saying I'm dull," I explain. "I'm explaining that my life is not exactly filled with adventure."

"And what's going on inside?" Ford leans forward. There is something a little unsettling about the intensity of his regard.

"The same as everyone else. Wild fantasies of espionage, horror and romance."

"Not the same as everyone, Delilah. Some people live their adventures and carry the dull emptiness inside." There is something in Ford's voice that makes the small hairs on the back of my neck stand up. But I ignore it, throwing back the last of the margarita.

"Time to return to active Mom duty," I say. We argue politely about who should pay; in the end, we go dutch, which isn't really fair, since I ate most of the nachos. As I stand up, Ford moves my stool aside and retrieves my coat from its hook on the wall.

"I'll walk you home," he says, putting his hand on the small of my back. The rain has stopped and I am aware of the sound of my heels on the sidewalk as we walk.

I stop in front of my building. "Good night." I want to get in quickly, before one of the many dog-walkers out gets a good look at me in my evening clothes, being escorted home by the plumber.

Ford looks at me as if he is dissatisfied with something. If I didn't know better, I would think he had been hoping for something to occur between us. "There are other possibilities, you know."

"Excuse me?"

"That car that tried to run you over. Maybe someone does have a reason to kill you."

"Like who? My soap opera storyline hasn't even aired yet, so it's not as if any lunatic couch potato's had time to fixate on me."

Ford actually looks angry. "Don't dismiss this out of hand. Think. Could someone have, say, a reason to want to keep you from writing any more episodes of your soap?"

I am very tired all of a sudden. "Listen," I say, "if I start to think like that, I'll never leave the house. It's like 9/11. You start believing the whole world's nothing but bad guys out to get you, you never get to lead a normal life. So unless there is some reason for me to get paranoid—"

"I don't think it's being paranoid to consider all the possible ramifications of a scenario—"

"I take Mr. Xanax when I start thinking like that."

Ford rubs his head as if it's beginning to ache. "So. I'll see you tomorrow?"

"On Saturday?"

"It's supposed to storm again, and I thought I'd come by and check on the pipes. Unless you and your family have plans . . . "

"No, it's fine. What time?"

"Around two. Maybe earlier—but I need to take my dog for a run."

"You can bring him, if you like. Jason will be out tomorrow." So will Sadie, but I don't want to sound like I'm coming on to him.

Ford smiles a little crookedly, but his eyes remain concerned. He brings his hand halfway up, either in a wave or in an aborted movement toward me. "Start asking questions, Delilah."

*   *   *

My neighbor, Kathy Wheatley, is already in the elevator.
She looks tense and pale and seems oblivious to my presence. Well, okay, she always looks pale—that whole blonde
eyebrowed, blonde eyelashed, not-enough-pigment-to-the-
personality thing. But right now Kathy seems distracted,
not at all her usual wholesome, determinedly cheery self.

"Everything okay, Kathy?"

Kathy looks at me as if startled out of a daydream of her
own. "Delilah! Sorry, I didn't realize it was you."

"Looks like you have a lot on your mind."

"Hmm? Yes." There is a moment's pause, and I find myself wondering just what it is that could be giving Kathy
Wheatley that haunted look.

"Is anything wrong, Kath?" This is just nosy, I admit, but
after years of being snubbed for playdates, I would get a
certain satisfaction from hearing that my neighbor has
some problems of her own.

"Oh, just silly stuff." Kathy waves a hand glittering with
antique Victorian rings. "Getting the country house reno-
vated is so time-consuming, and now Tamlyn's getting into
horseback riding, which is a huge expense. And David's
working on a book, which means lots of air travel, which
makes me a bit nervous."

I try to imagine Kathy sitting up nights worrying over
her bearded Mr. Potato of a spouse. But who am I to understand the ways of a man with a woman? Maybe, behind
closed doors, the man sheds his meek and spudlike ways
and thrills my neighbor down to her sturdy Scandinavian
toes. Or maybe David's starchy steadiness is precisely what
a hyper-motivated woman like Kathy requires.

I try to think how I would feel if Jason were always off in a hotel room halfway around the world. Not very different; distance is distance, and all it takes is a magazine in front of your face to create some. But still, some people fret over the miles.

"So David's away right now? How do your girls handle it?"

"Oh, goodness, they're far too busy to even notice what we do!" Kathy's eyes are too bright and I realize she has been crying. Suddenly I remember the pedicure and my suspicion that she may be having an affair.

"Well, my evening didn't exactly go well. First I thought I was going to Jason's Christmas party, and then it turns out that his big office do is Wednesday. Next I wind up nearly getting run over by a car."

"Hmm?" Kathy looks up at me, clearly startled out of a train of thought that has nothing to do with what I am saying. Why do I bother telling her about my life? Why do I always volunteer information that makes me appear to be an idiot? "Sorry, Del, I was just thinking about whether I booked Fleur's hair appointment. . . ."

"No problem."

We reach my floor and I turn to say good-bye. In the half second before my head is all the way around, I glance in the mirror behind me and catch a look of undisguised antipathy on Kathy's face.

"Good-bye, Kathy."

"Bye, Delilah!"

Discovering someone dislikes you while you stand in an elevator is just like discovering that someone has just passed gas, I suppose: The unspeakable is unmentionable. In any case, I am too fried to puzzle out the reasons why.

I know Jason is home because I manage to open the door to my apartment without using my key. My husband likes shortcuts and is forever pressing in the little button that un-locks our front door.

I walk in to find Jason carrying a frozen dinner into the living room on a tray.

"Where were you, Del? I let Hilda go at nine."

"Hello to you, too. I went to your office. As in, you never told me the Christmas party had changed dates."

Jason turns to me, and now I can see the chill of his anger in his eyes. "Yes, Delilah, I did. I told you we'd changed it to next Wednesday, because of setbacks with our big account. As usual, you probably just weren't paying attention. And now I suggest you let me eat in peace, as I have just spent this entire day in back-to-back meetings and I am exhausted."

So Madigan didn't say anything about our disagreement to Jason. "I may be disorganized, but it's because I'm disor-ganized that I always write things down on the kitchen cal-endar."

Jason's eyes narrow. "So now you're going to try to pin the blame on me, is that it?" He stands there, still holding the tray, and I can feel how badly he wants this conflict to disappear. He wants it so badly that if there were an exper-imental pill to take to make him invisible, he would take it. What he won't do, of course, is try to talk things through with me in a civil tone of voice.

"It's just that because I am so disorganized, I tend to write down important events on the calendar."

"It's not my fault if you forgot to write it down!"

I look at my husband. In the early days of our marriage, everyone remarked on how eager and practical and easy-going he was. I was the moody, difficult artist. His friends were certain he was getting the worst of the bargain. "Jason," I say softly. "What's going on with you?"

Jason's face reddens, either with embarrassment or with

anger. "Don't start in on me, Delilah. It's late, I'm tired, and you screwed up the date of the party. That's all that's going on with me. Not that you would notice if anything were going on with me. Not that I'm allowed to do anything but work my ass off all day long while you run around trying to express your creative side. God forbid you could spend the extra time making this house a place a man would want to come home to. Or extend yourself to cook a goddamn dinner."

My heart is pounding as quickly now as it did when the car nearly ran me over. "Are you trying to tell me your needs aren't being met in this marriage?"

Jason laughs, an ugly sound. "My needs! I don't get to have needs! I just get to be responsible all day long and frankly, I'm a little sick of it."

There is something dangerously taut in Jason's face and I feel I am within inches of colliding with it. A little voice inside my head is yelling, *Back off, back off.* But a hot flicker of anger flares up in me. No, I tell the voice, I will not stand here and get made out to be the bad guy.

"Well, maybe I'm a little sick of the way things are, too. If I'd wanted a long-distance marriage with huge expanses of emotional distance, I would have dated a spy."

"Yeah, well, try getting a paying job and dealing with all the bills for a change. I'll go fulfill my creative needs and then when *you* come home tired and stressed out, *I'll* complain that you don't make me feel like a man anymore!" Jason continues saying something about my numerous faults, but I find his voice fading into the background as I realize that it has come to this: We sound like some bad early seventies movie. And I know how that plays.

First, my husband will leave me for a younger woman with a daisylike face. Next comes the long shot of me in bell-bottoms and a sweatercoat, my hair looking like a halo through the soft focus lens as I walk through Central Park to some irritating instrumental music. I'll bump into some young guy with sideburns, we'll have cinematically experimental sex that will involve a lot of strangely sequenced jump-shots, he'll fall in love but I'll need to redefine myself, so I'll join a women's support group with one African-American woman, one Latina and another angry white woman with a gray streak. After the angry white woman yells at me I'll get a job that requires me to wear a fashionable mauve polyester suit with paisley cravat, and the soundtrack will actually acquire a hint of rhythm as I hit my stride. Finally in a position of power, I'll see my husband again with a very young, pregnant blonde, but he'll look at me with longing. I'll walk away poker-faced, not revealing whether I am gloating, grieving or merely constipated, while a pre-Islamic Cat Stevens sings convincingly about pain and new beginnings.

"Delilah? Christ, you're not even listening to what I'm saying!"

I turn back to Jason just as he throws his hands up and the tray with the lasagna lands on the floor. I get splattered by a bit of sauce.

"Mommy?"

We both turn and there is Sadie in her Powerpuff girls pajamas, blessedly nearsighted without her glasses. "You woke me up."

I move toward her first. "Oh, baby, I'm sorry. Daddy and I didn't mean to talk so loud."

Sadie looks at me. "Something spilled on you. Are you hurt?"

"No, no, honey, it's just tomato sauce. Daddy dropped his dinner."

Sadie looks up at her father. "You're not supposed to eat in the living room. It makes too much mess."

"Go on back to bed, Sadie." Jason's voice is tight with anger.

"Daddy's not feeling well, so he gets to eat in front of the TV. Just like you do when you're not feeling well, Sades." I put my hand between her birdlike shoulder blades. "Now off to bed."

Sadie yawns and I walk her into her bedroom, hoping I'm not dripping sauce. I hear a door slam but Sadie doesn't seem to notice.

"You okay, Sade?"

Sadie looks up and yawns again. "You still got sauce on you, Mom."

"I know. I'll go wash up." She gets back into bed and I kiss her on her little pursed mouth, just as I used to when she was a baby.

When I walk out of Sadie's room I find that Jason has cleaned up the mess and thrown the broken plate out the back door, so I wash my face and hair and put on a Victoria's Secret flannel nightgown. From the living room, I can hear the television warning about escalating tensions between somewhere and somewhere else.

I stand in the doorway. Jason will not look at me. I think maybe he is embarrassed by his own behavior.

"Jason." No reaction. "Jason." He turns and his face is full of spite.

"Well, that was a nice scene." His voice implies that I was the stage director.

"Jason, maybe we need to see someone. A marriage counselor."

My husband turns away from me, back to the news, where dislocated people are tramping from one danger into another. "I don't know, Delilah. You think words can change things. I believe in action. Do something. Don't just talk about it."

"But what do you want me to do?"

"Right now, I want you to leave me alone." With that, Jason turns back to the television. And then I go write a poem about rain and death and desire. It is not a particularly good poem, and I wonder if I have lost the knack for rendering the fat of things down to their bones. If so, what will I do with my mind, now that it's finally awake again?

Later, as I lie in bed beside my sleeping husband, I think about what I'd told my sister about not wanting an affair. I plighted my troth to Jason ten years ago, but I'm not sure he knew what my truth was. In that lovely old prayer-book language, troth has to do with intentionality as well as with action. Faithfulness is another word that comes to mind. It doesn't just mean to not go around *shtupping* plumbers, or even to not fantasize about shtupping them. It means to be full of the faith of the partnership, mind and body connected. With my body I thee worship, and thereto I plight thee my troth.

What did I think I was promising when I stood with Jason under the Jewish marriage canopy all those springs ago? My father had just had a heart attack and Jason was there for me, a constant presence, a comfort and a friend. When we made love, I could feel how I ignited Jason's imagination. He thought of me as something wild and creative and life affirming. We were going to draw strength from each other. We were going to invent a new family that wouldn't undermine us as our families of origin had done.

And then, at some point, I turned into scatty Delilah, and Jason transformed into the snide older brother I never had and didn't really require.

And now Jason's peeled back the mask of friendly animosity and shown me the wrathful, tantruming child behind. So there's not even the comfort of thinking, well, it's just bickering, it doesn't matter. I don't know if it's that he's changed or that he's showing me something that was there all along, but either way, I don't like it.

"Let me not to the marriage of true minds admit impediments. Love is not love that alters when it alteration finds. . . ."

I think Jason and I stopped being completely trothful with each other a long time ago.

Saturday, December 15
7 A.M.

Delilah Levine knew there were two kinds of hit-and-run drivers in New Terra City: The kind who had a little left-right confusion and the kind who did not.

She was pretty sure that the late-model black skycar that had nearly flattened her belonged in the latter category. Call it a hunch, but when a vehicle stops, turns, and heads back in your direction, it's probably not because the driver's eighty-seven and confused about which side the brake's on.

Pressing her hand against her front door, Delilah waited a moment before walking through the disabled forcefield. Fifteen minutes later, soaking in a warm isolation bath, she was still trying to dismiss the detective's concern that someone wanted her dead. Detectives were paid to be suspicious, after all, and just because a gruff ex-Earther cop was certain this was no random act of city aggression didn't mean a thing. All men were always convinced that their hunches were right, and men who happened to have been cops in an earlier incarnation figured their hunches were bigger and better than anybody else's.

The detective had a lot to learn if he still thought New Terra operated by Earther rules. Here, violence was constant, random,

meaningless. There wasn't a lot to be learned from crime scenes—
unless you wanted to learn just how far afield small body parts
could travel. As a barmaid at the Entropy Bar and Grill, Delilah
had learned that lesson all too well.

And besides, she had ways to protect herself. As she'd informed
the overly cautious detective, she wasn't some Earther female
with an electronic device for every task and a pack of mood-
enhancers dulling her senses. Delilah had grown up on New
Terra, where you thought damn hard about ingesting anything
that would alter your perceptions or slow your reflexes.

Sweeping her damp hair away from the back of her neck,
Delilah closed her eyes and leaned back, uncaring that her breasts
were now visible above the melting lilac-scented bubbles. After
all, there was no one else in the apartment to see her.

And then there was. Delilah's first intimation that there was
an intruder came with a prickle of awareness that tautened the
fine hairs at her temples.

"Who's there?" Her voice was sharp. She couldn't catch
much, just a sense of mammalian presence, so she let the fine
golden filaments rise out of the rest of her damp hair, probing for
more psychic information.

Warm, mammalian—male. That last impression was sur-
prisingly strong, and Delilah felt a charge of electric excite-
ment race down her scalp, tightening her body like a lover's
touch. Whoever this mystery male was, he was sending out
some kind of pheromone message that she was having no diffi-
culty picking up.

"Who's there?" This was the problem with being a glorified
empath. A true New Terran telepath would know who was there,
and if the male intruder meant harm, and what kind of harm he
intended. But Delilah, who had the serpentine tendrils of her fa-
ther's people, lacked the full range of their psychic powers. Her
human heritage had diluted her father's genes, and she was really

more empath than telepath, which meant that unless this male presence touched her, she wouldn't know what he was thinking.

"Sweetheart, I thought you said you were hard to fool."

"Detective Ford!" At the sound of the man's low, wry voice, Delilah sat up abruptly in the bath, realized her mistake, then sank back down into the melting bubbles. "What the hell do you think you're doing? And where are you?" Looking around, all Delilah could see were the pale terra-cotta walls of her apartment. The mirror reflected her own astonished face back at her, golden tendrils waving as she tried to locate the source of Ford's voice.

"What am I doing? Proving my point. You're easy meat for a determined hunter, Ms. Levine. And as for your second question—"

Delilah felt the whisper of movement in the fraction of a moment before hands clamped down over her wrists, pulling her out of the water.

"You bastard!" The moment his flesh touched hers, he became visible to her—his face broad and tanned and split by a wide grin, his dark brown hair just long enough to fall into his watchful eyes. The hands that held hers captive were large and calloused and she caught the smell of travel dust and woodfire on his leather jacket and then, against her will, she caught his impressions of her.

"Let go of me!" She struggled in his grip but the sudden spark of connection had stunned him into immobility. She had seen the look on the detective's face before, though not often, not since she'd gained control: She had linked with him, and he was now touching her as intimately as he had ever touched a woman.

"Christ." The word slipped out of his lips and Delilah watched his eyes widen. "You're wrong. This is more *intimate than I've ever been with a woman—not counting my mother, when I was inside her womb. Damn, I can feel your heart beating."*

"I know. I can hear you think." She had been nude and her an-

tennae had been fully extended when Ford had touched her, and this enhanced her powers. So instead of just receiving emotions— excitement at the chase, pleasure at the capture, a certain degree of male heat at the sight of her naked body—Delilah had linked their minds. Something that usually took a lot more than a touch of hands to effect. In fact, something that had never happened be- fore without full body contact—which made Delilah wonder: Was Ford psychically talented as well?

"I didn't think I was. A guy down in the Entropy Bar gave me an invisibility pill, which was how I got in here." Ford glanced down at Delilah's naked body, and she could feel his ab- domen tighten, could sense the rush of blood to places that weren't thinking about her safety or anything to do with the murder case.

"Let go of my hands. Break the link," Delilah said, in the most unfriendly tone she could manage.

"That's not what you're thinking," Ford replied, and his tone was huskier than usual. His eyes were as watchful as ever, but something in their darkness flared and sparked.

"Never mind what I'm thinking!"

"But I can feel what you're feeling," Ford said, and lowered his mouth to hers, and in that instant she stopped protesting, because she could no longer separate his thoughts from hers, and both of them were thinking pretty much the same thing: that his clothing had to go, and fast.

"I never knew you admired my chest so much," Ford said. "You were so very businesslike when you were sewing up that bullethole. If only I'd known how much you'd wanted to run your hand over the smooth, hard planes of my—"

"There is an etiquette among telepaths, you asshole! You don't go saying what someone else is thinking!"

"But I'm not the telepath, sweetheart. You are."

With an inarticulate roar of rage, Delilah tried to rotate her wrists to break Ford's grip. Unfortunately, this reminded her of wrestling with a certain towheaded farm boy back in elementary school.

Ford's dark eyes gleamed with interest. "Ah. So you like it rough, eh?"

"I'd like to kill you, yes," Delilah said, gritting her teeth as she tried to jam her knee between his legs.

"If I couldn't tell what you were thinking, you know, I'd let you go in an instant," Ford said. "As it is, though, I believe I'd rather do—this." And with that, he lifted her over his shouler and then deposited her unceremoniously on the bed, quickly straddling her naked, panting body with his trousered thighs. His right hand pinioning her wrists above her head, Ford traced the line of her breasts with his left hand. "And what does the lady think about that?" Ford shuddered as he felt the adrenaline-fueled intensity of her response.

"It's not what I'm thinking, you dickhead," Delilah snarled. "You can read what I'm feeling. What I'm thinking is, you're a dickhead."

Ford leaned over until his lips were within reach of hers. "So fight me."

Delilah caught Ford's lip in her teeth, but even as she twisted her wrists free of his grip, she felt her own control slipping. She felt the tension in his body, the unbearable weight of his uncertainty as he felt her hands slipping down his shirt to find the smooth, hard planes of his chest. . . .

Ford smiled as he caught that thought, and Delilah started to struggle against him for a moment, but just then his hands came around to cup her hips, bringing her flush against the hard bulge between his thighs.

"Shh, shh," Ford whispered into her neck. "No jokes now."

He pressed his lower body hard against her the moment she thought that she needed to feel him against her; his hand found the soft mound of her breast, still slick with moisture from the bath, the instant she craved his touch there.

"Oh, God," she moaned, and his mouth came down on her nipple, sucking hard, then harder.

"Please," she said in a voice gone almost hoarse, and he slid down her damp body, his hands spreading her, his breath ragged in the instant before he found her with his tongue.

"No!" She screamed when he caught her gently with his teeth, but he could hear the wordless pleading in her mind, and he found the perfect pressure to send her arching, her heels braced against the bed as he held her in his large, capable hands. He stayed with her, drawing the pleasure out until she collapsed on the bed.

She stared up at him, naked, sprawled with her legs apart. For a moment, she seemed unable to speak.

"Jesus," Ford said, "I never felt anything like that in my life. I could actually feel you coming. I never knew that a woman could feel so much—"

"Get out of here this minute," she snarled.

Ford just looked at her for a moment, an almost humorous expression of bemusement on his face. The bulge in his trousers looked almost painfully swollen. "I can't read you anymore," he said. "Not without touching you. So if you really want me to go, I guess I'll have to just leave. But—"

"Just go!" She launched herself off the bed and grabbed hold of him, intending to propel him bodily out the door if need be, but the instant she touched him, both their eyes went wide with wonder.

"Oh," she said.

"Shit, I didn't want you to know that." Ford's eyes met hers.

"But you always said you hated me." Her hands were still on his arms, and she could feel the tension in his biceps.

"I thought I did," he said, and then he was kissing her again, walking her back until she was flush against the wall.

The last thing she remember saying out loud was, "Don't get me pregnant," but by that time he was inside her, too large, too thick, too perfectly rough as he thrust too deeply inside her, slam-

*ming up against—there—sending shock waves of pleasure
through her body, each wave harder and stronger than the last.*

"Wait," he said, "don't move or I'll . . ."

"No," she said, "don't stop or I'll . . ."

*And then they stared, helpless, into each other's eyes, as the
wave crested and broke and carried them along.*

*For a moment afterward, they were too stunned to speak. Then
Delilah turned to Ford and punched him in the jaw.*

When I wake up I find my hair has reverted back to its
usual chin-length bob shape. Why is it that no matter what
I do to my hair it always winds up looking like it did in my
fourth-grade class photo?

I am brushing my teeth and wondering if I am constitu-
tionally incapable of change when Jason walks in, carrying
a mug of coffee.

"Here," he says, "with extra sugar to sweeten your temper."

"Huh," I say, "it's not my temper that went Prego on
the walls."

"Well, I used three in mine." Jason smiles his best blue-
eyed-boy smile. I spit out the toothpaste and accept the
coffee.

"You do good rueful, I'll give you that." And as easily as
that, we turn last night into a little contretemps, an awkward blip on the monitor but nothing major, nothing
marriage-threatening.

"I couldn't sleep last night. In fact, I almost woke you up
to apologize. I still can't believe I flew off the handle like
that. It's just there's a lot going at work right now, and you
picked the absolute worst moment to accuse me of spending my free time horizontal." With Jason, the apology always comes after the pardon. He likes to be sure of his
reception.

I would like to point out that I didn't actually accuse him, but this seems like the wrong moment to get picky with details. "So what's going on, Jason?"

Jason starts to rub a hand through his hair, remembers his receding hairline, and takes a deep breath instead. "It's this Biosensual thing—man, it's almost more trouble than it's worth."

I take a sip of coffee. "You want to talk about it?"

Jason closes the toilet seat and sits down while I perch on the edge of the bathtub. We discovered long ago that the bathroom is the safest place to carry on a serious conversation, as Sadie is always liable to hurtle into the bedroom at any moment.

"Okay, here's the situation. Basically, we have all the usual hurdles to getting a new product FDA approved, plus the fact that Irina's an ex-Soviet and used to work with some dangerous materials. Since a substance in the mold that's used to make Biosensual can destroy higher brain function if used in high quantities, the Feds have been driving us crazy with red tape."

"It sounds like they're justified. Who wants an aphrodisiac that Kentucky Fries your brain?" No wonder Madigan was so paranoid about bad press. Even Tarzan could figure out aphrodisiac good, no-higher-brain-function bad.

"Of course it doesn't fry your brain! The Spryngina mold that Irina's adapted has already been proven to help alleviate hallucinations in schizophrenics. With the side effect of disinhibiting them and making them, well . . ."

"Happy and horny?"

"Exactly. Now, in an even smaller dose, Spryngina's like a cross between a great margarita and Viagra."

Jason sounds a little too convinced of his spiel. "Have you tried it yourself?"

"Not exactly." Now he looks a little embarrassed.

"What do you mean, not exactly?"

"I tried it in a lotion, which turned out to be ineffective. Right now, it seems to do best in a suppository."

Which means only the French will want it, and they don't need it. But lotion sounds okay—I'm assuming a solitary application here, of course. "So let me understand this. You tried an experimental drug from this Irina person, who used to be some kind of mad Soviet scientist . . ."

"It's perfectly safe! Just because Bioscrub didn't work doesn't mean Biosensual isn't going to."

"Bioscrub?"

"An exfoliant that left some women looking as if they had leprosy. And there was Biocide, which was a spermicidal cream that did work, but had a few side effects. . . ."

I know all this perfectly well, of course, as it comprises my comic relief subplot for that coke-fiend actress with the frizzy hair. But I feel reluctant to pick this rare moment of accord to tell Jason about his project's role in my soap-writing career. Especially as this must lead into a discussion of my run-in with Madigan. "What kind of side effects, Jason?" I do everything but bat my eyelashes.

"It left a blue stain. All over the, uh, affected organ."

"And you definitely did not try that one out, because I certainly would have noticed if your *shmekel* turned into Old Blue." At least I hope I would have noticed. I haven't seen as much of Mr. Wiggly as I used to.

"I am pleased to report that Irina's blue period was before my time. She was with our competitors back then."

I stand up and start to wipe away the raccoonlike remnants of last night's mascara. "So your only problem is FDA approval? Doesn't sound too awful."

In the mirror, I can see Jason grimacing behind me. "Maybe before that whole anthrax scare, but these days, nothing makes the government more nervous than a scientist with the expertise to make scary germs."

I mull the problem over while moisturizing the dark shadows under my eyes, which turn out not to have been caused by mascara, but by stress. "So the food and drug people are dragging their feet and you're losing time and money?"

"It may be worse than that. I'm beginning to suspect the FDA isn't even going to allow us to do product testing." Jason drags his hands through his hair, a clear sign of acute distress. Usually he treats those last few follicles with a tenderness I can only envy. "I tell you, Del, I wouldn't be surprised if my office was bugged to make sure I'm not making secret deals with rogue operatives."

"Okay, now you're sounding like one of my fantasies."

Jason raises his eyebrows. "Something I don't know about going on in Delilah Levine's Theater of the Surreal?"

"Well, actually, there is something. . . ."

Jason leans over and kisses me on the lips. A good kiss. When he pulls away, his eyes are sparkling. "Tell me later. When we're alone. It's been a while since you regaled me with any of your racy plots."

We are grinning at each other and it is all so comfortable and so familiar that I decide, what the hell, just come out with it. Bare your soul, and other parts may follow.

"Well, turn on the TV Monday afternoon and you might just discover that you're not the only one who appreciates my talents."

Jason's face goes blank for a moment, and then he gives a whoop of pleasure. "You did it! You've gotten a script accepted!"

"More than that. A whole storyline. And—you're going to love this part—it's all because of you."

"Because of me?"

"Remember that Biosensual report you couldn't find? Turns out I printed a script out on the back of it, and when my producer saw the notes you'd made, he thought it was the best long-range storyline he'd seen in years."

"Tell me this is a joke."

"Now, before you get upset, I want to reassure you that I changed all the names and details."

"Oh, my God."

"Which is what I told your boss when he started having a similar overreaction last night."

"Oh, my God. Oh, my God. You took confidential corporate information . . ."

"I didn't do anything illegal."

"You didn't think of me at all, did you?" Jason looks at me with astonished disgust, as if I have turned right before his eyes into a massive Kafkaroach. It happens to all of us, you know; that's the real horror. One day you wake up and you're vermin in somebody else's eyes.

"I can't believe it. My own wife. You saw an opportunity and said to hell with my husband and his career, I'm just going to look out for myself? I asked you for those papers, Delilah. You lied to me. You lied. I always thought you were kind of careless and irresponsible, but this is worse. This is much worse. You're just completely selfish and self-absorbed."

My heart skips a beat. "How dare you?" My voice is trembling and even I don't know if it's terror or rage. "I am very sorry if I've done something that upsets you, but there are calm, respectful, adult ways to discuss this. You can't just speak to me as if I were—"

"Delilah." Jason has lowered his head into his hands. "I may be fired. I may be sued. I may be fucking unemployable right now. So do me a favor and just shut the fuck up."

And at last I understand how very, very not all right we are.

In a perfect metaphoric topper to the morning, I bite down on something hard at breakfast and crack a tooth. It's just as well; Jason and Sadie are taking a train to Larchmont to see his parents, and this gives me an excuse to stay behind and try to get an emergency appointment with a dentist.

Jason is impressively civil in front of our daughter. "Sure you don't want to come with us to see my parents? You know they'd love to see you."

They would, if only to impart religious lecture number 4,520. Why aren't we sending Sadie to a Jewish school, why don't we go to synagogue more often, why don't I consider taking that women's Torah study class. Jason's mother and father hold me personally responsible for the fact that their son eats bacon and plays tennis on Shabbat. Probably because Jason lets them believe that he'd be only too happy to kosherize our lives if only I didn't object so strongly.

Someday I may out him to his parents, but not today. "No thanks, Jason, I'd rather be the villain offstage than on. Besides, I have to see Dr. Eivvel about my tooth and do some Chanukah shopping."

"Dr. Evil! Dr. Evil! Come on, let's go, Daddy!" Sadie hops up and down on one leg, because the weather report has mentioned the possibility of snow and Sadie is excited at the prospect of sledding. Perhaps as a hedge against bad weather, Sadie has packed enough clothing, games and stuffed animals for a six-month stint in boarding school instead of the one night she will actually be spending with her paternal grandparents.

"Jason, you'll call me tonight? Sades, where are your glasses?"

Sadie touches her nearsighted face with surprise. "I thought I was wearing them!" She runs to fetch them and for a moment, Jason and I are alone.

My husband looks at me with such taut hostility that I am shocked. How mad is he, exactly?

"Jason, listen, about what happened . . ."

"Not now. This isn't the time to get into something as serious as this."

I try to read that closed, cold face. "How serious is this?"

Jason refuses to meet my eyes, and then Sadie scampers up with her glasses, chasing away the scary shadows with her presence.

Ten minutes later husband and daughter are on their way, and I am so late that I know Dr. Eivvel will refuse to give me the happy gas as well as the Novocain.

In the elevator mirror, I catch a glimpse of my flat hair, pale face and shadowed eyes. I notice that there is also a pimple forming on my chin. There should be a law preventing pimples and wrinkles from sharing the same face together.

"Don' worry, baby, you look fine," says Enrique the doorman over the intercom, proving that he is watching me on the hidden camera.

"Hi, Enrique." I pass him at a trot and he twirls his moustache at me. He was also very supportive when I was eight months pregnant: There's something to be said for an equal opportunity letch.

The sky is the cement-gray color of the sidewalk and my breath is visible as I careen down Broadway without catching sight of a single available taxi. All it takes is the threat of bad weather to make all the cabs and buses disappear from the streets of Manhattan.

Accepting the inevitable, I jog down the flight of stairs to the subway and actually manage to slam through the turn-stile without jamming my Metrocard in the slot. I am stam-peding down the passageway thinking I may yet make my appointment, when strong arms grab me from behind. A voice whispers in my ear: "Don't turn around."

It is a male voice, faintly accented, Spanish. My heart starts pounding furiously. There are only a few other peo-ple around, all wearing headphones and walking the other way. "What do you want?"

"You know what I want." Now the voice sounds familiar.

"Who is this?" To my chagrin, I still sound frightened.

"Baby! It's Diego!" I spin around and there is Diego Ramirez, ex-boyfriend and socialist playwright, looking lean and surprisingly polished in faded jeans and a leather trenchcoat.

"Diego! What are you doing here?"

Diego grinned, even more handsome with a trace of sil-ver at his temples than he had been twelve years ago. "Querida, I live here—well, downtown. I've been back in New York for three years."

"Why didn't you let me know you were back in town?"

"I thought I should see you at one of Marshall's readings. Or at the gallery, when Zohar had his show."

A little stung at the thought that my old crowd was still hanging out without me, I shrug my shoulders. "I have a seven-year-old daughter, which makes it a bit hard to get out most evenings."

"Of course. In any event, you look wonderful."

"You mean I look like shit. But I don't always. Just when I bump into ex-lovers."

Diego throws back his head and laughs. "Still sharp, my Delilah. Why not give me your telephone number?" His hair was still thick and full, I had to notice, and even if he did still have that one eyebrow thing going on, it didn't detract from his attractiveness.

"As long as you understand that I'm married now." Twelve years ago, Diego and I had the kind of relationship that gives you chronic urinary tract infections. We were so passionate that on the rare occasions when we had to spend a night apart, we would call each other up for endless heated conversations of the "what are you doing now" variety.

"But of course I understand you are a married woman, Delilah." Diego's dark eyes glint with suppressed amusement. "And I am afraid I am a little bit married myself these days."

I gape. I can't help it. Diego had always claimed that marriage was a bourgeois institution that limited and constrained an artist. "When?"

"Last year." Diego opens his wallet, producing a picture of a woman who looks flawlessly beautiful in the way only the very young can. Her face is like a flower. "This is Rhiannon. We are expecting our first child in March."

"How great! And she's just lovely!" Oh, Christ, I sound like Kathy Wheatley. At that moment, blessedly, I hear the rumble and screech of an approaching train. "Oh! That must be me! Well, we have to meet up again soon! Give me a ring!"

I charge up the stairs toward the platform as Diego tries to tell me I haven't given him my telephone number yet. Not that he would actually call me, he's just one of those compulsively charming people who can't let you go without winning you over. I leap through the doors just before they close, and as the express pulls away, I wish for two things:

That this actually is the train I need to take.

And that I hadn't asked Diego to give me a ring.

Dreams of losing teeth are really dreams about mortality, so I really don't think the dentist should have been so snide about my bursting into tears when he told me I needed two crowns. At least it convinced him to give me the other half of the Valium. I come home with two temporary teeth over my newly whittled stubs, but I'm still nicely woozy from the pill, so it's not so bad.

In the lobby, Enrique leers and hands me a small brown package that instantly fills me with guilt, as it means someone somewhere has sent me a holiday present and I have not yet sent anything to anybody. In fact, I am not aware of being on gift-giving terms with anyone outside the immediate family.

There is no return address.

Not that it matters. Whoever it is, I have not bought them anything. It dawns on me that I have not shopped for anybody in the family besides Sadie. The threat of a snowstorm coupled with the languor from the Valium discouraged me from braving the midtown crowds, but time is running out here.

Well, there's always the Internet—maybe I can do all my purchases while sitting at the computer in my underwear. (Besides causing all above-ground modes of transportation to disappear, the barest hint of inclement weather causes Manhattan apartment buildings to send great rippling waves of steam out of all the radiators. If you live in a pre-war apartment, you probably wind up wearing fewer clothes in December than you do in July, when your air conditioner's always going full blast.)

Sure enough, I open the front door to a sauna. Setting my mystery package down in my bedroom on the dresser, I strip down to my gray cotton running bra and underwear (a pair of Jason's discarded boxer shorts).

And then suddenly I am crying, thinking that maybe I shouldn't be wearing Jason's underwear anymore.

No. This is just an overreaction. We're going through a rough patch. This is what a rough patch must feel like when you're going through it. Like turbulence. It doesn't necessarily mean the plane is going to fall out of the sky. I must stewardess my way through this mess with a look of composure on my face. Everything will be fine or it will not be fine, but running through the aisles screaming never helped anyone.

I wash my face and turn on my computer.

Shopping takes me less than fifteen minutes: For Jason, a watch that astronauts tested on the moon; for both our mothers, really nice scarves and earrings that will never be worn; for both our fathers, expensive hardcover copies of a book about World War II that will never be read; for Hilda, a handbag, and for Tamara, a Happy Hummingbird vibrator from A Secret Place's selection of stocking stuffers. (Nowadays, everyone has a website, it seems.)

I hope Tamara will not be offended by my choice of a gift. Well, I hope she will be a little offended, and then I hope she will have enough fun flying solo to dump the married weasel who's been giving her the "morality's ambiguous" speech.

I mean, when it comes right down to it (no pun intended), partner sex is overrated and masturbation undervalued. Yeah, sure, partner sex can be an incandescent, timeless interlude in which one encounters the other with more intimacy than we can ever hope to find outside the womb, but it can also be a boring, discordant, deeply depersonalizing experience that leaves you feeling like reheated meatloaf.

That is to say, something that is sniffed twice, chosen because it is handy, and instantly forgotten.

So even if masturbation is not the stuff of song and story, hey, at least it usually leaves you with a smile on your face.

In fact, now that I think of it, maybe that's the answer to this pent-up howl of misery that keeps trying to claw its way out of my throat. I've done my chores, I've got the house to myself—what better time to dig the Happy Hummingbird out of its hiding place in my underwear drawer and take it for a test spin.

Fight pain with pleasure, that's the idea.

The bedroom seems the logical place, but when I settle back under the covers with my new toy, I find there is something . . . well, anticlimactic about the whole thing. Just hello, spread your legs, let's get to it. Part of what always arouses me is knowing that I am desired, and while the ingenious device I am holding is state-of-the-art, three-speed and multidirectional, it looks about as friendly as a fist and feels slightly clammy to the touch.

I try closing my eyes, imagining Ford standing face to face with me, our bodies so similar in height. I imagine the moment when I realize his body is reacting to mine.

But this is Jason's and my bed, and something about thinking about Ford and touching myself feels, well, wrong.

I try imagining myself tied hand and foot, a prisoner . . . Ford leaning forward, a gold earring glinting in his ear. Tight striped breeches straining over his muscular thighs, bare chest gleaming as he swings down from the rigging . . .

No, too Burt Lancaster. Try again. Maybe in the living room.

Ford, a cigarette dangling from his lower lip, regarding me balefully over a glass of whiskey as I saunter toward him, chin down, voice surprisingly husky as I ask him . . .

No, no, if I go the Bogart and Bacall route it'll take me hours.

I sit up, feeling antsy and irritated with myself. The change of setting hasn't helped. The Valium has definitely lost its punch and I find I am thinking about cleaning out these boxes. Won't Jason be pleased to come home and find the living room looking better organized?

I am still thinking in pre-catastrophe terms. It is entirely possible that Jason will only be pleased if he comes home to find I have moved out.

No, no, no. This is soap-opera thinking. One disastrous argument does not cancel out ten years of marriage. The best thing for me right now is to relax.

I can do relaxed. I am a lusty, sensual, earthy creature. Or at least I used to be. I look down at the vibrator. "Come on, Happy," I mutter. "We're going to get back in touch with our inner slut."

What I need is to loosen up, get the blood flowing. I need movement, I need wildness, I need to shed my inhibitions by unleashing my untamed gypsy spirit.

Recalling the sexy feeling I got from doing a Goddess-Within belly dance workshop right before I got pregnant with Sadie, I search for something evocative of the harem, but find the closest thing to Middle Eastern music I possess is a compilation of All Time Favorite Israeli Wedding Tunes.

No way can I Hava Nagilah my way to orgasm.

I settle on a seventies compilation that reminds me of my very early adolescence, and cast about for inspiration.

Got it. I'm the shy, young virgin with the nose of a Supreme Court justice and the hips of a cootchie girl . . . He's the guy with the sardonic gaze standing a little bit apart from the crowd. . . .

The stranger moved up behind Delilah so silently she didn't even know he was there until he spoke.

"I think you'd better dance with me."

Delilah whirled around. The man standing in front of her looked like a modern-day Attila the Hun, with flat, unreadably dark eyes and a cruelly sensual mouth.

"And why is that?" Her heart was already pounding before he had even pulled her into the solid wall of his chest, close enough to smell the faint, tangy scent of Dos Equis and lime, and the muskier, headier scent of his own heated male flesh. Her hand pressed against the black wool of his sweater and felt the tensile strength of the muscles beneath.

"Because," he said, his voice a whisper that raced across the sensitive skin of her ear and throat, "there are men here who want to kill you."

"K—kill me?" She tried to pull away, but his strong hands caught hers.

"Don't worry," he said, his voice a low growl, "I'm not gonna let them. Now laugh like I said something funny."

The pounding disco song carried her voice away as she attempted to laugh, looking around the dimly lit club at all the dancing couples, trying to imagine which one might be a murderer in disguise.

"Now look at me, Delilah."

Startled by the use of her name, Delilah's gaze caught with the stranger's, and she found something unexpected lighting his face; a look almost of tenderness, almost of concern. And then it was gone, and in its place was a clear, predatory intent.

"And now kiss me like your life depends on it." He was only about an inch and a half taller than her five foot eight, and when her mouth found his, it brought every solid, masculine inch of him flush up against every slender, feminine curve of her.

And there were a few more inches of him than she had been expecting.

"Don't stop now," the man murmured into her mouth as his hands came up to frame her hips more securely against his, *"I haven't got him in my sights yet."*

He was aiming his gun at someone? Unable to process what was happening, Delilah gave herself up to the unexpected intensity of his kiss, the wild intimacy of his tongue in her mouth, his hard body pressed boldly so that, despite the throngs of people all around, she could feel the length of his arousal all along her . . .

The front door slams, banishing all thoughts of dirty dancing. "Hello?"

Snapping upright, my chest heaving, I give a quick, involuntary scream and press four different buttons as the Happy Hummingbird oscillates and vibrates at three different speeds, in multiple directions.

"Delilah? Don't worry, it's just me. Ford." He has brought his dog with him and Fardles runs in ahead of his owner, sniffing my face and trying to grab the vibrator as if it were a bone.

Over the blare of the *Star Wars* theme (set to a disco beat), I yell, "Hang on a sec," finally find the off switch on the vibrator, shove the Happy Hummingbird under a cushion and arrange myself in a casual position the very moment that Ford comes walking into the living room. The damn dog is still nosing around the couch, doubtless hoping for a game of Fetch the Sex Toy.

"What's going on?" Ford leans down to grab Fardles's

collar, giving me his Spock look as I do my best to look un-ruffled. "I rang the bell but no one answered. Did you forget I was coming to check the pipes today? Down, boy."

"Sorry, the music was a bit loud. . . ."

Ford manages to look amused without actually moving any facial muscles. "Yes, I can hear that." He dials down the volume on the CD player while Fardles makes a sudden lunge for the couch. "Stop that, boy! I guess I'd better lock him in the kitchen with some water."

By the time Ford returns, I have slipped the vibrator all the way down into the couch cushions, to the nether regions where gold coins and contact lenses wait out the decades undiscovered. I feel marginally safer.

Ford strides back into the room, already in lecture mode. "By the way, Delilah, the front door was unlocked. I really think you should think twice before just leaving yourself open to any intruder who happens to . . ." Ford regards me suspiciously. "Delilah? Are you all right?"

"I'm fine!"

"You look like you're about to cry or something."

"No, really. I'm doing fine." Beneath the pillow, I can hear the vibrator giving a little rumble. Shit. I haven't turned it off. I've just dialed it into some strange new modality.

"But you're all sweaty and out of breath, and the shades are drawn." Ford comes closer, a frown furrowing his forehead.

For the first time, I can honestly imagine Ford as a science fiction nerd, and I am glad. And then I hear the Happy Hummingbird beginning to buzz at an alarming new frequency. It won't take a spaceship captain to figure out what's been warping my engine if I don't create a distraction, and quick.

I launch myself onto the floor at Ford's feet.

"I was exercising," I announce, doing a series of enthusi-
astic sit-ups.

Ford stares down at me, his hands on his hips. He is
wearing the same slouchy sweater as last night, and I can
see the smooth, muscled curve where his neck meets his left
shoulder. "You can't do them like that, Delilah. You'll kill
your back." Ford shoves a couple of boxes aside and hun-
kers down beside my ankles and grabs hold of them. "Here,
try not to move your head so much. And relax your neck."

Ford Carter Michaelovich is crouching between my legs,
and all I am wearing is a pair of frayed hamburger boxer
shorts. I don't know whether to laugh or scream. But I am
definitely not going to be able to relax my neck.

Oh, dear God, if I make it through this experience, I
swear I will never touch myself again. I start doing the sit-
ups in double time, to keep Ford's eyes above my waist.

"No, you're not engaging your lower abdominals." Ford
reaches out and puts a hand on my stomach. "You should
feel it all along here," he explains.

"I think maybe it's time for push-ups."

"Are you kidding? You should do at least sixty of these,
and then . . ." Ford stops, suddenly alert. "Do you hear a
buzzing noise?"

There is no time to think, only time to react. "Hiyaaagh!"
I scissor myself upright and begin making Kung Fu motions with my hands.

"Delilah, what the hell are you—"

"You said you do martial arts. I want to learn."

"But I just heard something that—"

I slap Ford lightly on the cheek, the way Tamara and I
used to do when we were playing "got you last."

Ford turns to me, a glint of something in his dark eyes
that reminds me of a cat sighting a mouse. "Listen, if you

want to learn about self-defense, the first thing you should know is never to get too close to your opponent."

I dance around Ford, nearly tripping over a box of old *Secrets* blueprints as the CD player begins to play "Freak Out." Ford is just standing very still, with his arms at his sides, looking poised and muscular and . . . smirking at me.

Now that makes me mad. It's not like I'm a total wuss here. I used to beat my sister up routinely. All I have to do is catch him off balance, and . . .

I rush at Ford, grabbing for his left arm with my right hand, and the next thing I know I am flat on my back and he is on top of me.

"Lesson number one, Grasshopper. Never drop your guard just because you're attacking." Ford is grinning at me, his hands pinning mine over my head.

"Lesson number two, try to bore your opponent to death by making like an old episode of *Kung Fu.*" I try to free my wrists, but Ford is every bit as strong as he looks. I attempt to buck him off, but his thighs just clamp more tightly around mine.

"The problem here is, no real muscle tone," he says, and I buck again, nearly unseating him.

"What you need is a regular routine of upper-body exercises that . . . Uh oh, illegal use of legs again. I think I may just have to punish you for that. . . ." He starts to tickle me on the ribs and I writhe.

"No, no, stop, Ford, stop . . ."

And suddenly I realize I am having way too much fun here.

"Delilah . . ." He is leaning closer, the teasing light gone from his eyes. And then the music stops and in the abrupt silence we both hear it. The bang of a door. The skitter of claws on wood.

"Fardles," I say. It sounds like a curse.

Clearly, the Labrador pup, hearing the grown-ups happily wrestling without him, could bear his isolation no longer. ("Who would Fardles bear," by the way, is the exact quotation from Hamlet.) Breaking free of his kitchen confinement, the dog barrels into the living room.

Frozen with horror, I watch as Fardles digs into the couch and, good bird dog that he is, produces his "duck": the Happy Hummingbird in all its pale pink glory.

Rolling off of me, Ford mutters, "What the hell . . . ?"

I run into the bedroom and slam the door.

Ford waits fifteen minutes before knocking and promising not to laugh if I will only please come out and talk to him, but when I do finally open the door a crack, I find him still crying with mirth.

"You realize I will have to kill you now."

"God, I hope so."

I throw the Happy Hummingbird at him and it begins to vibrate, sending Ford into a fresh paroxysm of laughter.

It is not the climax I was hoping for.

I emerge from the bedroom dressed in a black turtleneck, black jeans and a belt with a huge silver buckle, the closest thing I could find to a chastity belt. I find Ford in the kitchen, eating a bagel and egg sandwich out of a brown paper bag. The winter sun hits the pale yellow walls at a low angle, creating an illusion of warmth and peace.

Fardles looks up from the rawhide he is chewing and I find I cannot meet his eyes.

Ford gestures to the bone. "He says he's sorry. Feeling better now?"

"Fuck off." I watch him chew for a moment.

Ford takes a sip of coffee. "I got caught once. When I was in college. My roommate kept having girlfriends over, and they got . . . well, noisy. And I was just this shy science nerd, with no girlfriend. And then one day I got . . . excited, listening to them, and so I started . . . and anyway, the next thing I know, they come in through the door yelling, 'Gotcha!' The irritating thing was, they thought I was doing it all the time, but I wasn't."

Despite Ford's matter-of-fact tone, his face has that mask of scarlet again. He is not exactly the cool customer I took him for at first sight. Instead, he is surprisingly, engagingly boyish.

It's boyish that always used to tip me over the edge. That look of intense caution mixed with equal parts courage and desire. That air of expecting nothing of you, because it would be a miracle if you fell into bed. The lovely break of awe over the guy's face as you reveal—ta da—that you do, indeed, possess breasts.

To combat my wayward thoughts, I assume an expression that implies that I am a mature woman and Ford is nothing more than a nervous juvenile.

"Okay, now that we've established what we have in common with monkeys, can we drop the subject?"

"Sure." Ford looks at the cup in his hands. "Want some coffee?"

"No, I'll take some juice." As I reach into the cabinet for a glass, a thought occurs. "Ford? When did you go to college? After the navy?"

"Yeah. That's why I joined in the first place, to be able to afford an education."

"What did you major in?" I look up from pouring my juice to catch Ford's slight look of discomfort. "Engineering, but I had to drop out." Ford swallows a bite of egg.

I guess it's because I've created so many imaginary scenarios for him myself that I am puzzling over the reality. In most of my fantasies, I've seen Ford as a loner, because he seemed so taciturn at first. But the man I met in the bar last night was not so much aloof as shy, which fit with the story of Ford Michaels, geeky brain. Skinny, smart immigrant kid beefs up, joins the navy to get money for college, studies engineering and then quits school to become a plumber?

Something doesn't fit.

"So what happened that you had to leave school, anyw—" After all the fantasies, it happens so quickly I can't quite process it. One minute, I'm looking at Ford, and the next, he has moved to trap me against the kitchen counter and his mouth is on mine, tasting of scrambled egg and coffee.

At first, I'm not even sure if I like the way he kisses. And since I have imagined it lo these many times, I take a moment to figure it out, and then his hands come up to cradle the back of my head, and he angles his face to deepen the kiss. And oh, my God.

This is what I have been missing, this hungry pressure, this uncivilized contact.

I'm going to break it off right now, though. I'm not going any farther than this firm, delicious, close-mouthed kiss.

Then Ford opens his mouth and folds me against his body, his compact, muscular, deliciously firm body, and the tremors race through both of us. Oh, help, I really do have to stop this right now because he's got my combination and if I'm not very, very careful here, he's going to unlock me.

Then suddenly it hits me. He's *too* aware of me. I open my eyes and see the flicker of his gaze before his lids shutter closed.

Oh, hell, it's true. He's kissing me to distract me. I'm not being seduced here; I'm being played.

Which means I nearly guessed something he really doesn't want me to know.

Or else I'm simply having a crisis in confidence, having a bit of trouble believing an attractive man could still just want me.

I pull back and am gratified to see that Ford's pupils are dilated and he has the slightly glazed look you get when the kissing is good. He may be faking some of this, but at least he's not doing it entirely for the love of God and country.

"Okay," I say, "I probably sound like the world's biggest idiot, but is there a reason why you've got your tongue down my throat besides the obvious?"

"Delilah . . ." But the look on his face says it all. Yes, there is a reason, and it's not of the flattering overcome-by-lust variety. No, it's something sneaky or petty or just plain arrogant, like, I'm ashamed to tell you I'm dyslexic so I thought I'd distract you or I always wanted to nail a married woman or Baby, I could tell you wanted me, so I was just being nice.

So what's his secret? Not something embarrassing, like being caught flying solo. That wasn't when he started getting squirrelly. No, it was when he let slip that he attended college that Ford got all shifty-eyed.

The only reason for him to keep college a secret would be because it doesn't fit with his job as a plumber. Which means that his job as a plumber . . . is a cover for something else.

No, this is the kind of thinking that works for daydreams and daytime television, not real life. But Ford did tell me to start asking questions. And Jason mentioned the possibility of federal agents checking in on his projects.

And my gut is telling me something's weird here.

I try it on for size. "So, any chance you have an ulterior motive for hanging out in my apartment?"

"Yeah, that's me—plumber by day, secret agent by

night." He keeps his poker face and his coolly amused tone, but that telltale flush appears over his cheekbones.

"Okay, so I'm guessing not a Fed, because they probably train the blushes out of you at Quantico. But something secret agent-y, because you're trying the old ploy of saying the truth when the truth is so outrageous it's not really credible."

"Or perhaps I'm exhibiting traces of irony to call attention to the absurdity of your suspicions. . . ."

"Right. And the fact that you suddenly sound like a textbook convinces me that you're on the level." Suddenly I am so mad I want to hit him. Not playfully, like before. Solidly, with malice aforethought. I turn on my heel and head for my bedroom. I hear Fardles whining and, behind me, Ford yelling out, "Down, boy. Stay!"

He catches up with me in two long strides.

"Delilah, I'm sorry about what just happened. . . ."

"Save it." I try to slam my door in his face but he blocks it with one arm.

"I need to explain something. . . ."

"Find a therapist."

"Something I need to tell *you*." He shoulders his way into my bedroom and I turn my back on him.

"You don't need to tell me anything, Ford. We don't have a relationship. We're not going to have a relationship. I don't care what you think you're really doing here. Just go fix my pipes and get the hell out of here." Without thinking, I pick up the mystery package on my dresser and try to move past Ford, back into the hall. I'm not sure what I mean to do with the box in my hands; it's just one of those things you do when you're mad. Once as a teenager I slammed out of my parents' house carrying a toothbrush and the phone book.

"Wait. What's in that box?" Ford moves to block me, like we're dancing the avoidance tango.

"None of your business. Now, move."

"No return address. Do you know who sent it?"

"I know it's not for you, so if you don't mind . . ."

"Actually, I do."

I look up and suddenly it's all too much. "What the fuck is this? Who do you think you are?"

"You said you didn't care . . ."

"I changed my mind! What are you, a fucking blushing corporate spy? If so, I have to tell you—you suck at this gig. Shouldn't go into so much goddamn detail about your sick mom and your loser days in college, next time. Did you rig a problem with my pipes? Who else is in on this—Mrs. Kornislav and her flooded ceiling? Enrique the doorman?"

My voice rings out in the silent room. Ford just looks at me with an expression that mingles sympathy with extreme caution.

"Oh, my God." I sink down the wall till I am sitting on my heels. "I'm going crazy. I had a big fight with Jason and now I'm becoming a paranoid lunatic."

"Delilah."

I don't look up. Ford crouches down till our faces our level. "You're not going crazy." His voice is low and quiet.

"I'm just having a nervous breakdown."

"No." Ford tips my chin up. "But you do have to give me that box."

I stare at him, hard. "Are you going to explain anything to me?"

His eyes are completely dark and expressionless, as if he's thrown a switch and turned something off inside. "No."

And all my tamped-down anguish over Jason flares into a rebellious rage.

"Well, then, you know what? Fuck you, too." I stand up and throw the box down at him and he ducks to the left. The rest happens in strobelike flashes: the box landing in the closet behind Ford with a thud. The stark look of fear on Ford's face as he springs up and throws himself over me. The clap of thunder and flash of light as we hit the floor. The drops of moisture falling from Ford's face to mine as we turn toward the closet to see what's leaking.

The deluge from the broken water pipe as everything I thought I knew about my life explodes.

Saturday, December 16
5 P.M.
but my God it feels like
a lifetime has passed

A bomb did not just explode in my closet. I have not just discov-
ered a water-damaged cardboard box filled with some other
woman's clothing and two soggy, unsigned love letters.

I am actually on a train to Larchmont, anticipating a day and
a half of smiling tension with my in-laws, a pot roast, and possi-
bly some sledding.

Like most people, I've found that many of the most emotionally charged scenes in my life have taken place in
movies. Lauren Bacall absently massaging her knee through
her skirt until private eye Bogie pins her with his full attention and commands, "Scratch it." Burt Lancaster crouching
like a lion over shuddering spinster Katharine Hepburn and
telling her to believe herself pretty. The whole quaint Irish
town of Innisfree rolling out to see reluctant hero John
Wayne finally face up to his wife's bullying lout of a brother.

When I try to remember the most intensely felt moments
of my life, I usually find myself searching for the metaphors
of film and poetry: This was like that.

But as I sit here in Ford's arms and cry, nothing else

comes to mind. No fragments of verse. No echoes of cellu-
loid. It is all just what it is. My fingernails scrabble at his
arms, clawing for purchase in an unsteady world, and he is
rocking with me, his arms around me, one hand on my hair.

I don't say anything and he doesn't say anything. Except
at some point I guess I do say something—hold me tighter,
something like that. And he holds me tighter. I turn my
head into his body and take a deep breath. I remember
hearing that you can be bruised internally just from the
shock waves of a bomb, and I want to say something about
it but instead I close my eyes. I feel Ford's arms may be all
that's holding me together.

A couple of men in suits have just finished inspecting my
closet and bagging the fragmentary remnants of the mystery package. It turns out that the bomb wasn't really much
of a bomb at all.

I said it was the most bomb I'd ever been given, and one
of the suits, who looked too young to shave, laughed. The
other explained there hadn't been much explosive involved; whoever made this may have just been intending to
scare me. Or might not be very good at making explosives.

Both suits seemed to pay a lot of attention to Ford, even
though he didn't say much. I guess it's that old feminist
gripe; men like to talk to other men. I was too tired to complain. When they left, the suit who did look old enough to
vote told me that I would be kept under surveillance and
that all my mail would be checked.

It has only occurred to me, after they've left, that I have
no idea who they were. Local police? Federal agents? I
would ask Ford, but the cognac he gave me is having its effect and I'm too tired to get up from the bed.

I can hear him just a few feet from me, *bang, bang, bang-ing* away. I told him I didn't want to go rest in the other room. It's actually very reassuring to listen to him fixing the closet, except for the fact that the words to "Maxwell's Silver Hammer" keep running through my head.

Still can't sleep. This is what I find in a box in my bedroom closet, shoved far in the back, away from the open pipe:

One silk dress with a really awful, mimsy floral print, size sixteen.

One silk blouse, ivory, size sixteen, with an eighties-style bow at the neck.

A wool skirt, size fourteen.

Just My Size pantyhose, three pairs, beige.

A pair of simple black pumps, so large the owner must resemble one of Robert Crumb's cartoon Yeti women, with copious, shaggy body hair and breasts the size of European automobiles.

Love Letter # 1: In peacock blue ink, the lower half of it water-damaged.

Dear Love,

It's so strange, this thing between us—this forbidden passion between enemies. But despite your working for a company that poisons our food, soaps, tampons and makeup,

*and despite my work with CACA (caretakers against chem-
ical addivitives) I now realize that you and I are soul mates,
a Romeo and Juliet fighting the forces that keep us apart.*

*I know that if only your wife were not deluding herself
that she is a poet, you would not have to compromise your
morals by working for R. B. International in order to feed
and clothe your child.*

*I keep dreaming that there is a way for us to be together
in some more lasting way, although, I know, you said we
must not upset our families.*

*But, O, my love, the afternoon we spent together is like a
dream I return to again and again, the way you (too soggy
to read) and let me (too soggy to read) until I screamed
and screamed and screamed. I don't need assurances or
promises of tomorrow. All I need is to feel that I can dream
that dream with you again.*

K.

Love Letter # 2: In computer or typewriter font, wet but
completely legible.

Jason,

*You asked me to write you and I can only guess at your mo-
tives. Yes, the sex was great. Incredible. You are the first
man I have been with who seems to really care more for his
partner's pleasure than for his own. And yes, I have felt a certain amount of guilt, although since you explained that you
have been pleading with Delilah to acknowledge your sexual
needs and she has ignored them again and again, I do feel
that what we did was somewhat justified. You say you suspect that she has been unfaithful, and that excuses you. I am*

*not sure that anything excuses me, except for the fact that I
have received far more pain from my previous romantic relationships than I have inflicted, and somewhere there must be
some kind of universal balance sheet for these things.*

In any case, I look forward to your next "consultation."

Letter number one is clearly from a deranged Kathy
Wheatley. Oddly, I feel a momentary relief—so her not lik-
ing me wasn't completely personal! She was just shtupping
my husband! The second, oddly businesslike letter is the
one that really burns. Although it's signed only with a lipstick print, I know instantly who it's from. The only person
I know who can make a love letter sound like a legal brief.
My sister.

I light the first candle of Chanukah on the menorah Sadie
made in preschool. Jason returns half an hour later, irritated
that I did not wait.

"You said you'd be back before sundown," I say.

"Since when do you care about things like that? I thought
the point was family togetherness." Jason's tone is offhand-
edly aggrieved; the offhanded part is to slip the hostility
under Sadie's surprisingly good radar.

"Grandma gave me a Madame Alexander Doll," Sadie
announces. It is a pouty-faced Miss Israel with a white-and-
blue dress. To me, her little China-doll face looks disap-
proving, and therefore reminds me of my mother-in-law.

"Do you like her?"

"I wanted a blonde one." Sadie squints at me. "Daddy
told me not to say that I lost my glasses."

"Take Miss Israel into your room and go wash your
hands."

I look around for Jason, who has not yet been informed that I now hold the moral high ground.

When we talked on the phone late last night (Jason's parents don't answer the phone until the sun sets on Saturday, marking the end of Shabbat) we traded information in flat, emotionless voices: Yes, taking the 3-P.M. train. Sadie is fine but outside sledding. No, we don't have to make latkes tonight, we can wait until we see my parents on Friday. (My folks, who are not terribly observant, see nothing wrong with frying latkes on Shabbat to celebrate Chanukah, which basically means they're breaking one rule to follow another tradition. But then, Judaism's a legalistic religion and Dad practices law. It makes sense they'd find a loophole or two for themselves.)

I didn't inform Jason about the bomb, the closet, or the skeletons that fell out of it. I want to wait for a good moment to attack. Like when he's tired and defenseless and can't just hang up the phone on me.

I hear a short, sharp shout from the other room; sounds like Jason has just discovered Exhibit A.

"Delilah! What the hell happened?" Jason is standing on the threshold of our bedroom, pointing at the water-damaged walls and floor around our closet.

"The pipe exploded."

"It's that goddamn plumber, isn't it? I knew it! He's incompetent. We should sue the pants off him."

"There's more to the story, actually."

For a moment, Jason's face is almost boyish with surprise. Behind the receding hairline and sharpened cheekbones, I can see the outline of the nice young law student who let me debauch him on my futon in the East Village. "What?"

"Like I found a box in the back of the closet." Okay, so maybe I should have mentioned the bomb first, as a) people trying to kill me is probably a priority over Jason's cheating and b) learning that I nearly died would have made Jason feel sympathetic rather than threatened. But somehow it's Jason's betrayal that burns hotter in my gut. I have no idea who wants to kill me, but I know damn well who's been screwing my sister. I am aching to have it out with him. "Anything you care to tell me, Jason?"

"That box was not yours to open."

"The box was not mine to open? We're going to start by arguing whether or not what I found is admissible as evidence?" My voice is rising into operatic heights and I take a breath, slowing myself down to an angry hiss. "Listen, Jason, there are two letters in there that more than imply that you've been cheating on me. With at least two different women. And one of them appears to be my sister. So while I try to restrain myself from plunging something sharp and jagged into your pasty flesh, I think you'd better come up with something to say to me other than I shouldn't have opened the goddamn box without your written permission."

Jason's face is stiff and solemn, as if he were in court. "This isn't a legal argument. It's a personal one. You had no right to go digging around in my possessions."

"Whose clothes are they, Jason? Kathy Wheatley's? They look too big. My sister's? Or maybe they belong to the Russian lady. Are you screwing her, too? Is there anyone you're not screwing these days—besides me, of course?"

At that singularly awful moment—one of the three all-time awful moments of my life, as a matter of fact—Sadie walks in, still clutching the sour-faced Miss Israel. "What's wrong with you guys?" She looks from her father's frozen expression to my livid one. "Are you fighting again?"

"Very nice, Delilah. Perfect timing, as usual." Jason holds

my gaze; part of me knows he is acting wildly defensive, but all I can read in his face is anger and disgust.

I inhale deeply, bend down, and prepare to initiate damage control. "Sadie, Daddy and I are having a disagreement, and I'm sorry you had to hear any of it, but . . ."

I hear the pounding of Jason's angry footsteps and the slamming of the front door.

"Are you going to get a divorce?" Sadie sounds surprisingly composed, the way she did when she discovered that her pet gerbil was dead.

"We aren't deciding on a plan of what to do right now," I say. "We only know how we feel. And we each feel pretty mad at each other. At the moment. But we both love you and neither of us is mad at you, Sades. And you're not the reason we're mad at each other."

I look into my daughter's nearsighted gray eyes and wish I weren't still so angry at Jason. I need calm and I need distance so that I can be sure I am choosing the right words, the words that will comfort and yet not lie, the words that will shape this experience into something bearable.

"It's okay, Mommy," she says, stroking the hair back from my forehead. "I'm getting really good at magic. I can cast a spell that will get Daddy back for us."

"Oh, Baby, you don't need to get Daddy back. He hasn't left you," I say, my voice breaking a little.

Sadie gives me a crooked smile that is so like mine I am shocked to see it on her unlined face. "He's not here, though, is he?"

"He's just embarrassed, Punkin. Remember when you hid in the closet because you made the baking soda volcano on Mommy's bed? Daddy's sort of feeling like that."

Too late, I realize I have just admitted that Sadie's wonderful Daddy has done something very wrong.

"So he'll come back to say he's sorry?"

There must be a hundred books on how to tell your children if you and your husband are having marital problems. I would sell my soul for a glimpse at one now.

In the end, we make latkes for dinner. I grate the skin off my fingertips and there's probably blood mixed in with the potatoes, but Sadie is distracted by all the beating and mixing and frying and tasting, so it's worth it.

I let her sleep in my bed, on Jason's side.

Monday, December 17
1 P.M.

On a brisk spring day two years after her divorce, Delilah Levine strode past Columbus Avenue's artful boutique windows looking as if she herself had stepped out of one of the displays. She was every inch the urbane cowgirl in her turquoise and snakeskin cowboy boots and fringed suede jacket. A careful observer would have noticed that the elegant man's watch on her narrow wrist was a Patek Phillipe, and that her hair, with its mingled shades of dark copper and burnt honey, had the jubilant bounce and shine that only a great deal of money can buy. A few men turned to watch her as she loped across the street, because she had the kind of confidence that is innately seductive. A few women turned to watch her as she rearranged her handbag across her shoulder, because it was the kind of bag women always covet—large enough to contain the overflow of a busy life, its leather as gracefully well-designed as a horse's show saddle.

What the bag implied about Delilah was true. She had a gracefully busy life, the direct consequence of turning a fairly generic soap opera into a cult favorite; the entertainment magazines were calling her "the woman who revolutionized daytime."

Sadie now went to a school where all the children of rich bohemians went, learning math in conjunction with music and reading Animal Farm *before visiting an organic farm and feeding the free-ranging hens. She was the most popular girl in her class, and this, above all else, gave Delilah comfort.*

If there was a lingering sadness in her eyes, her lightly tinted sunglasses concealed it.

"Delilah?"

Delilah turned, the sun glinting off the fiery highlights in her windblown hair. For a moment, she didn't recognize the wan, hollow-eyed man in the gray business suit. "Jason?" He looked like an insurance salesman down on his luck; the past twenty-four months seemed to have aged him in dog years.

"I can't believe it's you. I meant to call as soon as I'd straightened myself out, but . . ." For a moment, the faded blue eyes steeled into something like their old shade. "When the soap aired I felt I had to disappear."

"We needed the money, Jason. Sadie and I had no idea where you'd gone, or whether you were coming back."

"Yes, well . . . how is Sadie? Does she . . . does she ever talk about me?"

Delilah looked at the man she had shared a bed with for ten years and felt nothing, not even contempt. "We adopted a puppy from the pound. She asked about you for a few months, and she needed some therapy, but now she's fine."

"Oh. I . . . That's good, I guess." Jason shrugged, and a faint odor of mothballs and failure came off of his suit.

"Are you planning on getting back in touch with her now? Because it'll just be awful if you dip back into her life for a month and then take off again."

"I guess it's better if I just disappear, then, isn't it? I mean, it's not like I deserve to see her, after what I've done . . . to you, and to her. . . ."

Delilah looked at Jason, who seemed to have shrunk into his

clothing. He had lost weight, she realized; he looked like a man re-
covering from a long illness. "She's still your daughter," Delilah
said. "You're still her father. Decide what you want, but whatever
you do, don't just walk out on her again."

Delilah turned and walked down Columbus, her ex-husband's
gaze hot on her back.

"Hey," he called, and she stopped but did not turn around.
"That plumber. What happened with him? Did you ever . . . were
you ever . . ."

Delilah spun around. "He fucks me every night. He's sound-
proofed the walls so Sophie doesn't wake up when I scream his
name at the top of my lungs. Wasn't that thoughtful of him?" The
cowboy boots made a satisfyingly harsh sound on the pavement as
she turned on her heel.

A sudden blaring of car horns covered over any response Jason
may have made, and by the time Delilah reached the end of the
block and turned, he was gone.

I don't know why other women want chocolate when
they're depressed. Personally, I want salt, spice and oil.
French fries, onion-ring loaves the size of small dogs, really
crispy calamari with a spicy dipping sauce. I also like really
thin, almost crackerlike Tuscan pizzas with lots of garlic
and almost no cheese.

I'm not indiscriminate, either; I'll walk two miles to get to
one of those little midtown Belgian Frites stands where you
can get really fresh, thin fries and some vinegar to pour on
them. Forty blocks: That takes a lot of motivation.

It's important to set goals for each day when you're depressed.

I have told Sadie that Daddy had an unexpected business
trip that had nothing to do with our argument.

I have called his office two times, but am no clearer about

whether he has gone in to work but is ignoring me, or has run off to Katmandu.

I have not said anything to Kathy Wheatley, and have blessedly not run into her in the elevator. Yet.

I have not called my sister or my mother.

It is actually a nice, clear December day, sharp and sunny. It's the kind of day English people say they prefer to gray and overcast, but I know what would suit my mood better. I am walking down Broadway, my hair carefully arranged, my face made up. Now that I know my husband has cheated, I'll be damned if anyone catches me looking like a slob.

I am going to buy myself a black suede knee-length coat and matching boots. I have decided that if I were to have these things, then I would be more capable of coping with my new, unpleasant reality. It hit me when I saw a picture in a magazine of a woman who might, in some alternate universe, be me; a taller, thinner, younger, handsomer me, with the kind of authoritative chic that proclaims, I am not a loser. Men want me. Women admire me. Cross me and I'll kick you with my daggerlike, three-inch heel.

When I was younger, I used to get this way about a particular doll or tiara or toy. If I have this, I will become transformed into the kind of person whom life treats well.

Even now that I know that this kind of magical thinking is false, I can't help but respond to the siren's call of shopping. And really, walking out in the fresh air is good, having other people around is healthy. When you are in danger of being sucked down into a whirlpool of melancholia it's important to lift your face up to the sky and see that the sky is still blue, the sun is still shining, and the brick is still falling toward your head.

Oh, Jesus. I jump out of the way just in time. A chunk of

sidewalk cracks at my feet, and a little gaggle of onlookers congregates around me.

"Shit, man. That shit nearly hit your head," says a huskular young man in a plaid hat.

"You okay?" This from a guy in baggy white worker's overalls on some scaffolding twenty feet over my head. "You okay?" He shouts it louder the second time.

I grunt something that means, You nearly brained me, and I'm going to sue you, your company, and the entire anarchic city of New York for being negligent and deceitful and immoral.

Maybe I'm getting some of my feelings toward Jason mixed up here, but still. A person should be able to go out to belabor her credit card without incurring grievous bodily damage.

"Can you walk? I think you need to come sit," says an elderly lady in a bright yellow Dolly Parton wig. What she says makes no sense, and I am about to tell her this when I realize the lady is my cantankerous neighbor, Mrs. Kornislav.

Then she throws her head back, nearly dislodging her hair. "Hey," she shouts up to the worker on the scaffolding, "did you see where that came from?"

"Yo, lady, it wasn't me. It came from that roof over there." The man points to our building. "Don't touch the brick, when the police come they can measure trajectory or whatever. Prove I didn't drop it. Last thing I need is to be sued. You okay, lady?"

God, does everyone watch cop shows these days? I grunt that I am all right. Speech seems beyond my capabilities.

Mrs. Kornislav takes me by the elbow. "I think," she says firmly, "that we had better take you home."

"Shouldn't we wait for the police to come?" A whole sentence. It comes out a little thickly, but still—coherent, pertinent, calm. I am proud of myself.

"We'd do better to call that plumber of yours right away."

I do not even puzzle over the oddness of this pronouncement. I simply nod, glad to finally have someone else in charge.

The layout of Mrs. Kornislav's apartment is a perfect duplicate of mine, and I feel as though I have come home to a parallel universe in which all the furniture is very formal and dark and everything has a Jewish theme. Even the cushions on the couch have little Jerusalem scenes on them. I feel guilty just sitting my bacon-eating *tuchus* down on her kosher furniture.

There is a strong aroma of dill and chicken stock in the house, a familiar soupy smell that makes me feel about four years old.

"Here," says Mrs. Kornislav, bringing me cup of milky tea with two hard-looking cookies on a plate.

"Thank you." What I really would like is some of the soup she's making, but it doesn't seem polite to ask.

"Ford is coming right over."

"Is he? Why?" I stop sipping my tea. Mrs. Kornislav shakes her head. Her features appear pinched and small inside the nest of Rapunzel hair, but her eyes are bright and clever and ever-so-slightly malicious. She reminds me of some small, resourceful, unexpectedly ferocious animal—a wolverine in grandmother's clothing.

"So, you're telling me he still has kept his cover? Well, good for him. A bit embarrassing for you, but then, maybe you weren't thinking with your head, eh?"

I look at her blankly. "His cover?"

"Well, yes, dear. I mean, did you really think the building was paying to have a plumber work for this long on your closet? Drink your tea."

I obey. "I'm not sure I understand." Or want to. It's one thing to suspect someone in a burst of free-floating paranoia, and another thing entirely to hear your suspicions confirmed.

"Delilah, you are aware that your life is in danger, aren't you? I mean, I know this has all been a bit of a shock, but you are a smart girl, really. At least Ford says you are."

Does he? That's flattering. Right now I'm a sucker for praise, especially since I am suddenly waking up from my stupor. How can I have simply stopped worrying about the fact that someone sent me a bomb?

I know the answer—denial—but still I feel an infuriated concern about whether or not I can trust myself. It's the same way I feel when Sadie does something thoughtlessly dangerous, like sticking a lit candle on a paper plate or walking right up to some mental case in the subway.

Okay, so let me think my way through this. Before the closet erupted in skeletons I was mad at Ford because he kissed me. No, I was mad at him because he was kissing me to keep me from wondering what he was keeping from me.

Like, how did someone motivated enough to join the navy in order to get a college education wind up as a plumber?

Answer: He didn't. Which explains his remarkable lack of progress in my closet.

I look at Mrs. Kornislav as she eases herself into a large chair. "So Ford is undercover. Which begs the question, who or what is he investigating? Not me, clearly—I haven't done anything to interest the feds in years. So he's investigating Jason. Because of that aphrodisiac thing that he and the former Soviet scientist are cooking up?"

"You're referring to Irina Skulnikovna, a former chemist from Vladivostok. She was the number three in command at Biopreparat, the old Soviet Union's bio-weapons program."

"Oh."

"Frankly, we're not in quite as trusting a mood as we used to be. If she'd agreed to work directly with the government, then fine, but for some reason Irina said she wanted to go into the private sector."

"Well, there's more money to be made . . ."

"Selling biological agents to rogue nations, for example."

"But why are you investigating Jason?"

"He was behaving suspiciously. Our surveillance caught him leaving work at odd hours with Irina, once to go to a hotel room, and once to shop at a boutique for plus-size women."

"I knew it! The bastard's having an affair with this Russian woman, too."

Mrs. Kornislav gives me a look of grandmotherly compassion. "Bubeleh, believe me, if they were just meeting in secret for that kind of funny business, the government would not be getting involved. Besides, have you seen the woman?" She hands me a picture.

"Oh, God, my husband is sleeping with Janet Reno!"

In some ways, this makes me feel worse than knowing he slept with my neighbor and my sister. That might have been a simple case of proximity lust, or a tidy attempt at revenge for some imagined slight, or boredom. But to choose an ugly colleague as paramour! This must be how Princess Diana, Patron Saint of Unhappy Marriages, felt when her husband left her for an older, plainer woman. No reassuring fantasy that your spouse just wanted a bouncy new ride—no, he just felt you lacked something in the personality department.

"Are you all right, dear? Have some more tea."

"I'd rather have schnapps."

Mrs. Kornislav gives me a sniff of disapproval before lumbering off to pour me a very stingy shot of whiskey.

"Thanks." I spend a moment warming the inside of my throat. It's not enough, but I can see that Mrs. Kornislav is not the type to offer seconds of alcohol. Which leads me to my next question. "Mrs. Kornislav, if you don't mind my asking, what's your role in all of this?"

"Well, I used to be a personnel psychologist at Quantico, and since Ford's usually more of a lab rat than a field agent, it was felt he could use some backup."

My brain is hurting. "You're saying that you are Ford's backup?"

"I didn't say it, dear. I implied it."

"And you're both FBI as in Federal Bureau of, could have done more chasing down leads before September 11, guys in dark suits and glasses, don't play well with CIA? That FBI?"

"We don't really enjoy being stereotyped that way, and I disagree about the validity of your second statement, but yes, I suppose that you're not completely wrong."

I lean back on the couch, which is completely unyielding. Not furniture for slouchers. "So Ford is a lab worker and you're a shrink, and they chose you two because everyone appropriate was off learning Kurdish dialects?"

"Here's a pillow for your head—hair tends to leave greasy stains on the fabric. We needed someone who could actually do a bit of plumbing, as well as someone familiar with biochemistry. We told Ford to try to keep his mouth shut as much as possible, but lately he kept hinting about how he felt your life was in danger and that you needed to be warned."

And then there are three sharp knocks on the door.

"It's open, dear," says Mrs. Kornislav, which seems a bit lax for an FBI agent, but still, what do I know? Maybe most of the higher-ups in the CIA are also little old Jewish women with big wigs.

Ford comes in, looking a little sweaty in a dark gray sweater and black Levis. He barely glances at me, but there is something flustered in that brief glance. "What happened, Bella?"

"The sky is falling, only it seems to have singled out my head." I shrug as two sets of eyes look at me as if I'd stolen someone else's line in the school play. "Well, it did."

"That's about the size of it," says Mrs. Kornislav. "Where were you, anyway? I thought you were supposed to be keeping tabs on her."

Ford takes a breath, and is once again his imperturbable Spocklike self. "I had to run an analysis for the lab. Marco was supposed to be watching her."

"Well, if so, he watched her nearly get conked by a brick. Any luck on getting something from the clothes?"

"Only traces. We need a larger sample to work from. But I'm more concerned with Delilah's situation." Ford's jaw is clenched, and a muscle flexes in his cheek. Well, that's nice. I've never made anyone's jaw spasm before. At least not while I was sitting six feet away.

"Bella, this kind of incident is the reason I was arguing that we needed to make a full disclosure. . . ."

"Like you've been thinking with your head, boychik."

"That is entirely uncalled for. . . ."

I glance at my watch, suddenly reminded by all the high drama that it's time for the debut of my *Secrets* plotline.

"I hate to interrupt," I say, "but would it be possible to turn on the television? I'm recording at home, but I'd like to catch my soap."

Both Mrs. Kornislav and Ford look at me as if I have lost my senses. Ford recovers first.

"You mean the soap with the plotline you borrowed from your husband's top-secret memo?"

Doesn't anyone understand that all fiction writers use real life as an inspiration? It never fails to infuriate me that nonwriters do not understand the key is how facts are embroidered, shaped, and made to fit into an aesthetic whole. "Actually, I only used Jason's memo as a starting point. As with all fiction—"

"Well, we're recording it, too, but yeah, we can watch it if you want."

Ford leans over and reveals the TV, which is hidden, hotel-like, in a cabinet. It may be the shock of recent events, but I notice the lean line of his muscled torso when his sweater rides up.

We all turn to the television. There is a sudden swell of violins, and Ford fiddles with the volume as the image of a treasure chest appears onscreen. A skeleton key turns, the box opens, spilling out the images of the cast members.

"I can't hear," Mrs. Kornislav complains.

"Shh."

"Turn it up!"

Ford glances over his shoulder, looking a little irritated, then complies.

Blackjack, gagged and bound hand and foot (with his shirt off, for some reason) is squirming manfully as Ruby, dressed in a trench coat and fedora, is holding a gun and forcing Skylar to drop two glowing orange pills into a glass of water. The water fizzes and bubbles orangely.

(The fizzing pills were my suggestion. My bosses wanted it to be a potion, but I thought that seemed fake. I also happen to know from Jason's marketing research that Americans, given a choice, like taking their medicine in pill form. Germans prefer injections, and the French take almost anything they can in the form of a suppository.)

"I won't drink it," Skylar says, as blonde and wholesome as the saleswoman at the sex shop, and with a similar air of coy possibility.

"Oh, but I think you will. You see, a bullet in the brain—that's certain death. But I have every reason to believe that this dosage of the Mulanga flower isn't fatal at all. In fact, it probably won't even hurt you. You may even find it . . . surprisingly pleasant."

"I don't believe you would actually shoot me! Not now that we know we're sisters . . ." (This seems almost prescient, considering what I now know about Tamara.)

"All the more reason for me to treat you like the whining obstacle you are. Now open wide."

Close-up of Skylar's perturbed face. "What will it do to me, Ruby?"

"Well, that depends. If I got the dosage right, it should make you feel . . . shall we say, a certain affection for this gentleman here?"

"Our father's assassin! I'd rather die!"

"And if I didn't get the dosage right, you might. So what's it going to be, dearie?" Ruby does something to the gun that is supposed to make it click, but doesn't. Everyone pretends that it has, though.

"*Mmmffmm,*" says Blackjack, writhing manfully again. Close-up on the anguished expression in his eyes, and then fade to a man in a business suit, saying he knows what it's like to have credit problems.

"Well," I say, "they certainly repeat the word 'dosage' a lot."

"That's kind of unfortunate, actually."

I turn to Ford. "Why is that?" Onscreen, a really happy mommy is dancing in a meadow with a lot of clean laundry.

"How much of Jason's memo did you understand?" Ford looks at me with his opaque gaze, and I realize that behind his calm expression there's a gathering storm.

"The bare bones. That the active ingredient in Biosensual is something the FDA is awfully squirrelly about."

Not even a ghost of a smile. "We're talking about a potential level-three health and safety hazard."

"Lock-your-doors, grab-your-Hazmat-suit level three? And some of this stuff might be in my apartment?"

Ford pauses, as if making a decision. "Yes, but it's not dangerous unless ingested. Otherwise it would be a level-four."

"Ah."

"And even if it is ingested, it's all a matter of the dosage. Take some botulinum toxin A, some of the most poisonous stuff around, and dilute it enough, and you can inject it into rich women's foreheads to keep them from frowning."

"Botox." I realize I am wrinkling my brow in concentration and make an effort to smooth my expression out.

"Okay. So Irina Skulnikovna is working with a mold that can destroy higher brain functions. In smaller doses, it seems to be a simple disinhibitor that produces a release of endorphins."

"Like ecstasy," I say, remembering a few long-ago happy

nights at Le Bar Bat, when I thought everyone was my glossy, happy, huggable friend.

A crease appears between Ford's eyes. "Delilah, have you tried any of this . . . any of your husband's drug?"

"No, I haven't. Why?"

"Because the difference between a dose that makes you feel . . . disinhibited, say, and a dose that might destroy your higher brain function, is only a few milligrams."

I seem to recall Jason telling me all this, but with a decidedly different spin. "Okay, I'm beginning to see why the FDA wants to bury this particular nut."

Just as Ford opens his mouth to respond, the soap opera's theme music announces the return of the show, and we all turn back to the set.

"Oh, God, Blackjack, take me, please take me!" Skylar undulates like a maddened ferret across the floor.

Bound hand and foot, Blackjack is, alas, in no position to take anybody.

"Maybe I can help," says Giacomo Ferrigamo, the sleekly evil clothing mogul, appearing at the door wearing a designer suit with a sinister metallic sheen.

Blackjack struggles with his ropes, but it's no good; Skylar is already eyeing Giacomo as if he were the first hot dog at the barbecue.

"You know, this really won't be good for Biosensual sales," says Mrs. Kornislav.

"Are you kidding? Sales should go through the roof!"

Ford looks at me, then back at the TV, where Skylar is now moaning as Giacomo traces one finger down her bare arm. "You think watching a woman moaning like a retriever in season will make a mostly female audience want to purchase your product?"

"You're one of those people who never did drugs in college, aren't you?"

Ford raises one slanted, dark eyebrow. "I've never felt the need to experiment with my brain's chemistry in order to experience stimulus," he says.

"Nerd."

"Do you have any idea what effect this mold has on the hippocampus?"

"Did you even try a few mushrooms?"

"I think you're missing the point, here. . . ."

"Smoke the occasional joint?"

A flush, either of irritation or anger, has appeared on the tops of Ford's ears. "Delilah, forget the non-issue of whether or not I was a nerd in college. I've already told you I was. I admit to being the biggest, straightest, deadly dull science nerd in the northern hemisphere."

"But you did drink, didn't you?"

"Delilah." Ford grabs me by both shoulders, giving me a little shake. I can see out of the corner of my eye that Mrs. Kornislav is half scandalized, half captivated. "Has it occurred to you yet that this show is the reason bricks and cars keep heading straight for you?"

But of course, like all things that are perfectly obvious once they are pointed out to you, it hadn't occurred to me.

"Are . . . are you saying that some rogue government has sent terrorist operatives out to get me?"

It's a strange, strained moment. There is something in Ford's face that says he is thinking about shaking me harder, or possibly kissing me. There is a buzzing in the back of my ears that might be the TV set, or might be residual damage to my pineal gland. Ford's hands tighten on my shoulder for a moment, then release.

"Actually," says Mrs. Kornislav in what I feel is an inappropriately upbeat tone of voice, "we seem to have a rather long list of people who might like to see you dead."

My mother opens her Tudor-style door with a dramatic chatelaine's gesture of welcome, and then mimes shock, pleasure, concern and great joy at seeing me. Then she bends down to enfold Sadie in a smothering bosom-hug of homecoming.

"How's my beautiful baby girl? Look at you, so tall. Gorgeous."

"Hi, Nana. I missed you. How's your yeast?"

Look of maternal confusion, replaced by look of dawning horror as my mother recalls the colloquial term for *candida albicans*.

"From the bread you were baking, silly!"

My mother oversmiles like an actress about to launch into a testimonial. "Oh, that yeast, that's done, we're working on potato latkes now. And big, fat doughnuts. Have you ever made a doughnut from scratch? No? You'll love it—it's dangerous, it's exciting, and you have to eat everything immediately. We're going to have so much fun!" My mother hugs Sadie again, then looks up at me. For a moment, I catch a glimpse of Tamara in Mom's plumply pretty, blue-eyed face with its neat helmet of hair, and something of what I'm feeling must show in my expression. "What's wrong, Delilah?"

I inhale a familiar breath of home. Lemon floor wax and evergreen air freshener, the passing whiff of gardenia perfume, and overlaying everything, a hint of fried potato in oil. The self-conscious refinement of suburban New Jersey. I exhale. "Nothing's wrong, Mom."

"The kind of nothing that stands six feet tall, weighs seven pounds more each year and leaves the toilet seat up? I've got that kind of nothing trouble, too. Well, don't just stand there thinking up something to lie to me. Come in, take off your coats. Sades, I've fixed up your mother's old room for you. How long can you stay? I wanted to take you over to my flower-beading class tomorrow. . . ."

"Mommy, can I stay at Nana's for tomorrow, too?"

I look down at my daughter's eager, upturned face, and think about falling bricks and runaway cars. "You can stay for a couple of days, Bunny. At least."

"Great!"

"Ah, Sadie, that gives us time to go to the temple's big Chanukah fair. We can introduce you to my friend Marnie's granddaughter, who belongs to the local Girl Scout troop. . . ."

It is one of life's great ironies that the very same things that made my childhood an unending torture—my mother's cooking, silly arts and crafts projects, synagogue functions and gender-discriminatory activities involving the wearing of psuedo-military unforms—are now the cause of my daughter's expression of unmitigated pleasure.

"Girl Scouts—great! Why can't we live in New Jersey, Mom?"

Dinner is a nightmare. I have not had time to tell my mother anything other than the bare bones of my predicament— Jason and I are arguing, and I need someone to look after Sadie while we sort ourselves out—so naturally I come downstairs to find my sister carrying out a big platter of pot roast to the dining-room table.

"Hi, Del," she says. Just like that. Just like she's not guilty of betraying me with my husband.

"Auntie Tammy!" Sadie barrels into her, wrapping both arms around my sister's middle.

"Careful, Punkin, I'm loaded down." Tam beams down at my daughter's head—which is at breast level—just as if she had never had Sadie's father in a similar position.

My father comes in to witness the lighting of the second candle of Chanukah with an air of having been called out of a very important meeting. "Aren't you even serving the food yet? Why do you tell me you're ready when you're not? Is the idea that the food tastes better if I have to sit around waiting for it?"

"Barry, please, let's have a nice dinner."

My father, who has the short graying curls and angry jowls of a Republican businessman, is actually an ex-Peace Corps hippie type turned divorce lawyer. Like my mother, he is wearing an expensive, inside-out-style sweatshirt. "Let's define our terms, then. By 'nice', do you mean aesthetically pleasing? Do you mean organized and precise? Or are you trying to imply a kind of forced pleasantness?"

"We're not in court, Barry." I stare at my mother; for twenty-five years, she worked as my father's legal secretary, and Tam and I had always gotten the impression that at home as in the office, Dad was by far the more senior partner. I half expected my Dad to announce he was holding her in contempt of court, but instead, his eyes just sort of slide away from hers.

"I was just saying let's agree on terms, Adele. Isn't that right, Sadie? Hey, kiddo, I got another law case for you."

"Great, Grandpa."

"Sit by me. Mommy, hurry up already, half the dishes are getting cold. All right, Sades, so there's this sailor on a ship who starts arguing with his friend, and the ship goes through a massive patch of fog. There's a scream. When the fog clears, the first sailor is still there, but his friend has vanished—*poof!* No bloodstains, no body, nothing."

As my father launches into his double indemnity case, I try to catch my mother's eye. But since Mom keeps disappearing into the kitchen with her usual air of trying to keep one step ahead of impending nuclear disaster, this proves impossible.

I follow her into the kitchen, where she is decanting kasha varnishkes onto a platter. Despite my inner turmoil, I find myself reaching for one of the shell-like noodles, which is flaunting its delectable little self on a savory beach of buckwheat. The smell of it is as regressive as melted Crayolas or heated latex balloons. Maybe I can just pretend everything is normal so that I can sink back into being a sick seven-year-old in need of rest, a humidifier and lots of stodgy, reassuring food.

Unbidden, an image comes to me of my sister straddling my husband. No, not even kasha varnishkes can take away that sour taste.

"Mom, can we talk for a moment?"

"First take this in for me." She hands me the platter.

"Mom, it's about having Sadie over. And it concerns Tamara."

Of course, that is the moment my sister walks in, carrying five butter knives. "Dad says we need something sharper for the meat."

My mother puts her hands on her hips. "Oh, God, the meat must be tough." She doesn't sound so much upset as annoyed, and this, too, is something of a sea change for my mom. Some tide has shifted in the marriage; something has eroded her usual deference to my dad, and now it comes back to me, Tamara's question from two weeks ago—maybe it's not Dad who's having the affair.

But there's no time to loiter on that particular train of thought, because steam-engine Tamara is already huffing down another track.

"So what concerns me, Del?"

"I'd rather not be having this conversation right now."

"Tamara! Delilah!" My father's voice causes us both to give a little startle, I notice. "Get those knives in here, would you?"

We bring the sharp knives out and sit down for tough meat and legal argument.

"All right, verdict time," my father booms at Sadie. "Should the sailor have been tried a second time for his friend's murder, or not?"

I've been down this road before with my father. Whatever you say, he argues the opposite, until you beg him for the real answer. Tamara went to law school so that she could finally produce the correct response, only to discover that my father just likes arguing, the way some men like sex with plump interns.

I turn from my father only to see that my sister is glaring at me while sawing away at her entrée.

"So, Del," she says in a combative I-know-you-took-my-Go-Gos-album tone, "what was it that you were about to say to Mom in the kitchen?"

Before I can answer my sister's question, my mother prods at her beef, apologizes for its quality, and we all take turns to taste it and compliment it, except for my father, who is too busy playing devil's advocate.

When I look up, my sister is still looking at me, her face filled with all the hostility of unacknowledged guilt. "Well?"

"Certain evidence has come to light," I say, forking a piece of meat, "that has caused me to believe that Sadie would be better off staying here for a few nights. But I would prefer that Mom and Dad keep her close to home."

"What kind of evidence?" My sister's blue eyes narrow.

"The kind of evidence that careless people leave when they believe themselves to be above certain laws."

My father, smelling a legal case, stops badgering Sadie. "What's this about someone breaking a law?"

"Yes," says Tamara, looking completely unrepentant as she sips a glass of Mom's truly awful zinfandel, "and are we talking laws here, or are we more in the realm of societal conventions?"

"Laws," I say, holding my sister's gaze. I am still chewing the piece of rather fatty roast in my mouth, and so am prevented from saying more. Which is probably a good thing. Even I do not know if I mean the kind of laws that say you shouldn't go around killing people, or the kind of laws that say you shouldn't go around screwing their husbands.

My sister gives me a tight smile. Clearly she thinks she knows which laws I mean. "And how does Jason feel about all of this?"

"Ask him yourself. If you can locate him." I throw back my head and down half my glass of zinfandel, grimacing like Clint as the taste hits my tongue.

"My daddy's run away from home," says Sadie, as if making a general pronouncement about the weather. "I'm staying here so that Mom can find him and have a fight without me hearing and getting all upset."

Yes, indeed, I'm doing a marvelous job of protecting my child. At least she doesn't seem to be aware of the unknown-homicidal-maniac aspect of the situation.

"Oh, honey!" My mother reaches out her arms to me, upsetting the gravy. "You never said anything."

"Oh, please." Tamara stands up. "You and Jason have been in a marriage of inconvenience for I don't know how long, and now it's a huge shock to everyone that things aren't working out. I'm sorry, Del, but I don't believe in lying to children to make them feel better."

"I don't get it, why are you mad at Mommy?" Sadie looks like she's about to cry. "Why is everyone mad at Mommy?"

"Oh, sweetie, no one's mad at your mom." My mother rushes out of her seat and wraps her arms around Sadie. "It's just that your auntie Tam is an older sister and sometimes sisters fight. Sometimes Auntie Tam gets jealous of your mommy and she forgets she isn't four or six or even sixteen, but a grown-up woman who ought to know better."

My sister stands there, holding the back of her chair, her eyes flitting from Mom to Dad and back again. "I don't really think you're in a position to throw stones, Mom. I mean, for years you've just taken whatever Dad has dished out, and now all of a sudden you're some expert on relationships. What's changed all of a sudden? Or don't you care to talk about that?"

"Tamara Ilana, at your age I'd been married for eighteen years and already had two children. I also worked outside the home, and even if you've had more education than I did, you sure don't have the life experience to go with it. So before you go embarrassing yourself in front of your niece anymore, I suggest you apologize, go home and think long and hard about who needs to get a lesson from whom."

My sister just stands there as the silence thickens and grows, her eyes swollen with unshed tears. Even I can see she is holding on to the back of the chair for balance, and for a moment I feel sorry for her. Adolescent rebellion must be like chicken pox: That much harder and more awkward when you experience it for the first time as an adult.

"As if your life experience has anything to do with mine, Mom! I'll have you know I spend half my time covering up Dad's mistakes, with no thanks and no respect. Maybe it's time I just let you all work it out by yourselves!"

Then Tamara starts crying and runs out the door.

"I don't understand," says Sadie, two fingers in her mouth. She hasn't done that since she was three. Her flyaway hair is almost standing on end and her eyes are enormous behind her new purple spectacles and she is suddenly, poignantly pretty in the way of waifs and orphans.

"It's okay," says my mother. "It's just like a flu going around, except instead of sniffles everyone's breaking out in strong feelings. We'll get through it. What do you say we cast a little spell for peace and everyone getting along after dinner, huh, Sadie? I think I saw something in your book where you braid some threads together. No frogs, no newts, no spiderwebs. We should be able to handle a bit of thread braiding, right?"

My daughter stops crying, not noticing the snort of disgust from my father. "Will it work, Nana?"

My mother strokes the flyaway hair back from Sadie's eyes. "As I understand it, Bubbie, believing is what gives magic most of its power."

Tuesday, December 18
10 A.M.

"What I don't understand is, why do you let that ridiculous mortal dictate to you, Delilah? It's unseemly." Adele snapped her fingers and was instantly perched high atop the kitchen counter, her billowing purple caftan obediently arranging itself in neat folds. "Really, Delilah, letting Jackson order you to stop using your witchcraft is barbaric. Why don't you trundle him off to a nice therapist and have him work out his inadequacy issues? It might even help him function better in bed."

"First of all, Mother, his name is Jason, as you well know."

"Who cares? He could be replaced by an entirely different mortal husband and one would be hard pressed to notice. He has no personality!"

"Now, Mother, you know there's a difference between the suspension of disbelief and not noticing." Delilah had, in fact, suspended her disbelief quite a few times in the course of her marriage. She willingly accommodated the fiction that Jason wished he could spend less time at work, for example, when she knew very well that he would rather be at the office, where everyone had assigned roles and didn't deviate from them unless officially given permission.

Delilah also accepted the story that they had only had one child because of technical difficulties, while the truth was that deep down, they both suspected that their marriage probably couldn't weather the intrusion of another infant, with all its mindless demands and its inability to suit anyone else's schedule.

Like most reasonably contented wives, Delilah was a master of suspended disbelief. She chose to believe that she was happily married to a very nice man, and that belief smoothed the lines from her brow; it made her recite her wifely lines with conviction.

As she calmly continued cutting carrots into the pot in her cheery modern sixties kitchen, no one would have suspected her of harboring a secret bohemian past. There was something Grace Kelly-ish about her, a kittenish aristocracy to her fine features and smooth, dark blonde bob, that made her seem like she was slumming it a bit in her little navy sleeveless top and capris pants.

There was none of her mother's theatrical sulkiness about her; Delilah radiated the kind of self-satisfaction that would have been irritating had she not possessed a glint of something self-deprecating, even mocking, in her warm hazel eyes.

"And by the way, Mother, Jason doesn't have any problems feeling . . . adequate. It's just that he believes that anything worth doing is worth . . . well, doing. He thinks magic makes everything too easy."

"Darling, magic is what freed our sisters from the drudgery of stew making and housecleaning back when all the other goodwives thought it was the height of creative expression to stitch a paisley quilt. I mean, when you look back at history, where are all the great women artists and writers and scientists? Chopping carrots, that's where. Except for the few, the brave, the witches, who dared to use magic to free themselves—to create!" Adele made a wild flourish with her right arm, and her trailing sleeve landed in her daughter's gravy.

"Have you been having a little liquid lunch, Mother?" Delilah arched one eyebrow, looking suddenly a good deal older and more sophisticated. Without that look on her face, Del might have passed for twenty-five or -six; with it, she might have been given ten or twelve years more. The truth, of course, was that she was pushing two hundred and fifty, but even back in Old Salem, she'd always been very careful about the sun.

"And what's wrong with a little juice of the grape, I'd like to know? Frankly, darling, your mortal life is turning you into something of a bore. And when I think of all the lovely covens that wanted you as high priestess, and all the lovely men you could have had group sex with . . ."

"Mother, I got tired of performing the great rite with a bunch of guys in reindeer masks a hundred years ago. Jason gives me something different. A home."

"You know you sound retro even now, don't you? Smart women are burning their bras these days."

"Yes, well, that'll go out of fashion, too."

Adele huffed a disgruntled sigh, dipping one vermillion fingernail into her daughter's stew. "Ugh, speaking of bland. Don't you believe in using herbs anymore?"

Delilah gave her mother a quick, knowing glance out from beneath her long eyelashes. "Not your kind of herbs, Mother."

"And where, may I ask, is my darling witchy grandchild?"

"She's off at a friend's, for a sleepover."

"Hope she doesn't try that Sleeping Beauty spell I taught her last time she was over . . ."

It was at that moment that Jason Green walked into his house, with the eager step of a man who does not know that his five-hundred-year-old mother-in-law is visiting.

"Delilah, I'm home!"

Delilah ran to give her husband a kiss. "You're home early! Mr. Madigan usually keeps you till six."

"Well, honey, I told him I had to be home early, because tonight we've got something to celebrate."

"And what's that?"

Jason beamed at his wife. "Do I need to remind you about last night? Last night when you gave me the best present any man could ever receive? Last night when you blew my mind—and everything else, I might add. Baby, I take back what I said about not using magic. If last night is anything to go by, then there are definitely situations where anything worth doing is worth doing with an extra pair of arms."

Looking over Jason's shoulder at her eavesdropping mother, Delilah made a shooing gesture; her mother stuck her tongue out and then made a sweeping gesture with her arms, and disappeared with a tinkle of bells, which Jason did not appear to hear.

"What about last night? You were working late."

For a moment, an almost comical look of befuddlement crossed Jason's features. Then he smiled. "Oh, I get it, you little tease. You want me to pretend that it wasn't you in my office, giving me the best sexual experience of my adult life."

Both of Delilah's arched eyebrows shot higher. "It wasn't."

"Sure, honey. There just happens to be a woman who looks exactly like you, but in a brunette wig, who appeared at my office wearing your trench coat over that hot little bra-and-panties set I bought you last Valentine's Day."

"Brunette? You mean, like my sister Tamara? My developmentally arrested sex-addict sister, I might add, whom you know hates me and is wildly jealous of me, and is also a witch?"

Jason's jaw dropped, and then his face turned pale, then red, then pale again. It's all well and good to marry an immensely powerful sorceress, until, of course, the day comes when you piss her off.

"Sweetheart, either you've just been very stupid or very naughty. And I'm afraid there's really only one sure way for me to find out which." Delilah gave an adorable little twitch of her nose, and the next thing Jason knew, he was hanging suspended

*from his wrists, and a very muscular man in a black hood was
doing something behind him that made a sizzling noise. "Aw,
honey, I thought it was you. Honey? Delilah? Del!"*

*Back in suburbia, Delilah Levine was calling up a few old
friends, and telling them to bring their reindeer masks along.*

There are three calls on the answering machine congratulating me for yesterday's hugely successful *Secrets* program, although I am not sure what "successful" means.
Does it mean a poll of two ladies from Wichita who liked it?
Is it the opinion of our corporate sponsors or merely our
own creative team being self-congratulatory?

And, the burning, unspeakable question underlying all
these others: Does this mean that I will now be able to afford to raise Sadie in Manhattan on my own?

I climb back into bed with my coffee and a bowl of
Sadie's favorite chocolate-and-sugar-coated cereal, and
channel surf. Channel 10 has trouble in the Middle East.
Channel 9 has a woman who thinks her husband is cheating on her with her sister. Hey, I could invite Tamara to join
me on the program so a licensed therapist can watch us
scream at each other! Channel 7 has a crusty, decaffeinated
man trading bon mots with a chipper, caffeinated woman.
Both of them manage to drink from their mugs and talk
without mishap, which is more than I can say for myself; I
have somehow oversipped and dribbled coffee all down
my chest, staining my favorite Buffy the Vampire Slayer
T-shirt. Channel 20 has a young man singing while he digs
a grave for his mother. From what I can see, her crime
seems to be that she dragged him by the arm at some point
in his childhood. Oh, God, I have dragged Sadie by the arm,
not as a daily occurrence, but every once in a while when
we really need to get out the door and she can't tear herself

away from some *Animal Planet* program. What if Jason brings this up when we're in court while we're divorcing? What if I'm found to be an unfit mother?

Channel 36 has the weather.

The front door slams and I realize this is Hilda's house-keeping day. She is expecting to tidy and do laundry while I work, and then she is supposed to pick Sadie up from school.

I do not want to work, but I cannot just lie in bed while someone else cleans my mess. I mean, I can, I used to do it all the time as a teenager, but only if the mess cleaner is my mother. Hilda will not ask me if I am sick and can she fix me something more substantial to eat, Hilda will ask me if I am sick and look at me as if I am the lazy, louche, unpleasantly puerile product of a decadent society.

Is it too late to send Hilda back home? Yes, of course it is, she lives a million miles away, in Queens.

"Hello, Hilda," I call, dragging myself out of bed. "I seem to have overslept."

Hilda shrugs out of her coat, which is a light camel color and impeccably clean and pressed. She exchanges her very nice beige pumps for embroidered house slippers. Her dress is made of dark purple wool with pearl buttons and she smells like night-blooming Jasmine.

"You look nice," I say, wishing I were wearing under-wear and hoping that my Buffy T-shirt covers all bases.

"I believe appearances count," says Hilda. "In my country, even the poorest woman takes pride in looking her best." The unspoken corollary to this, of course, is *Unlike in your country, where the richest woman takes pride in letting her flesh fall out of some expensively ripped and frayed* shmatta.

"Well, you do look great, Hilda."

She doesn't look at me as she unfolds her apron. "Also,

Sadie and I are planning on going to the Met after school. We wanted to look at the Egyptian temple on the first floor."

"Oh, gosh, Hilda, I'm really sorry about this, but Sadie's not here. I mean she's not at school. She's staying at my parents' for the next few . . . well, probably through the winter break. So on the bright side, you'll get to have a bit more free time to get ready for Christmas."

Hilda is not amused. "I already got presents for all my friends and family. I brought them over to my country when I took my vacation early, because you told me you needed me until just before Christmas."

Yes, so sorry, Hilda, but that was before people started attempting to kill me and my husband abandoned ship. Meeting her unfriendly dark gaze, I say out loud, "I'm afraid a couple of unexpected things have happened. There was really no way for me to know ahead of time that I would have to leave Sadie at my folks' place."

"Uh-huh. And what about Mr. Levine?"

"What about him?"

"This don't have nothing to do with the fact that I won't do toilets and floors? He ask me, I tell him, housekeeping means I sweep, I dust, I do laundry and I fold, but it does not mean I stick my hand down somebody else's toilet."

"No, really, it has nothing to do with cleaning."

" 'Cause I do plenty here without sticking my hands down your toilets."

"You do tons! You're indispensable!" I am trying for cheery, upbeat and normal, but there is a shrill note in my voice which could be mistaken for sarcasm.

Hilda takes a deep sniff, as if she could say something, but is thinking better of it. "So," she says carefully, "this week, you gonna need me, or not need me?"

"Not need you, I guess."

"And this vacation's gonna be paid, or not paid?"

"Paid, Hilda. Of course." But I am sweating a little. I hadn't really thought about the ramifications of giving Hilda a second paid vacation, but I am, after all, responsible for her income. Besides, maybe I am now a rich soap-opera writer.

"And do I still get to choose a week off that's convenient for me this summer, or is that suddenly changed, too?"

"I, uh, hadn't really thought that through yet. . . ."

"You don't think too much, now, do you?""

Okay, this was a bit much. This wasn't just rancor, this was spite. "Listen, Hilda, I know you're upset about the change in plans, so maybe you need to take the rest of the day to get used to it." There is a belligerence in my tone now, but I can't help it; I feel like there's an unofficial club of Delilah-bashers forming, what with Jason, Kathy, my sister and now Hilda all lining up to give me my lumps.

Hilda's eyes narrow. "Maybe I just take the rest of the year off, huh? Only reason I stay so long is I feel sorry for that poor child of yours." She unties her apron.

"Excuse me?" I say it the nasty way.

"You heard me, lady. That child don't have a proper mother, what she have is one lazy slut who don't clean, don't cook and half the time don't know what day it is. Girl wears patent leather to school on gym days, sits out while her class plays ball. You too busy foolin' with the plumber to go volunteer at Sadie's school book sale, so what do you do? You send Hilda."

"That was once, when I was sick! I go to almost every parent thing you're supposed to volunteer for! And I do tons of things with Sadie—arts and crafts, science projects . . ." I run down the list of insults. "And I am not screwing the plumber!"

Hilda rolls her eyes and waggles her head like Aretha reaching for a power note, ready to shame all the other divas. "Whatever. Then there's that man of yours, dresses like a Carnival Queen. You got him so mixed up he don't know if he's a boy or a girl!"

"Excuse me?" I say this the completely thrown-for-a-loop way.

"Oh, I catch him at it one time when you and Sadie were out. Said he was doing research for his job. I said, honey, not unless that's some new job you got, because he was wearing a silk dress and heels."

That awful silk dress in the closet! Those enormous pumps! No wonder Jason ran away. Not because he couldn't handle my learning about his extramarital hijinks. Because the explanation for the affairs was something he's more ashamed of than affairs themselves.

My husband is a cross-dresser. It explains so much.

"Thank you, Hilda, that was very useful information."

"Yeah, well, you can kiss my ass, too. Just be glad I stayed as long as I did, 'cause if Sadie turns out all right, it's no thanks to you."

I don't try to explain that I wasn't being sarcastic, because there are some arguments that there is just no coming back from. The door slams behind Hilda and although I am sorry for Sadie, I am also relieved. If I survive this next week, at the very least I will no longer be surrounded by people who are only pretending to be my friends.

It is the good side of learning all the dirty secrets that have been festering inside of everyone's smiles.

Losing Hilda and discovering she really always loathed me is a positive development, a kind of emotional exfoliation. And if there is a residual layer of burning discomfort, a nagging worry that Hilda may be right about my being a deficient mother, I dismiss it. All of us breeders are tested in the crucible of parenthood and found wanting. Even the best mother fails her child in some ways; it's the built-in obsolescence factor that will help Sadie walk away from me to build her own life when she's twenty-one.

In fact, I am so pleased by this new turn of events that I fix myself an emergency Screwdriver, put on my favorite old Abba CD, run an extremely hot bubble bath, sink down and try to drown myself in self pity.

I wake to find the bath cold, the bubbles gone, and Ford sitting on the closed toilet seat, looking down at me.

"Hello," I say slowly. I try to raise my leg and arm so that I am not so very completely naked, which is silly, because it seems that my personal FBI man has already seen every last goose-pimpled inch of me. I want to say, This isn't my breasts' best angle, but I figure the best way to play this is cool. I do so hope I haven't done anything unseemly in my sleep.

"What are you doing, Ford?"

"Thinking about how to wake you up." He keeps looking at me, his eyes black on black, leaving no clue as to what he is thinking. For a moment I wonder if he has even noticed that I am naked. Then I notice the dark flush on his high cheekbones and my nipples tighten until they sting.

He lifts his chin, and for a moment I swear his nostrils flare; then he tugs at the laces of his left hiking boot, pulling it off with the sock attached and throwing it behind him without looking where it lands. The second boot follows and then Ford pulls his shirt out of the waistband of his jeans and starts unbuttoning. He doesn't look at what he's doing, but I can't stop. My mind wanders down the ladder of his ribs, across the tightly ridged abdominal muscles. He moves like a dancer or a fighter, as if he is really inhabiting his body.

And now his shirt is undone and he is standing, his hand at the top button of his black jeans, and somehow I have missed the part where we agreed that this is what happens next. This is not like my fantasies. Things are going on in his head, decisions are being made, conclusions drawn, and I don't know what he's thinking or feeling. I feel chilled and raw and vulnerable. What if I can't relax? What if I am tense and unyielding and he tells me to just go with it, and I can't? What if I don't like it and I wind up just going along with it to be polite, or because everything is going to hell and Jason did it with someone else and I might die without knowing who killed me?

And as if he can sense my indecision, Ford stops undressing and kneels down. "You think too much."

"How can you tell?"

"I've spent some time studying you."

I stare at him, trying to take this in. I have been aware that he has a slight crush on me; now I think I have understated the matter. Waves of heat and tension are coming off him, and I know if I were to touch him at all, anywhere, he would shudder.

And I realize that I want to touch him. His shoulders are wonderful, laced with long muscle, as understated as a poem. His capable, long-fingered, work-roughened hand moves along the rim of the tub, near my arm, stopping just short of contact.

"I'm not supposed to be doing this."

"Why are you, then?"

"I figured if you hadn't wanted me to see you, you wouldn't have been alone in the house, naked in the bath."

"It wasn't meant as an invitation. I just forgot you were coming."

His hand, approaching my upper arm, stills. "I want to touch you." He waits, his gaze intent on mine. "I want to climb inside of you."

My eyes dip to the front of his jeans; yep, that's what he meant. "The water's cold."

Ford leans over until his mouth is less than an inch from mine. "What do you want me to do, Delilah?" His voice sounds gruff, almost angry.

I slosh slightly downwards. "Hand me the towel, please."

Ford stands up and holds it out for me. As I step out, he folds his arms and the towel around me from behind. "What now?"

"What now?"

He braces his legs and I can feel his erection against my back and bottom, through his jeans, through the towel. "What now, Delilah?"

"What now?" Oh, I do not want to have to tell him what to do or what not to do. I want him to sweep me off my feet, fight off my resistance, still my racing brain. I want to be seduced, ravished, made not responsible for my actions.

"I told you what I want." To be inside me. "Tell me what you want."

I start shaking my head, and the movement grows wilder as his arms tighten around me. "I don't know," I say, still whipping my hair from side to side like some overwrought debutante.

Ford spins me around to face him, his shirt undone, his hair falling into his face. "Tell me, Delilah." His hands gripping my upper arms. "Tell me to get lost. Tell me you don't want me."

"I can't!"

And now he is kissing me, not gently, thank God, giving no more time for thought. He has his tongue in my mouth as if this were sex, not a preamble, as if you could come from the taste of someone if you tasted them enough, and his hands are dragging through my hair, pulling, but I can feel the wild specificity of his desire, the loss of control, and my hands are on his face, his jaw, running over the trembling muscles of his arms.

He lowers his splayed hands to the cradle of my hips and pushes, and just as I had suspected, we are perfectly aligned. I can feel the rigid length of his arousal through the layers of his denim and my terrycloth, and then he looks into my eyes and brings my hips flush against him again. I open my eyes to see that his eyes are now clenched shut, the cords on his neck standing out, and I inhale sharply at the sensation. He pushes again and I sink my teeth into the hard muscle of his shoulder.

"God." Ford scoops me up in his arms as if I weigh nothing and kisses me, bumping into walls and off doors. I start to laugh but he is kissing me again, his mouth moving down my neck, to my ear, then back to my mouth. He makes a sound like he's in pain—his hip has caught the corner of a dresser, but there's no smile, no acknowledgement of the absurd aspect to all of this. He's just looking up for long enough to navigate the doorway and now he's looking down at my breast. "Christ." He dips his head down and this time he nips me, not too hard, just over the left nipple.

I can't remember the last time a man was at me this way, with no room for talk or humor or suggestions. He's like a force of nature, like a stallion in rut. He's like Mr. Spock when he goes into that Vulcan Pon Farr madness and has to get to his planet to get laid by his one true mate or die trying.

"Ford?"

He looks up, his eyes glazed. "What?"

"You're scaring me a little."

This time he does smile, a rueful lift of his eyebrows. "Shit, I'm scaring me. Just let me get the first time over with, I promise I'll be better after that."

Something about the thought of that, his nervousness and his desire, catches the breath in my chest and makes me pull his head down to mine. I slide my legs down his and I can feel how hard he is against my belly. We're still in the hallway but I don't care, my towel is sliding away and I am pulling down Ford's jeans and—Christ, the man doesn't wear any underwear, and I try to lean over and take him in my mouth but he grabs my wrists and shakes his head no.

"Sorry," he says, "I, uh, need a second."

So we just kneel there on the floor for a moment, breathing hard, looking at each other. After a moment, I reach out to him, but he shakes his head again. "I can't. I can't move. I want to—I planned on—I think if I even touch you right now, I'm going to explode."

I stare at him. "Has it, uh, been a long time?"

He gives me a crooked smile. "I, uh, yeah. And also there's the, uh, you factor." He takes a deep breath, like a diver preparing to brave the ocean, and reaches for me slowly. Our bodies press together from shoulder to thigh, and he gives a long shudder. "Maybe one more moment would be . . ."

And then, I don't know why, I just feel so fed up with everything and I don't want him to be all boyish and sweet, I want him to take me, God damn it, so I sort of half punch him in the chest.

"What?!"

"Stop worrying about losing it and just do something!" And then I hit him again, because honestly, it feels kind of good. And then I stand up and try to kick him and he does something with his arm to deflect it and now I am running into the living room and he is right behind me, and now I am whirling and trying to hit him again and he is catching both my wrists and now I am pinned on my back with my hands over my head.

"What are we doing here?" He looks almost predatory, his thick, dark hair hanging in his face, the muscles of his shoulders bunched. "Are we fighting?"

I lunge up and kiss him, using teeth, and now he gets it, no more questions, just his knee spreading my thighs and his hips driving him deep inside me, and the power of his stroke nails me to the rug. He slams into me so roughly that by the third stroke I am mindless with pleasure. He rears over me like a barbarian prince, his chest gleaming with sweat, his hands never loosening their hold on my wrists, and I can feel the tension bunching the muscles in his thighs, each thrust now taking him a little further into animal consciousness. No thinking now, just flesh sinking hard into flesh, just the battle to reach the summit and leave the self behind. But then his hands tighten on my wrists and he says, "Say it," and I understand this isn't just my fantasy, he has his fantasy going, too.

I don't know what he wants me to say and I don't want to fail him and then he plunges into me again and the seismic waves ripple over him and through me and I shout his name.

I can feel the pulse and surge of him inside me, and he says my name and pushes again, his back arched and his eyes screwed shut for what seems a very long time.

He collapses on top of me as if someone's shot him. I

don't mind; he's not that heavy, and it gives me a chance to run my fingers through his hair and compose myself. I blink my eyes a bit, because it's always embarrassing if you look like you've been crying right after, but when Ford looks up, I can see tears in his eyes, and he doesn't seem to mind.

"Hey," he says, stroking the side of my face.

"Hey yourself." I don't know what to say to him. It occurs to me belatedly that we didn't have the safety talk, even though I use an IUD so pregnancy isn't an issue, and then Ford moves slightly so he can rest his head on his right hand. His left hand is still cupping my cheek.

"Delilah, I don't want to sound like a B-movie lover here, but . . . I was kind of out of control, usually I'm more, I mean, it doesn't usually happen that quickly for me, and . . ."

"Ford, I've been fantasizing about this since the first moment I saw you. I've had so much mental foreplay that you probably could have said Hello and that would have done me fine."

His grin is pure boychild. "So you *did* come!"

Oh, argh, not this again. "Okay, well, if you mean did I get to the top of the mountain and plant my flag there, then not exactly. It was more like, I made it to the observation deck and took the cable car down. But it was some mountain."

"You took the cable car?" The look on his face is almost comical.

I sit up a little and roll onto his chest. Early on in our relationship, I tried to explain this once to Jason, and failed. Years of semi-faking was the unfortunate result. "I mean I wasn't left stranded up there, I got a very nice ride down, but not the skiing-at-full-throttle-down-Everest ride."

"Oh."

"But it was incredible." I grab his face. "Really incredible. It's just the way I'm built, it takes me a few times to get the rhythm exactly right with a new man. To, I don't know, let myself go completely. It's me, not you, and please don't make me feel bad about it."

"So it was with me like it was other men." Ford says this very slowly, as if rolling the words around in his head.

"No, stupid. It was better." I can feel my eyes tearing up and I blink hard. "Look, I'm sorry I'm not one of those orgasmatron women who just fly off to nirvana at first touch, but if you stick around, you'll find out that by the third or fourth time . . ."

What am I saying? Now I sound both emotionally needy and like I'm trying out for some hot new porn contest.

"Are you crying?" He tries to move my hands from my face.

"Only from frustration."

"Delilah."

"I mean, not that kind of frustration, not the help-me-out-here kind, more the boy, am-I-bad-at-talking-about-this-kind-of-thing kind."

"Delilah."

I look at him, and it's that awful post-coital thing where the man is relaxed and tousled and has just become ten times handsomer and more desirable, and you've turned all red-eyed and sniveling. But he reaches out and folds me into his chest, which seems to have a place designed just for the shape of my head.

"Listen, Delilah, I've been fighting this like hell, told myself at first it was just some weird psychological reaction to being in the field, but I have to tell you, I'm crazy in lo—"

"Shhh." I turn and kiss his mouth, his damp face.

"Too soon?" He strokes my hair.

"Too soon. It's always best to wait till your pants are on and your brain is working again before you go making the big 'this is it' speech."

"You're just a cynic." In a lightning-quick movement, Ford rolls me over so that he is on top of me again, flexing his lower body. "Too soon for this, too?"

"How old did you say you were?"

"Old enough to know it doesn't feel like this all the time." He rolls his hips and then says, "hang on a sec," and starts sliding down me. I start to protest and then I feel his mouth, startling and tender, on my surprised and sensitive flesh.

Ford leans up on his elbows. "I used to be considered fairly good at this, but of course one woman's delicacy is another woman's loathsome dish of snails. Let me see if I remember anything . . ."

"Oh!"

"Okay, so that's one that you like, I'll keep that in mind, and how about when I do this . . ." he does something with his tongue that I believe I read about once in a book called *Secrets of the Harem.*

"Oh, my God!"

"Good, okay, and if you don't like something, let me know, but since you seem to go for a bit of rough I was wondering if you might just want me to . . ." and now there are teeth, and suction, and his fingers as well, and this time he doesn't stop and when I try to move away he actually growls.

Ford changes the angle of his attack and the feeling builds, my thighs quaking as I start my ascent again. His eyes open, and I am afraid and I do not want to let go like this, with him watching, without him incoherent with lust, too. I pull back from the edge and he looks up, his chin slightly damp, smiling the smile of Satan to the nearly damned. "I think we need to come back to this when you're not so self-conscious."

"I'm not self-con—"

"Yeah, right." He moves up my body to grab a hank of my hair in his fist, baring my neck. "You forget, lady, I'm a trained FBI agent, and I can tell things about you from the pulse in your neck to the level of tension in your jaw."

"So tell me something."

His hand tightens in my hair. "You talk too much." His mouth skims over my neck, down to my breasts, and he gives a little sharp inhalation before he collects himself and is back in character. "But I can tell you this . . ."

"Yes?"

His mouth closes over my left nipple with the faintest pressure of teeth, sending an almost electric jolt of sensation through every other erogenous zone. "You've been think-ing about doing this, too."

"Well, actually . . ."

"Sorry, FBI regulations stipulate no interruptions during interrogation." His mouth moves to the other breast and then he suckles, hard. My fingers tangle in the rough silk of his hair and I can't help it, I start laughing with pure hap-piness, and Ford smiles as he raises himself over me again, poised at my entrance. It is what I've dreamed of, until, un-permitted, the sound of the door opening interrupts us.

Life is not the movies, and Ford and I are not so carried away by passion that we do not hear the click of the lock. Yes, for once the front door is locked, and in the extra few seconds it takes for the person on the other side to locate, insert and turn the key, we have time to scuttle away from each other like frightened beetles, so that by the time the person walks in the door, we are hidden behind boxes.

See, I think to myself, sometimes it pays never to put things away.

"Delilah?" I give a nervous start at the sound of my husband's voice. I can see Ford, holding a finger to his lips, and I wonder if the bloom is already off the illicit rose. FBI agents are not in the habit of skulking naked behind cardboard cartons, after all, and what happens right after sex often determines whether or not a repeat performance is in order.

"Delilah? Sadie?" A pause, footsteps. "Hilda?"

I close my eyes, because I read somewhere that something about eyes draws people's attention. And then the footsteps carry on, into the other room. I hear my name called again, as Jason stops, then moves on a few steps, then stops. I hear the sounds of rustling and thumping. Have I left something incriminating that will alert Jason to the fact that Ford and I are in the house?

Well, duh, yes, a trail of clothes. Which, from the sound of it, Jason just threw into the hamper. It takes me a minute, and then I realize—only one set of jeans, no incriminating male underwear, and a towel. Jason probably thinks that in his absence I am just more slobby than usual.

Which leaves only Ford's hiking boots. I glance at his feet, which are curled under him. He looks at me inquiringly, and I point at his feet. He looks at them uncomprehendingly, but the slight change in position gives me a clearer view. Not frighteningly large, but not dainty, either. Will Jason notice if my shoes have suddenly gone up four sizes?

Which brings me to the thought of large women's shoes, Jason's cross dressing, and his multiple cheatings on me.

He's the guilty party, not me; I didn't break our vows until he did. So why am I lurking in the shadows like a criminal? I should just just stand up, naked and proud and, woops, slightly drippy, and march right out there and say . . .

"No. She's not at home. Nobody is. And it's a land line, so we can talk."

Ford and I both widen our eyes simultaneously.

"Uh-huh. That's what I thought. So I'm just taking all the samples and bringing them over to my hotel room—uh-huh . . . Uh-huh."

There were samples of this hazardous sex aide in the house? Where? I look at Ford—this is not news to him, I realize.

"I'm not sure, Irina. Christ, I know, I forgot to make that call. It's been a little hectic at home this past week, which is why I decided to rent the hotel room. . . . Yes, at the Christmas party tomorrow night. You'll have the new formulation by then? . . . Perfect. The people I told you about will be extremely happy to hear that."

I hear Jason hang up the phone and start walking again. Shuffle, rustle, thump, thump. Which people he told what? Is it possible that my cheating transvestite spouse is also an international black market dealer?

The toilet flushes. More rustling. I can see that Ford is getting impatient. He probably figured fieldwork meant jumping out at people with badges and guns, shouting, Halt! FBI! Clearly, there's never going to be a television series featuring this lovely little scene.

"Damn. Papers."

And now Jason is heading straight into the living room. All right, so we've moved beyond ridiculous straight into dangerous, and Jason is looking at boxes, and my eyes are shut, no, open, I can't bear not to know if he's spotted me.

"Christ, Delilah, you are such a pig."

At first I think he's speaking to me, as in, Hey, you, naked unfaithful wife, you're a pig. But then I see that he's looking in the opposite direction.

It seems that in the throes of passion, Ford and I knocked over one of the boxes.

As Jason kneels to rearrange the papers and rights the carton, I hold my breath. "Script pages, script pages . . . perfect, there's my report, hidden right in the middle."

Actually, the report was printed on the B-side, as it were, but I am so relieved that Jason has found what he's looking for I am afraid I might start to laugh. It's one of my least-endearing qualities, nervous laughter. In just about any crisis short of life or death, I start giggling hysterically.

I bite the inside of my lips as Jason finishes gathering his papers, rustles into his coat, and slams the front door.

I am about to say, That was close, but Ford motions for me to remain silent for an extra moment, and then, right on cue, the door opens again.

"By the way, Delilah, I'm assuming that you're hiding here somewhere based on the overwhelming smell of sex in the living room. I can't say I blame you entirely—the fact that one of my samples of Biosensual is half empty probably has something to do with your loss of control. It also goes a long way toward explaining why the plumber seems to have taken up permanent residence in our closet. In any case, I'll have my lawyer contact you in the next couple of days, and you can have a little think about which weekends you'd like to visit your daughter."

This time, when the door slams, I don't feel like laughing at all.

*   *   *

"So."

"So."

Ford and I are standing awkwardly at the front door, like a Victorian message painting: In the Aftermath of Illicit Carnality. God, I hate this part. If only you could just cut to black in real life and pick up two days later, different setting, different scene.

"Where was Jason hiding his Biosensual samples, anyway?"

"In his underwear drawer. Where most people hide things."

I make a mental note to move the Happy Hummingbird.

"You okay?" He reaches out to touch my cheek and I lean into it.

"I will be."

Ford looks at me as if he'd like to say something but didn't get his script in time. Which is nice, because it means he didn't completely expect me to have sex with him. "You'll stay put?"

"I'll be queen of home delivery. When will you come by . . . I mean, will you be doing plumber things tomorrow?" It has to be asked, but I do my best to deliver the line with a semblance of insouciance.

Ford shakes his head, and I can tell from the look in his eyes he doesn't like this any better than I do. "Not unless Jason comes back. As things stand, there are other things I need to do."

"It's probably best."

"I'll get in touch as soon as I can."

The elevator arrives.

I smile. He smiles. My brain says I'm being stupid, even high-school crushes last longer than this, but my gut tells me it feels like good-bye.

"See you," he says, but I'm already heading back into the apartment and pretend not to hear.

I am sitting, damp-haired, on my bed wearing the bathrobe I had on the first time I met Ford. I've just told my father everything. He went all legal on me, which was what I expected, reassuring me that there is absolutely no judge in the land that will remove Sadie from my custody on the basis of my having an affair. Especially as Jason was first to jump on the infidelity bandwagon, and likes to wear dresses.

I asked my father if he was having an affair, too, and he said not anymore.

We didn't really discuss Tamara. I mentioned her name, and my father said, "I see."

I'm glad I didn't have to talk to my mother.

I think I'm going to be sick now.

Wednesdsay, December 19
7 P.M.
First Full Day of P.C.C.
(Post Coital Crisis)

Delilah the Demon Destroyer, anointed warrior against the forces of evil, feared adversary of all the hosts of Hell, lay in her lover's arms, her light brown hair spilling like silk over the muscled chest of her sworn enemy.

A full moon was rising just outside their bedroom, and even though the demon idly playing with Delilah's hair could see perfectly well in the dark, he admired the way that Delilah's skin gleamed in the pale light.

"What are you thinking, Ford?" Delilah lifted her head and gazed up into her lover's dark, hooded eyes. He smoothed a lock of her hair away from her forehead.

"About how you used to say the only way you would touch me was to draw blood."

"Well, that was when I thought you were evil . . ."

"Yeah, well, instead I drew your blood." A look of boyish satisfaction crossed the demon's face. "I've made you blush."

"I guess I should clean myself up . . ."

"No." The word, sharp and commanding, brought Delilah's chin up. Ford smiled with just a hint of wolfishness. "You forget—

I like blood. The smell. The taste. And virgin's blood is best of all. It has such a delicious tang of innocence lost."

Delilah raised her eyebrows. "And is that all I am to you, Ford? A tasty snack?" She stroked fingertips over the taut muscles of his abdomen. "I might just have to make you pay for that . . ."

"You need to trim those nails." Ford sat up, both Delilah's wrists manacled in his right hand. He watched her as she struggled and could not free herself from his grip.

"What'd you do," she said with a little laugh, "sap all my strength?"

"Well, now that you mention it—yes." Ford brought his fanged face closer to Delilah's. "Oh, don't look so confused. I'm an incubus, not a vampire. I don't need to actually drink blood to receive its power. And the maidenblood of the Destroyer is pretty potent stuff."

"I'm not sure I like being the weaker sex." Delilah twisted in her lover's grasp. "How long till this effect wears off?"

"A few days. Long enough to have a bit of fun without you getting in my way."

"What?" Delilah stared at Ford, suddenly aware of the change in his tone. "What's happened to you?"

"Why, nothing, my sweetmeat." He released her hands with a little shove that sent her stumbling back.

"Then why are you acting so cold?"

Ford shook his head as if bemused by the question. "What did you think would happen after we did the deed—protestations of undying love? Proposals of marriage? Not to mention that all you did was lie there like a bit of liver on the mattress. I would have thought with all that lovely fighting muscle tone you would have been able to be a little more—how shall I put it—interesting."

Delilah inhaled sharply. "But you said—you said you loved me. You swore—you said—"

"Good grief, woman, has it never occurred to you that demons

*lie? What have you been going around killing us all for, then—
lousy table manners?"* Ford reached over and grabbed the filmy
white silk nightgown, which he had reverently removed from
Delilah's shoulders not an hour earlier.

"But it couldn't all have been lies! You swore by all the old
gods . . . you cried for the first time in a millennium."

Ford wiped the blood from his upper thighs with the nightgown
and then sniffed it appreciatively. "Well, maybe I did. I was kind
of worked up over the thought of poking you, and for a sex demon,
that comes pretty close to love. But unless you work up some new
tricks, you're just going to be one of those one-hit wonders, I'm
afraid." He stood up, then chucked her under the chin. "Cheer up,
honeybun. I'm not terribly interested in you anymore, but that
doesn't mean the other, lesser demons won't give you a try."

Ford turned to pull on his trousers and for a moment, his sup-
ple, beautifully masculine back was turned to Delilah. With a
growl of fury, she grabbed her silver-bladed dagger from the
dresser and launched herself at him.

Ford grabbed her wrist and, with his newly increased strength,
bent the fragile bones back until the knife fell from her fingers
with a clatter and Delilah was kneeling at his feet. "Now, if you're
a good girl and run along, I won't snap your neck. This time."
And then, with a sharp tug, Delilah's first lover broke her wrist
in two places.

Delilah moved back, cradling her fractured limb. "You take
those few days and you better run and hide, Demon. Because I
will tear your heart out for this."

Ford gave her a look that was almost compassionate. "But
sweetie-pie, that's just the problem. You might kill me—though I
doubt it, others have tried—but you won't have my heart." And
then he walked out her door with a casual backward wave, not
needing to look over his shoulder to know that she was watching
him leave.

*   *   *

Here's my problem; I can't seem to get past the first seduction without my daydreams turning dark. In real life, I know, the first time usually just greases the wheels for the second time, and things don't usually get going properly till the third or fourth, but in real life, good sex is also followed by arguments, stress, commitments, so-so sex, house-hunting, gradual disenchantment, childbirth and then no sex.

So in my fantasies, it is always the first time, astonishing and new, when these pleasures that we so lightly call physical, as Colette said, have the power to shake the soul.

I wonder how this fling with Ford will end. Sure, he thinks he's in love with me. That's because we haven't had much of a chance to talk yet. He still thinks I'm witty, sophisticated, game for a little unsanctioned sexual activity. So far, any evidence to the contrary has been chalked up to charmingly vulnerable. But how long till vulnerable becomes neurotic, and woman of the world gets recategorized as woman with baggage. At that point, even my willingness to bring out the furry handcuffs and plastic doodads will become beside the point. There will be fewer phone calls, more excuses, and at some point the change will come, ardent lover to soulless demon, and I will wind up attending square dances at the local synagogue while Sadie informs me she's going to be a flower girl at Daddy's wedding to Auntie Tamara.

Which is all to say, Ford, that shape-shifting snake, hasn't bothered to call me yet.

So I'm going to Jason's office Christmas party tonight. Because, in the end, it's not about Ford and me, and it's not about biological agents and the FBI. It's about Jason and me finding a way to conduct ourselves like reasonable, mature adults.

And if we can't manage to do that, well, then it's about my getting a chance to scream at him in public before the lawyers get involved.

For this, my first social occasion as a separated woman, I have chosen to wear low-rider jeans that make my ass look terrific (for when I make the big exit), a ripped Madness sweatshirt from the mid-eighties (to show I don't care what I look like and to remind Jason of the days when he thought I was cool) and more eye makeup than Liz Taylor doing Cleopatra. I have gone spikey with the hair, and all in all, I look like I might do some damage with the studded belt around my waist.

Tamara walks in just as I am sliding the dangly earrings through the hole, causing me to miss and draw blood.

"Jesus Christ, Tam, what are you doing here?" And what's the point of having a doorman in the lobby if he never announces that someone's coming up? I really must start locking my front door.

My sister sits down on the bed. Her hair is flat and dirty, and she is wearing a sweatshirt and jeans. There is no makeup on her face, and she looks pale and tired and surprisingly young.

"I wanted to talk to you."

"Try calling next time." I dab alcohol on the new hole and decide to go earringless, even if it does cut down on the Goth Mistress on a Rampage effect.

"Dad told me you told him."

"What is this, you're mad I snitched? It's not like we're in high school and I told on you for smoking, Tamara. I needed legal advice."

"Dad told me that, too."

This time I turn to look at Tamara. "I can't believe you did it, Tamara. What was it? Were you jealous of me? Are you in love with him? Are you on drugs that diminish your ability to make rational decisions?"

"No. There just aren't . . . that many men who are interested in me. And Jason was, so I thought, if he's willing to break the rules, maybe I should be, too." Tamara lifts her red-rimmed eyes to meet mine. "It almost seemed like something you would do."

"Have sex with my husband?"

"Adultery."

"Well, sorry to tell you, but you both managed to beat me to it."

There is a long moment of silence. Then Tam pushes her hair back from her face. "I'm leaving Daddy's practice."

"Okay."

"But I can't leave the family."

I don't say anything.

"It's the only . . . you and Sadie and Mom and Dad are all I've got." She is red-faced now, crying.

"Ah, shit, Tam. I'm not going to sit here and tell you it's all right."

"I didn't come to ask for you to forgive me." She sounds angry.

"Well, why the hell not? You should!"

And then, absurdly enough, we are both laughing. I sink down beside her on the bed.

"It's still not all right," I tell her, close but not touching. As soon as I say it, I want to get away from her. The need to be forgiven is emanating from her like a wet-dog smell.

"I know that." Wet-dog eyes, too; pathetic and listless.

I inhale, stand up. "Listen, I need a drink before I go off to confront Jason, and frankly, your being here doesn't help."

"I'm leaving." Tamara stands up, then reaches into her handbag. "Here," she says. "Take these."

I look at the packet of tiny, square transparent papers in her hand. "What are these? Those new breath mints?"

My sister just shrugs. "Some things only a sister will tell you. And if you're going to go shout at Jason . . . maybe these will come in handy."

"Yeah, after a Bloody Mary or two."

Tamara looks at me. "It's not my place to say anything, but . . . you're planning on going dressed like that?"

"You're right, it's not your place. And things between us are still not all right, Tam. I want you to leave."

She nods.

"Now."

She stands there.

"Fuck off, I'm going to speak to you again, all right? It's not the end. I'm sure there will be lots of family dinners to endure this winter and I'll still let you take Sadie to Rockefeller Center to ice skate. But it's not forgotten, I'm not over it, and I'm still allowed to get overwhelmed with the shittiness of what you did and yell at you. So thank you for the breath mints and please just leave now."

She does, and I make myself a Bloody Mary with lots of Tabasco. Then I play "Earl," the Dixie Chicks' snappy, vengeful anthem of kill-your-husband sisterhood.

Somehow the song worked better before sisterhood got so complicated. I've chosen the soundtrack to the wrong movie. There's no Thelma to my Louise. My life isn't shaping up to be the story of a woman who's unlucky in love but finds solace in the company of her girlfriends, because, hey, those are the folks that stick by you come hell or high water. This isn't going to end with Tam and Kathy Wheatley and me all plotting a delicious revenge on Jason and then sitting around some fabulous Manhattan nightspot sipping Cosmopolitans.

This is going to end with me pretending to be sanguine when Sadie rips into me for kicking her daddy out of her daily life.

This is going to end with my entering some brave new world of dating where every available man I meet has already been rejected as defective, deceptive or destructive by some other, wiser woman.

This is going to end with a messiness of lawyers and therapists and the predictable, desperate purchase of unconditional four-legged comfort.

Assuming that my friendly neighborhood FBI man can catch whoever's trying to kill me before they hit a bull's-eye. But I never had a single fantasy in which I cowered in my apartment because something nasty was outside, so I guess I'm going to take my chances and face my dragons.

That said, I ask the doorman to hail me a cab and I look left, right and overhead before I scurry into the yellow taxi's backseat and curl up inside my coat. The heater is on, but my hands and feet are freezing. I wonder vaguely where all my blood has gone—not my brain, that's for sure, or I wouldn't be doing this.

I manage to get into the party with no difficulty. Both the guard in the lobby and the haughty receptionist are well lubricated with drink and the perennial Mardis Gras promise of office parties: that rules will be broken and ties loosened and secret desires given license for an evening.

Despite the fact that I am the only person not wearing either a suit or a cocktail dress, no one seems to notice me at all. The hivelike hum of conversation is punctuated with

words like "branding," "clueless," "London office" and
"analysis." Two blonde women are laughing like hyenas in
a corner, and then someone turns up the music, an old
Rolling Stones song that soon has a few of the men shuf-
fling around while their colleagues clap and cheer them on.
I see one short, balding man walk out of the men's room,
apparently talking to himself. Then I notice a small earplug
and realize he is probably conducting some sort of phone
conference. Or maybe he's faking it.

What a perfect solution to finding no one to talk to at a
party! Stick a headset on and phone your mother. Or just
mumble to yourself and pretend you've got someone on the
line.

Phone-call man catches me watching him and starts
making deliberate eye contact. I turn the other way, because anyone who carries on long-distance conversations
while going to the toilet can't be washing his hands properly afterwards.

A woman in stiletto heels steps back onto my toe and I
change direction again. No sign of Kleat Madigan or Jason,
and so far no one trying to drop anything on me. The crowd
parts and I spy an open bar set up against one wall, so I
walk up to it.

"Martini, please." I figure it'll be less messy than a
Bloody Mary if I lose control and spill it on myself.

"Flavored or regular?"

The voice is familiar, so I look. The bartender is Ford, almost unrecognizable in a tuxedo with his hair cut shorter
and spiked up.

"What choices do I have?"

"Lemon, chocolate and mango." There is a silver earring
in his left ear. He looks at me as if he's never seen me before.

"Regular, please."

I watch him as he mixes and shakes. "What are you doing here?" He keeps his head down, and even I am not sure he is talking to me.

"A girl like me? A place like this? Looking for my nemesis. Or nemeses. Assuming you can have more than one archenemy at a time. Looking for my husband, at any rate, and trying to avoid his boss, who may be trying to kill me."

"You've been drinking."

"And you're going to blow your cover if you keep up with the lecture."

Ford hands me the drink, anger implicit in the movement. "Go home, Delilah."

I sip my drink and watch him over the rim, aiming for a film noir kind of attitude. "So are you the only man your company has these days? Plumber, waiter, Indian chief?"

"Listen, I made a mistake getting personal with you, Delilah. But right now I need you to use your head. You need to go home where you'll be safe."

He looks at me and I can't quite believe I had this man inside of me. There is no trace of boyishness on his face now. If there were, I might have been able to tell him that there is nothing that feeds fear like hiding from danger. I feel calmer stalking my adversaries than sitting in wait. Yes, someone might attack me, but at least tonight I'm expecting it.

"You know, it's a really nice martini, Ford. Shaken but not stirred—kind of how I felt the other day." I toast him with my martini and then saunter away, thinking, Shit, I've really blown it, maybe he was just too busy to call before and now I've made fun of his sexual prowess. There's rarely a way to come back from that.

But the truth is, no one's ever too busy to call when they're in the heat of first passion. Pon Farr is over, Mr.

Spock is back on the *Enterprise* and it's time for me to focus on finding my errant spouse.

Suddenly the music changes, and someone new must have seized control of the CD player, because the song that blasts out of the speakers is one of those angry hip-hop soliloquies that seem to be all about taking your clothes off and driving your car into a wall.

Half the crowd cheers, the other half boos, and a heavy hand comes down on my shoulder. I spin, spilling my drink, and find myself looking into the florid, Brando-esque face of R. B.'s military C.E.O.

"Delilah Levine," he says, stepping in close. And unless he's just very happy to see me, that's a gun I feel pressing into the small of my back. "Just the woman I was hoping to talk with."

"Well, I'm here, talk away," I say as loudly as I can, spilling the rest of my martini as he moves me through the crowd and into a corridor.

"I'd rather go somewhere private."

"Would you? Look, I need another drink. Let's go back to the bar for a second." In the sudden quiet of the hallway, my voice sounds shrill and panicked.

"This won't take a second." Kleat Madigan prods me in the back again and then frog marches me into a smoked glass office. He doesn't turn the light on, which is probably for the best. I think I am calmer without actually having to see the gun.

I take a deep breath and turn around slowly. "Okay, so what's this all about? Did Jason tell you not to let me near him? Or are you still harping about that hopeless legal matter?"

Madigan's laugh rings out in the small space. "Oh, God, I love the feistiness of you!"

"Yeah, that's me, lovable and feisty. So how about we go back to the party and discuss all this—"

Madigan's large body blocks the exit. "I'm not angry about the soap opera anymore, Delilah."

"You're not? That's good."

"In fact, I'm actually very pleased." Madigan rakes one hand through his graying brush-cut hair. "Lord, it's hot in here. Are you hot?"

"If you're hot, maybe we should just go right out and get a breath of fresh . . . what are you doing?"

Madigan moves his bulky body so close to me that anyone watching would think we were about to make out. I can feel the gun again, this time poking me in the stomach. "You see, Delilah, we did a little marketing research and found that the exposure from your scripts was actually extremely beneficial to our product."

"That's fantastic, so why exactly are you sticking a gun in my ribs?"

Madigan pushes the gun harder against me. "I may be hard as steel, Delilah, but this particular piece of military equipment is designed for pleasure."

"Oh . . . oh, my God." I try to inch away from the man, but he slams both meaty hands into the wall, pinning me.

"Do you know how long it's been since someone's stood up to me the way you did? Talked back to me?" Madigan rubs his sweaty face into my neck. "I find it refreshing."

"Then I'll do it some more. Back off!" But there isn't enough force in my voice, I am still so dazed with relief that Madigan doesn't intend to shoot me.

"Yes, yes, fight me." He is rotating his hips now.

"Have you been drinking? Because I need you to hear what I'm saying right now. And what I'm saying is no, no, no, No! Get the hell off me!"

"Baby, I'm not on you—yet." He starts fumbling with his fly and I gasp. Madigan's grin widens at the sound. "Are you ready for greatness?"

"GET THE FUCK AWAY!!!"

"God, you're hot. Put your hands on my dick now."

Do men really think this kind of talk is arousing to women? They have really got to stop reading their sex magazines and start reading ours. "Mr. Madigan, I'm married to one of your most important employees."

"Jason's not here tonight. Just one touch. Just for a moment."

"I am a non-willing participant in this scenario. Now I am just going to walk out that door. . . ."

"No! No! You mustn't leave. Baby, I haven't felt like this in years." Suddenly Kleat Madigan, billionaire C.E.O. and ex-Special Ops commander, sinks to his knees, grabbing me around the waist and burying his face in my stomach. "Hit me! Beat me! Punish me, Delilah, make me bleed."

Or maybe he's saying make me bleat. Either way, I must admit that this is a positive development. He wants a dominatrix, which means I can control this. I assume my best Madonna voice, part Detroit street, part English bitch. "Down on your knees, Scumbag! No touching without permission!"

He complies with a thud.

Now, I have two hundred and fifty pounds of crazed ex-commando at my feet. So let's think this out: What would make a man turn into a lust-crazed animal without any sense of consequence or embarrassment?

Answer: Pharmaceuticals.

"Mr. Madigan, try to remember if you've taken a drug recently. You do not want to be caught attacking the wife of an employee."

"Yes, yes, I'm bad, I must be punished!"

"I told you to get down."

"Just grind your heel into me and I will."

But of course I'm wearing ankle boots with flat heels.
"Please stop thrusting against my leg."

"Can I use your breasts?"

It is at this moment that Ford crashes into the dark
room. It takes him only a moment to take stock of the situation, long enough for Madigan to stop gyrating against
my stomach, which means there probably is no pressing
need for Ford to haul back and punch the larger man in
the jaw.

Still, I have to say I enjoy seeing Madigan land in a heap
against the far wall. In my pre-Jason dating days, I tended
to go for narrow-shanked, pasty-faced musician types, and
with the exception of one summer when I was fifteen, I
have never dated a guy who could actually fight.

"That was impressive. Especially given the fact that
you're wearing a tux."

"Yeah, well, I seem to have impressed the wrong party."

I turn and sure enough, there is Madigan, hauling himself up with a low growl, tucking himself in, and beginning
to circle Ford.

"Shit, watch out, Ford, he used to be one of those guys
who can kill using just their thumb and index finger."

Ford gives me a quick, bemused glance before returning
all his attention to Madigan. "So your advice to me is . . ."

"Don't let him pinch you."

And then there is a quick flurry of action as Madigan
lunges and Ford spins, and then Ford kicks and Madigan
blocks. They circle again.

"Aren't you the fucking bartender?"

"I'm on my break."

Madigan punches, Ford blocks and spins, then kicks out and knocks Madigan down. But Madigan has gotten hold of Ford's ankle and pulls Ford down, and then both men spring back up like combatants in a martial arts movie. For a big man, Madigan has moves.

"What's your problem, kid, you don't like watching the grown-ups have sex?"

Ford cocks one eyebrow. "Was that what you were doing?"

Madigan straightens out of his troglodyte warrior hunch. "What the hell did you think we were doing?"

Ford looks at me.

"I thought he had a gun."

"It wasn't a gun?"

"It was Mr. Happy. Seems Mr. Madigan's been getting all Biosensual over me."

For the briefest of moments, there is an expression of dismay on Ford's face. "Well," he says carefully, fixing his bow tie, "in that case, I guess I should wish you both a pleasant evening and—"

"Ford, you are a complete and total shmuck and—watch out!"

Madigan slides into Ford feet first, as if he were home base, but even as I'm flinching in sympathy, Ford is flipping backward, away from the force of the blow. He comes up with a phone in his hand and slams the instrument into Madigan's jaw, sending him down for the count.

In the ensuing silence, I can hear that the Rolling Stones faction has won, because "Satisfaction" is blaring loud enough to be audible inside our glass-walled office.

"Well," says Ford. He is still in a fighter's stance.

"Well."

"Do you have anything else to say for yourself, Delilah?"

Actually, I am at a dead loss. Should I be angry, cool, conciliatory, or some strategic combination of all three? Stalling, I reach into my handbag. "Breath mint?"

Ford looks at them for a long moment, then at me. "Thanks," he says, taking one of Tamara's whisper-thin sheets. And then he winces and pulls up his shirt, revealing a foot-shaped abrasion just under the flat plane of his left pectoral. "Man, that hurts."

"I thought he didn't connect."

Ford meets my eyes. "He did."

"Still convinced I was overcome with lust for the big guy?"

"I'm not stupid, Delilah. I was bluffing to catch him off guard."

"Uh-huh. Do you want me to take you home?"

"Yes. And maybe you should stay there with me."

My heart starts thudding, and I tell it to slow down. "Your ribs are going to be fit for the barbecue by this time tomorrow, Ford. Why not give the he-man thing a rest?"

Ford rolls his shoulders, grunting softly with pain. "Because if Madigan wasn't the one who wants you dead, then we have to look at the possibility that your husband is the one who's been trying to kill you."

"He wouldn't do that."

"Wouldn't he?"

I open my mouth, then close it. The truth is, you don't get betrayed by people you don't trust. By definition, it's the ones you think will never hurt you who wind up doing the most damage.

I insist on going home first, to get my cell phone and toothbrush and a change of clothes. Plus I need my own nondrying facial soap and moisturizer, and something silky to sleep in. Surely there must be something silky somewhere in a drawer, dating from the late eighties, with snaps in the crotch. Not that I'm intending anything to happen, but I would like Ford to want something to, even if it doesn't.

Also I would like my mascara, under-eye concealer, and a little bit of blush, although I can't say these are necessities, like my special neck support pillow and soothing chamomile supplement tea.

Ford looks disgusted when I finish getting the last item on my packing list. "Christ, woman, haven't you ever roughed it?"

"Life is rough enough as it is, thank you very much." Since Ford seems to be in a rush, I forego brushing the mixed drink funkiness from my mouth and settle for one of my sister's mints.

"Are you quite done, Delilah? Because unless there's some other vital object that you can't spend a night without, I'd like to get home before my vision blurs completely double."

I turn to face Ford. He is slumped on my bed, his face so white he looks like a mannequin.

"You're seeing double?"

Ford swallows. "I'd nod, but I'm concerned my head might fall off."

I sit down beside Ford. His eyes are even darker than usual, and I realize that his pupils are enormous, almost eclipsing the iris. I put my hand on his chest and feel his heart racing wildly under my palm. "Is it your ribs? Maybe you need to go to the hospital, Ford."

He closes his eyes, then opens them. "Your shirt."

I look down. "What?"

"It's too loud."

"My Madness sweatshirt is too loud? But it's black."

For once, I have no trouble reading Ford's face. It is anguished. "It's like a steel drum, pounding."

Well, Madness was a Ska band, so that makes some sense. No, wait, it doesn't. I put my hand on Ford's forehead. "Are you hot? You're sweating."

"Just take it off, all right? Before my head splits open."

I pull the shirt over my head, revealing my good black lace bra, not that Ford seems to notice. "Ford, I think you're having some sort of shock reaction to your injury."

"I can't breathe."

"What?"

Ford is tugging at the buttons of his collar. "Can't. Breathe."

I slap his hands away and unbutton his shirt. He bends over, gasping, and I think, this is weird. I might be back in my old apartment share, helping one of my roommates through a bad trip.

But Ford doesn't take drugs. At least, not on purpose.

"Ford?"

He is sitting on the bed. "My legs are tingling." He runs his hands up and down his muscular, black-trousered thighs. "Bad tingling. Burning. I think I'm having an allergic reaction to something. I've got to get these pants off." I help him unzip and pull the slacks down to his black ankle boots, which, amusingly enough, match mine. As I've said before, my typical response to a crisis is demented laughter, so as I stand there with his feet in my hands, his pants tangled around his ankles, I start giggling.

"I think we need to get your boots off first," I say.

"Stop moving in the strobe light. I think I'm having a seizure."

"Ford, did you drink anything at the party? Could someone have dosed you?"

Ford shakes his head. I get his second boot off, and the

pants follow. God, undressing an uncooperative man is hard work. I am panting myself by the time I have Ford naked, and he is shivering.

"Get under the covers."

"Still cold."

"Move over." I slide between the sheets with him, but the moment I touch him he gasps. "What's wrong?"

"You're burning me."

I move away, trying to puzzle this out. But Ford groans, and something about the sound of it contracts every feminine muscle in my body.

"What was that, Ford?"

"I think . . . I think I know what drug I've been given."

"Acid? Coke? Smack? Ecstasy?"

Ford's dark eyebrows knit together. "Not unless Ecstasy gives you a raging hard-on."

I make a small noise and yes, I look. I'm not sure what makes an erection angry but there's definitely a big lump under the covers. Well, it's a two-boner night for Delilah Levine, folks. Which would be more flattering if everyone weren't under the influence of a brain-addling mold.

"So I take it you're feeling a little Bionsensual?"

"I'm feeling like I could fuck my way through the hull of a ship!"

I glance at him. He appears to be in some distress. "So the symptoms are intense?"

Every tendon in his neck seems to be straining. "You know that fine line between pleasure and pain? I think I've crossed it." Ford takes a deep breath. "I think . . . I think I've been under the influence of this drug . . . for some time. Working with it, I wasn't always sufficiently cautious." Ford's eyes are fixed on mine.

"Which would explain last time, I'm assuming."

"I lost control."

We stare at each other, two strangers, one naked, one nearly so. "I didn't think it was undying love, don't worry."

"Delilah."

"What?"

"I think I'm having a heart attack."

I sigh. It seems very unfair that Ford has just told me he never really wanted me and that I am not allowed to just scream and punch him. "You're having a panic attack. Relax." My tone leaves something to be desired in the way of sympathy, I suppose, but given the circumstance, I feel I'm performing above and beyond.

Ford, however, seems to disagree. His hands reach up and grab my upper arms. "You don't understand. I fell in love with you before I got a sample of the drug. But the drug's a disinhibitor." He swallows, hard. "And I think I've just been given the mother lode."

I find myself distracted from what he is saying by the muscular column of his neck, the inviting pad of muscle between shoulder and . . . shit. Tamara. "The breath mints," I say. "My sister probably thought she'd effect a little husband-and-wife reconciliation." Which means Jason gave Tam some of this stuff.

I am distracted from the unseemly images this thought conjures by the sound of Ford moaning in agony. Well, I think it's agony. He rolls over until he's on top of me, pressing his narrow hips forward as if his lust could sear a hole through my jeans.

"I'm losing it," he says. He's sweating again. His eyes aren't completely focused, but the musky, male scent of his heated body and the feel of him hard between my legs is making a convincing argument to the reptilian center of my brain.

"Let me get my pants off," I say slowly.

"No!" A muscle is jumping wildly in Ford's jaw. "I don't feel . . . I don't have enough control, Delilah."

I place my hand alongside his high Tartar cheekbone. "You don't have to make it good for me this time, Ford. Just ride this out. No pun intended."

But his arms are braced, shaking with emotion or the drug, I can't tell. "I'm not scared I won't make you come, Delilah. I'm scared I'll hurt you."

"I'm not exactly a blushing virgin, you know."

"I'm a martial arts expert, Delilah. If I forget and put my hands on you the wrong way . . ."

Now I know I'm sick, because the thought of all that masculine strength barely held in check does not make me want to run and hide under the bed. Quite the opposite, in fact. It makes me want to unleash something wild and primitive, something that will slam me up against the wall and take me like a soldier.

Without actually hurting me, of course.

"Well, maybe if we had a safe word . . ."

Ford grabs my hand and suddenly I'm holding his shaft in my hand and he is trembling from head to toe. "I keep thinking I'm going to explode but the feeling just builds." My fingers contract on him and he buckles.

"Delilah!" I stroke him once more and Ford gives an angry shout. The next thing I know Ford is straddling my thighs, shackling both my wrists with one hand. "You don't want a safe word, do you?"

"What are you talking about?"

But now Ford is looking down at me with grim certainty. "You want me out of my mind, because that's where you want to go."

"I do?" Because suddenly I'm not so sure I trust this guy looming over me with the feral glint in his eyes.

"Jesus, I've been an idiot. Worrying about pleasing you. Driving myself insane because maybe I wasn't experienced enough for you."

"Ford, what are you . . ."

"You don't want expertise. You want crazed passion. You want an out-of-fucking-body experience."

"Well, it depends on what you mean by—"

He silences me with a kiss. "You know I love you, right?"

I nod.

"Good."

I have seen drugs make men do many improbable things, but never in my life have I seen a man take a pair of jeans and rip them down the middle. But that is what Ford does. He unsnaps my jeans and tears them down the zipper and along the seam. The veins and muscles in his arms stand out and he pauses over me, breathing so hard I can see his nostrils flaring like a stallion catching the scent of a mare in season.

"Jesus, Ford, your ribs . . ."

"Not feelin' them. But I can taste the smell of you."

Which is probably better than hearing my Madness sweatshirt. At least I hope it is. Ford spreads his thumbs into my ripped jeans and tears them again. Then he puts his head in my lap and takes my silk panties between his teeth and yanks, hard.

"Ford . . ."

He rubs his face against my inner thighs. "I thought I could make it happen like this. With the right touch. With enough patience." His tongue finds me, and it's as if someone has drawn every nerve ending to the surface. I nearly buck him off the bed, but his hands come up, clamping me into position. "But this isn't the way into you, is it? It's nice, you like it, but it isn't the key."

"Ford, you're new to this, but all these thoughts you're having, you've got to realize that they're not really—"

Ford moves up my body, and there is something about the way he is moving that reminds me of how he fought Madigan. I am aware this time, as I was not the last, that his graceful athlete's body, so near mine in size, is also a weapon.

"Like a soldier, that's what you were thinking, isn't it? And something . . ." Ford looks confused for a moment. "Something about turning into a sex demon . . ."

"How can you know that?"

There is a thunderclap of connection as our eyes meet, and suddenly I feel as if I can see into his mind, too. I can feel him inside my head, the younger version of him, which feels like his true self, not a chemist or an FBI agent but an asthmatic boy in a female household, coming into adolescence in a guilty rush of sexual longing.

It's like Ford's coming into focus for the first time, the science nerd and good son rebelling against his dying mother to fulfill that other, less easily satisfied desire, the yearning for some kind of physical test, the testosterone urge toward the release provided by sports, cars, fighting. I can see the dating past he's never discussed, the ex-girlfriend who was a born-again virgin, the secret stash of pornographic comic books. Am I making these things up, jumbling together what I know of him and what I surmise, or is this some wild intuitive leap, am I reading Ford as he thinks he is reading me?

"If you're going to say no," he says, abruptly sitting back on his heels, "then do it now. Get up and get out of the room."

I start to sit up, but I myself do not know why. Perhaps it's because he's frightening me. Or because *I'm* frightening me. Or maybe it's just that in my fantasies, you don't need words to get what you want. Vampire, acrobat, mercenary, changeling, whatever mask he wears, the man of my dreams is always a mind reader. He knows what I don't say, what I can't say; he can look into the secret heart of me and give me what even I don't know I desire.

But isn't that everyone's secret fantasy? I am moving off the bed as if in a dream, still holding Ford's gaze.

"Wait." His hand shoots out and tangles itself into my hair, dragging my face on a level with his. "I'm not wrong, am I? Can you feel it, too?"

But I won't make it easy for him. I just look into his eyes and then he makes a low sound of despair and suddenly some new part of the drug must be hitting my brain, because I seem to have a complete, unprecedented point-of-view switch.

Ford knows the moment it happens. It is as if the flickering circuit between Delilah and himself has just been switched on. He can feel her eyes on his body, his compact body with its overly-muscled, nomadic horseman's legs, and suddenly he sees himself as she sees him, lean and athletic, almost hairless, his erection longer and thicker than she recalls from their first encounter.

Tracing his hand along the lace of her black brassiere, Ford breaks the gold clasp open with one hand. As her astonishingly beautiful breasts spill out, out he feels himself harden even more. Delilah does not have the gym-toned, sinewy body that hardly seems naked without clothes. She is slender and lithe and deliciously, shockingly pale, her pubic hair a wild thatch shades darker than the hair on her head.

With a grin, Ford uses the broken brassiere to lash her wrists to the bedpost. She isn't fighting him, but she is resisting, and if he weren't in her head, if she weren't in his, he would stop now to make sure this was all right. Ford pauses, momentarily unsure.

Is this all right? He thinks he thinks it. Maybe he says it.

Oh yes, this is all right. He knows he hears it, but isn't sure how.

Jesus, she is gorgeous right now, her eyes huge and dark and her mouth an open invitation to sin. He would like to thrust into that mouth, he thinks, but then he sees how the position of her arms pushes her breasts out, and he traces one work-roughened hand across that creamy flesh.

And he can feel it, her skin so much more sensitive than his own, the lightning connection between nipple and groin. His heart is thudding as he straddles her legs so he can nuzzle his silky hair (her thought) against her breasts, and she would like to tangle her fingers against his scalp but it's wrong, he is the enemy, he is—what? An Apache, a Mongol, possibly a demon. He laughs as he catches that thought. She thinks his teeth look very white. She wonders whether he will bite her.

Ford bends his head and suckles at her pebbled, dark nipples, using his teeth to the very edge of pain, to the place where pleasure shorts out the brain and what is left is ragged and wordless and raw. He hears her sob and releases her wrists, and now her arms are around him, clawing down his back, struggling to find purchase against the sleek play of his muscles. She is parting her thighs and he thrusts blindly as she tries to get her hand between their bodies.

"Wait," she says, wanting to guide him, but he thrusts again, not caring if it hurts to batter against the wrong spot, beyond any consideration beside this primal need to get in there and pump himself dry inside her.

He pulls back and on his third thrust he sinks into the wet muscular grip of her, and that first penetration stuns them both into immobility.

They pulse inside, two creatures operating now from a knot of nerves low in the spinal cord, brain bypassed completely. Delilah throws her head back and wraps her legs around Ford's taut waist. Her heels dig into the small of his back, driving him forward.

When he moves she gasps, a sound just this side of pain. He is in pain, too. The drug has heightened every sensation to the point of blackout. When he starts to withdraw that small, necessary distance, he sees minute pinpoints of light, like stars, against the inside of his closed eyelids. When he slams into her again, the stars implode.

He becomes aware that she is speaking, pleading with him to go on, go faster, to *move*. Her head whips back and forth on the pillow. He knows he is meant to be finishing this off now, but some small part of him is aware that his heart is beating like a jackhammer, and he is just the tiniest bit concerned that he might go into cardiac arrest.

Then he catches the clean, seashell scent of female desire, and suddenly he can feel her fingers tracing the sensitive skin at the base of his scrotum and then slipping inside and pressing somewhere that sends a jolt of pleasure through him. For a moment, he thinks he has lost it.

"Shit," he says. Then he slides out of her and realizes that he is still hard, even harder than before, his erection so engorged it is painful. He puts his hand down and feels himself pulsing in time with his own heavy heartbeats, and for a second, as he begins to push into her, the room shimmers red around the edges. He watches himself slide into her, slide out, and once again he is in her mind as well as his own, filling and being filled, his senses bleeding into hers.

It is like nothing he has ever known before. It is as if other sex was a tune played on a single flute and now he is standing in the middle of a full, orchestral concert, and the music of it swells slowly, building low at the base of his spine, a rising tide crashing more and more forcefully.

Ford's next thrust pushes Delilah back until her head nearly hits the headboard, and she reaches her hands back and braces herself as he thrusts inside of her again. It is more than pleasure now, it is a compulsion, a salmon-spawning instinct to fuck her as he has never dared with any woman before, using all his strength, holding nothing back. He wants to send his sperm into her so deep that it can't come out. He wants to come so hard he knocks her up.

Her legs lift up again, impossibly high, her ankles on his shoulders, and he is slamming so deep inside her that he is a little scared but no, she is climbing with him, he can feel the tense internal constriction of her muscles and he wants to say, *Don't worry, I'm taking you all the way this time,* but instead he growls and manacles her wrists with his hands. He stares into her eyes as she starts to quake beneath him, shaking and shaking, and still he can't let go and inside he can feel her muscles squeezing him and the feeling is so intense that he can't breathe, and suddenly there is a stab of pain in his side, the injury to his ribs finally making itself felt. He can't catch his breath and the old fear hits him, I can't breathe, pleasure and panic stretching the moment until her finger slips inside him again and he claims her mouth with his own as the world goes black.

Thursday, December 20
9 A.M.

Ford sleeps with his body wrapped pythonlike around Delilah's. When she opens her eyes, she sees him watching her.

"Good morning, cherie." The look in his eyes is lit by equal parts tenderness, amusement and desire.

"Good morning, Lieutenant." She says it as she says everything, with the poise of an aristocrat ten years at court. The truth is, she is a little embarrassed. She has never lost control the way she did last night, except possibly in the throes of childbirth. The panniers from her hoops, the multiple layers of petticoat and underskirt, are all strewn across the canopy of the bed like victims of an explosion.

Delilah has opened her thighs to spies and courtiers, captains and kings, but she has never greeted the sun with her skin unpowdered and her hair in tangles down her back. Should she excuse herself and recostume? It seems almost an act of cowardice.

"You have me at a disadvantage, sir. I should attend to my toilette before any further . . . conversation."

"And give you time to armor yourself with artful subterfuge, Comtesse?" Ford nuzzles his dark head against her bare breasts. "Stay. I come to you weaponless. Even my wits are gone."

Delilah tugs at his hair, wanting to see his eyes. In a world where every word has a double meaning and every gesture is a kind of code, she has learned the impact of being direct. "You, sir, have never had an unguarded moment in your life."

His face is impassive. "Except for last night."

She nods, accepting this. "C'est vrai. But the drug must have worn off by now."

Ford moves against her. "It has," he murmurs, "I'm under a different kind of influence."

"And what is that?"

He moves into her as if they were born to be one flesh. "First, I'd like to know how you feel about the idea of having another child. Because I think Sadie might quite like having a little sister or brother. . . ."

"You must be out of your mind," she replies, but her body has a completely different reaction.

"Totalment," says Ford, raining kisses down her collarbone. "But I believe half of you is also mad. Let us see if I can meet with your complete approval."

"But you are an agent of the king, and I work for the queen—"

And then Ford moves his hips, almost without volition, and the wave of desire pushes them apart and then crashes them together again.

I open my eyes to find myself lying on the bare mattress. The sheets have slid off the bed in the night, and as I sit up to pull them up again, I hear a low grunt. I turn and find Ford curled up in a ball.

"Are you okay?"

"I think I did myself permanent injury last night."

"Your ribs?"

"I believe one's broken."

I sit up, running a hand through my hair, trying to clear

my head from the remnants of sleep, drug and desire. "Do you want me to call an ambulance?"

"I say don't bother. Neither of you is going to need it."

Ford and I turn toward the sound of Kathy Wheatley's voice. She is sitting on my old nursing chair, as blondely wholesome as ever, wearing a pair of dark blue velvet overalls that show just how much weight she's gained this winter. She has a gun pointed at my head.

"Delilah, look out!" Ford is off the bed and airborne in the blink of an eye. It's an incredible feat of martial arts athleticism for a man who is barely awake and already injured. His foot's about an inch from the gun when it goes off.

And then he is on the floor, groaning, and I am thinking, Okay, tackle her now while she's distracted, but it's already too late; she's looking at me with a half smirk on her big pale mouth.

Ford looks me in the eyes the whole time I'm tying him up, but I haven't the foggiest idea what he's thinking. Probably some brilliant plan for how to overpower the crazy woman with the gun. Or maybe he's just trying to apologize wordlessly for being a bit premature with the kung fu. But now that we're not having sex, he's a closed book to me.

"Put him in the closet. And remember, no talking."

This being New York, no one calls or comes up to investigate the sound of a firearm going off.

I scoop another measure of ground coffee into the filter, thankful that Kathy allowed me to put on my bathrobe. Something about being naked really puts you at a disadvantage.

Not as much of a disadvantage as being unarmed, but I do feel a little less desperate without my *tsitskes* hanging out.

"I don't quite see why you want to kill me." I pour the water into the back of the machine and rest my hands against the sideboard. "It was you trying to kill me all those times, wasn't it?"

"I find it a little insulting that it took you so long to figure out. How many enemies do you have, anyway?"

"I'm not sure. Sometimes you think someone hates you and it turns out they really want to jump your bones. I sort of thought you were coldly indifferent to me, Kathy."

"Well, you were wrong. I loathe and despise you."

"Thanks for clearing that up—actually, the gun was my first clue."

"You know, you're not really that funny."

I open my mouth and Kathy gestures with the gun.

"Actually," she says, "I think I get the last word."

The truth is, I think she needs the silence to figure out what to do next. It occurs to me for the first time that maybe she wasn't terribly good at her high-powered job. Ford's presence upset her plans and she doesn't seem too good at thinking on her feet. Which means I could get lucky here.

Or I could get shot. The problem, as I see it, is this; we're both improvising, and I'm probably better at coming up with good lines, but she can kill me if she doesn't like the way the scene is playing.

The familiar sound of coffee brewing trickles through the kitchen.

Unfortunately, the dripping coffee reminds me of the fact that Ford, who is still naked, may be bleeding to death slowly in the closet.

"So, Kath, isn't this where you let me in on your reasons for wanting me dead?"

Kathy raises her pale eyebrows, and for a moment I think she isn't planning on answering me. "Actually, I don't so much want you dead as I want to change the balance of power between us. Right now the scales are tipped in your favor. I'm all about restoring the balance."

"By killing me. I have to say, that sounds a little . . . unbalanced."

"Let's just say I'm adjusting your timetable. I mean, quite frankly, you're killing yourself with the stuff you eat and drink. I've never even seen you in the Health Food store. You never bother to buy organic. And Jason says you actually have an IUD corroding your insides. No, don't turn around. Keep your eyes on what you're doing. Making the coffee."

"With a gun pointed to my head. How are you planning on killing me, Kathy? A bullet's awfully messy." Tough talk, but my hands are shaking, and so are most of my internal organs.

"I was thinking poison."

Now I am light-headed with fear. I swallow, and there is no saliva in my mouth. "What kind of poison?"

"I don't know, Delilah. There are so many possibilities. So many things I could put in your nice cup of morning chemicals and heart-jolting caffeine, sweetened with a little dietetic additive that causes brain cancer in mice. Something that will dissolve nicely in your hormonally engineered milk? But you look pale. Maybe you'd like a little liver-damaging acetaminophen, in case all this is giving you a headache? Take two if the pain won't go away. Take three, even. Acetaminophen can kill as nicely as anything else, which is why you can't buy these nice big bottles in Europe. Nine out of ten suicides prefer them."

I take a deep breath. "So you're going to try to make it look like suicide. What about Ford, Kathy? There's an FBI agent bleeding in my closet. You'll go down for double homicide if you don't stop now, and you know how the courts treat cop killers."

"Don't be ridiculous. It'll look like a homicide-suicide. Don't you give me credit for having any imagination?"

So much for her lack of improvisational skills. "Please, Kathy, can't we talk about what's really bothering you?"

"I don't like the sound of your voice. Move away from the knives."

I walk toward a stool and sit, watching Kathy closely. "I told you that Jason and I are getting divorced. Why kill me to get me out of the way?"

"You think I'm in the throes of some kind of mad passion?" Kathy's laugh reminds me of a teenager's. It has that same high, forced note of contempt.

"Are you pregnant?" I say it as gently as I can. "Is it Jason's?"

My neighbor looks at me with enough venom to fell an ox. "I've only gained ten pounds, Delilah."

"Sorry."

"Maybe fifteen. I've been under a bit of strain, so I ate a little more than usual."

"Perfectly understandable."

"But it doesn't happen to you, does it, Delilah? Some of us watch what we eat and exercise and slave for hours to try to make healthy cookies that don't taste like cardboard and what happens if we forget and eat the tiniest little bit of fat? Instant cellulite. But not you. You run around with your skinny little body, happily cramming any kind of garbage into your mouth."

I try to think of a way to level the playing field. "Probably just means I'll get osteoporosis when I'm older."

"You may be right, but I can't wait twenty years to be sure. There's a principle at stake here, Delilah. How can I teach my kids right from wrong when you're here, screwing up my example? I mean, here you are, the worst kind of sloppy, irresponsible parent, sticking your only child into a dirty, overcrowded, weapons-filled public school, neglecting her crucial years of development in order to write your silly, smutty soft-porn fluff, and despite all this, your daughter's healthy and well-adjusted."

"Well, she *is* into witchcraft—"

"Shut up. I was always so careful with my girls. From the moment I discovered I was pregnant I stopped having coffee, chocolate, alcohol and bleached flour. I piped Mozart into my womb and gave up my career to devote myself full time to their needs. Custom designed their furniture so it would spark their budding aesthetic senses. Childproofed the house down to the last sharp table corner. Researched to get them the best doctors, books, educational toys. Washed their new clothes by hand before they wore them. Never used chemical detergents on the furniture. Sanitized their hands a hundred times a day and peeled their fruit and never, ever let them eat those awful, processed candies at Halloween."

"What do they eat?"

"Rainforest-friendly carob when it's seasonally appropriate. I have never stuck them in front of the TV. They don't even know TV exists. I have two nannies, one to speak French to them and the other to speak Castilian Spanish. They go to piano lessons and gymnastics and horseback riding, and every other week they study Kabbalah or swim, and each and every day they get two hours of exclusive one-on-one Mommy time. Not a token fifteen minutes. Two. Full. Hours."

Poor mites.

"And since September eleventh I make sure the girls have emergency kits of Cipro and potassium iodide in

case of anthrax or a dirty bomb. I tell them that if the terrorists strike, they have to call me on the cell phone and
I'll let them know what medication to take. And what do I
get? Learning disorders. Nervous tics. Behavioral problems.
Seizures!"

Kathy's gun hand is shaking. "All I want," she says, "is
for them to live up to their full potential. You want to know
about working mothers? Well, I am the hardest-working
mother I know."

"Kathy. You can't control everything. You can keep your
kids from the evils of sugar and food dye for only so long,
and then they grow up and rebel. They eat Twinkies. They
try controlled substances. They mix body fluids with other
surly teenagers. And we just have to cross our fingers and
hope we haven't made ourselves so abhorrent to them that
they don't feel they can't tell us when they're in trouble."

She looks up at me and her face reminds me of my sister's, bloated and miserable. Jason's women. "I gave up
everything for them. My job. My friends. I stuck with a
marriage to a personality-deficient invertebrate because I
knew he would be a good father. For seven years there
hasn't been a spare moment that hasn't been about my
kids. About finding the right school. The right camp.
About volunteering for the Fall Fair and the Winter Auc-
tion and the Spring Fling. I've been on every goddamn
committee to make sure the damn teachers know which
kids to pay the most attention to. And what do I get? What
thanks do I get? My husband telling me that *I'm* what's
screwing the girls up!"

"Maybe," I say carefully, "the problem is you haven't let
yourself have a life of your own. Because the thing is, it's a
child's job to grow up and separate, and if you haven't left
a little corner of your mind for your own dreams, then you

don't have anything left when they start becoming people with dreams of their own."

Kathy's mouth twists oddly; irony doesn't suit her broad Scandinavian features. "You don't need to lecture me on the virtues of being selfish, Delilah. But you can't manufacture a passion for something. I did think sleeping with your husband might be a nice little treat. I was angry at him, you know, because of where he works, and it turns out being angry is one step away from being aroused. But you know what? I don't really think he cared about the sex that much. After ten years of being faithful, I broke my vows to be with someone who wasn't really there."

"I'm sorry, Kathy." I look at her flushed face, her overly bright eyes. "You have medication, don't you? Mood stablizers? Maybe something stronger—something anti-psychotic?"

Kathy shakes her head sharply, as if she's just stepped in something nasty. "More chemicals. And they were making me gain weight. Not to mention ruining my sex drive. I thought going off the pills might help me feel more with Jason."

"I see." Yes, so much better to be thin, lusty and a homicidal maniac.

"But once the chemicals stopped sedating me, Jason seemed to lose interest. Now. Enough talk." Kathy opens her jacket and starts pulling out two bottles of prescription pills. "Pour yourself a cup of coffee. Or would you rather have a little alcohol? It might go faster with alcohol."

"Coffee's fine, thanks." I try to think how Ford, bound hand and foot, might be able to free himself from the closet in order to save me. If this were a movie, it would be obvious to anyone that he would be able to save me in time. What's a little rope and a blindfold to an experienced FBI agent? Besides, you know the heroine's not going to die abruptly, unless the film's French, or maybe German.

Unfortunately, this is my life, and life tends to go for abrupt genre shifts. Drama to farce. Action/adventure to tearjerker. Romantic comedy to thriller.

And suddenly it strikes me that I don't have to stay in character, either. Even if you don't get a choice about what's going to happen, you still have the choice of how to face it. "Kathy?" I take the pot of coffee in my hand.

"What?"

"Fuck you." The words hit her at the same time as the scalding coffee. The glass pot hits her a second later, as the gun goes off, discharging into the ceiling.

And the next thing I know we are rolling around on the floor, yelling and screaming, and she's taller and heavier than I am, but not quite as mean. And she hasn't seen as many movies.

I cock my head back like Gerard Depardieu and slam her with my forehead, and for a moment we both see stars.

I recover first. I haul off and slug her in the nose. Once you get over the shock of actually having someone hurt you, it's not that hard to hurt them back.

And then it's over. She's out, and I'm not. Wait, I am. No, I'm conscious again, and she's still lying there. So I win. Nyah, nyah, na—nyah, nyah.

It seems even two gunshots aren't enough to alert the neighbors. I have to call 911 with my broken index finger and try to give my address through my bloody nose and lip. When the police come they find two semiconscious bodies on my bed and start handcuffing me before I get the whole story out.

"Jesus, lady, which one of them called us?" The officer looks very young and slightly nauseated.

"I did. Can you check the tourniquet on the man's leg? I don't want to give him gangrene."

The older officer inspects my handiwork. "So what happened—you catch your old man cheating and just shoot the shit out of him?"

"Not exactly. Call Mrs. Kornislav in apartment 3C. She can explain everything."

The two officers exchange looks. "What is she, your psychiatrist?"

I close the eye that isn't already swollen shut. "No, she's my FBI agent's psychiatrist."

But Mrs. Kornislav's not home. So we wait for the ambulance to come for Ford and Kathy and then down I go in the elevator, scuffed, bruised, handcuffed and escorted by the men in blue. Naturally the elegantly gloved and scarved Caroline Moore is present to witness my humiliation.

"Delilah? Can I help?" I can't help but notice that the police officers are staring at her glowing, dusky prettiness. And then I remember that my husband paid this Amazon for the privilege of telling her what he should have been telling me.

"Yeah. First of all, if you talk to Jason, tell him that his insane ex-mistress just tried to kill me, and could you call my father at Levine and Levine in Teaneck because I need a lawyer, and the ex-mistress is in no condition to corroborate my story. Second of all, I think you'd better quit Kathy Wheatley's little guerrilla mom group, because she'll probably have to hold the meetings in jail."

"Wait, let me get my Palm Pilot out so I can get this all down."

I watch as Caroline reaches into her deliciously fashionable pale camel handbag, which gives off the scent of new leather. And then, maybe because she is wearing gloves, maybe because of her unexpected connection to the chaos of my life, Caroline spills the contents of her purse all over the elevator floor.

"Oh, God," she says, getting down on all fours. It's not until she looks up that I realize that she's crying.

"It's okay," I tell her. "Slow down. Deep breaths."

One of the officers bends down to help her, but it's me she's looking at as the doors open to the lobby. "I guess it's the pregnancy hormones," she says. "I can hold it together when I'm working, but then the minute I'm done, I fall apart. And Kathy and her group are the only mothers I know, and they kept telling me how I needed to stop working and childproof the house and learn what the emission standards are for that building across the street with the smoking chimney. . . ." Her face crumples. "I'm just so overwhelmed."

"Don't worry. It gets easier," I tell her as the police escort me out to their car. "Call me if you need to talk."

She gives me a little wave. I do hope she remembers to call my dad about getting me a lawyer, though.

Friday, December 21
10 A.M.

Agent Delilah Levine knew that people don't get betrayed by people they don't trust. By definition, it's the ones you think will never hurt you who wind up doing the most damage.

Which was why, even as she limped up the driveway to her parents' pleasant suburban home, she had her right hand resting over the butt of her service revolver.

A middle-aged woman with Angelina Jolie's lips and a dog that looked like a bad wig glanced over at Delilah and pulled her cell phone out of her mink. It wasn't really the neighborhood for black leather and thigh-high boots, but Delilah had learned that cowhide deflects knife blades better than fabric, and ever since the Biosensual debacle, she'd learned to keep her flesh well barricaded.

For the battle-hardened veteran of too many close calls, the clear, wintry brightness of the morning and the tantalizing hint of her mother's potato kugel perfuming the air didn't mean all was well.

It only meant she hadn't identified the danger yet.

"Mom?" I decide to pat my face down with powder while I wait for the door to open. I've already Maybellined the worst of my bruises, and my folks have prepared Sadie for the fact that Mommy had a little accident, but I don't know how my daughter is going to react when she sees me.

Then the door opens and I snap my compact shut. For a moment I think I knocked at the wrong house. The woman standing in front of me is not my mother, although she does look familiar. She's not my sister, either, although she has sharp blue eyes and a similar style of shellacked dark brown hair. But her face is rawboned and angular, and she's wearing the kind of ruffled Laura Ashley dress favored by the less fashionable *Little House on the Prairie* fanatics.

"Oh, God, your face." The woman reaches out her hand to touch my cheek. Her eyes fill with tears. "I'm so sorry."

I stare at the woman blankly. I pull her hand away and it seems much too large. Her knuckles are . . . She's a man. I look at her features again. She's my husband. "Jason?"

He nods. His cheeks are flushed with embarrassment. No, I'm wrong—that's rouge. "You didn't have to wait long at the police station, did you? We sent Harvey as soon as Caroline called your dad."

"No, it was just a couple of hours, to handle the paperwork. After Ford regained consciousness he cleared everything up."

"Ford's the plumber?" The way Jason says it I know he's thinking of a different word.

"Actually, he's FBI. You were under investigation. Seems the feds thought you were up to something suspicious." We stare at each other like two dogs meeting for the first time in a long while. Jason looks away first.

"You have to know, Delilah, it wasn't about Kathy. Or about . . . It was about me, trying to understand what this all meant. Whether or not I was gay."

I stand there, just trying to take it all in. I hadn't even realized that my husband had been in touch with Sadie and my parents, but from the look of Jason's eye makeup, my mother has been a major influence. "Do you mind if I come inside?"

"Oh, gosh, sorry, of course. You must be freezing." Jason ushers me inside and leads me to the most comfortable couch.

"Where're my parents?"

"Upstairs."

"And Sadie?"

"Watching TV." Jason reaches out for my hands again. He's wearing coral nail polish, along with his wedding ring. "Delilah. I wish . . . I'd give anything to go back and change what happened. But when I first started to get the urge, I couldn't accept it. I thought wanting to wear women's clothes meant I wanted to be a woman. And I guess I had a bit of a midlife crisis."

I look pointedly at his dress. "But all that's over now?"

"Well, in a way it is. I've accepted this part of me now. I'm okay with it. And Sadie's okay with it. Even your mom and dad seem to . . ."

"You told my dad? Why am I the last one on your list?"

This new, kinder, gentler Jason gives me a long look of sustained empathy, like Olivia de Havilland comforting the higher-strung Vivien Leigh. "I am sorry, Delilah. But don't you see why you'd be the hardest one to tell?"

"I guess."

"But now I can share this with you. And I'm not alone. There are a lot of us. Heterosexual men. Good husbands and fathers who have discovered a feminine aspect to our personalities. It's not a disorder. It's a gift. And it's just as freeing for me to put on a dress as it was for women to put on a pair of trousers a hundred years ago."

This sounds suspiciously like a spiel. "Have you been seeing someone? A counselor or psychiatrist?"

"I've found an organization of cross-dressing men." Jason smiles at me with a hint of irony, and for a moment I recognize my husband under the thick layer of foundation and lipstick. "You know, Sadie thinks it's like beauty and the beast. She says I'm nicer like this."

And the funny thing is, I can see that she's probably right. "Oh, Jason."

"It's going to be better, Del. Now that I have embraced this, you'll find me calmer. More centered. And this is something we can have fun with together." He gives me a little wink. "I still can't walk in heels, you know."

I put my hand on my husband's smooth, closely shaven jaw. "No, Jason, I'm sorry. I'm not going to play dress-up with you."

"Is this about my being gay? Because I can assure you—"

"No, believe me, I don't think you're gay, and you didn't even have to screw my sister to convince me. It's just that this isn't my fantasy, Jason. And I can't find a way into it. I'm glad you're getting in touch with your feminine side, but honestly, this kind of elaborate costuming doesn't have a lot to do with how I feel myself to be female."

I can see the man inside the wig bristling. "Well, Delilah, for once maybe this isn't about you."

My face hurts, and not just from the beating I took. It's hard to sit here with Jason, but I realize I have to make the effort. Having a child means staying connected to a man long after all the other bonds of intimacy and love have dissolved. "No, Jason. It's about Sadie, and about us being the best parents we can. But not together. Because you have an erotic compulsion to dress like a Republican politician's wife, and I can't go there."

I don't know what Jason's about to say and I guess I never will, because at that very moment we hear the rapid thud of little feet pounding down the stairs.

"Here we go," I say. "How's my makeup?"

Jason inspects me for a moment. "Fine. How's mine?"

I wipe a smudge of lipstick from his tooth and we turn to face our daughter with a united front.

"Mommy, Mommy, did you see Daddy's wearing a dress now? He said I can put on makeup with him but that we have to wait before telling all our friends."

I wrap my daughter's sturdy, small body in my arms and, for just a moment, she melts into me the way she did when she was younger and I inhale the delicious little-girl smell of her. Then she pulls back again, too excited by the reappearance of her transfigured father to remain in the circle of my embrace.

"Isn't it great, Mommy? Now we can all play dress-up together." I notice that she is wearing a purple silk kimono over flannel long johns. Maybe she can give her father fashion tips.

Sadie smooths her father's wig. "I want a black one, like Mulan."

"Well, Chanukah's not over, honey."

"And a puppy."

This new, feminine Jason does not answer her with a blunt acceptance or denial. He just smiles and Sadie's joy is palpable; anyone can see that she believes that her magic has wrought a wondrous transformation; her grumpy, impatient, volatile father has become a calm lady, with the application of false eyelashes and a big flowered smock.

"So, when are we going home, Mommy? Can we stay another night here?"

"I suppose we could spend one more night, sweetheart," I say. "Daddy and I have a few things we need to figure out together before we go home." I turn to Jason and watch as a small spark of rebellious anger flickers and then fades in his gaze.

"That's right, Kitten. Mommy and I need to do some talking. But we won't argue anymore. We're done fighting. And we both love you and that is never going to change." Jason in a dress really is a much better husband than he was in a cowboy hat.

"Why?" Sophie's sharp eyes search first my expression, and then her father's. "What's going on?"

I glance upstairs and out of the corner of my eye I can see my mother opening the door to her bedroom a crack. My father's gray poodle hair is visible just over her shoulder, and they both look like they're wearing scarlet robes. The smell of incense is strong enough to reach me half a house away.

Mindful of our audience, I hold out my hand and Jason takes it as we begin to construct the mutually agreed upon fiction of the amicable divorce.

I arrive back in New York City twelve hours later. I'm not sure why, but I just couldn't fall asleep in my parents' house. I'll let Jason have the dubious comfort of my childhood home for tonight. I guess it's a good thing that my mother has managed to redress the imbalance of power in her marriage, but it's a little disconcerting to discover that your folks are giving up Hadassah synagogue dinners for a pagan tour of Great Britain.

On the other hand, I have to admit I find it oddly satisfying to listen to my legal expert father having to get my mother's help on the arcana of another system of beliefs.

As for Jason: Well, soon enough he'll have to face his own

mother and father, so I don't mind if he borrows mine for a little while longer. For myself, I choose a night of wound-licking solitude.

It is cold and dark inside the apartment. I guess I forgot to turn the radiators on.

And then I sense it; a presence in the house. I am not alone. I stand stock-still for a moment and then someone grabs me, palm muffling my startled cry.

"I'm going to take my hand off your mouth if you promise not to scream. Do you understand?"

I nod my head and start to shout. It's not a logical response, it's just shock and anger and now I am fighting for all I am worth, arms flailing, legs kicking, until I hear a hoarse grunt of pain and suddenly the light flicks on.

My attacker is hunched over, gripping his side.

"Ford?"

"Yeah." He looks even worse than I do. He is wheezing painfully until he gets an inhaler out of his jacket pocket.

"Can you breathe now?"

He nods. I notice that his crutch has fallen down and hand it to him.

Naturally, the sound of our violent altercation has not aroused any of our neighbors' curiosity.

"What the hell were you doing? Trying to kill me? Or trying to get me to kill you?"

"Neither. I had more of a . . . different scenario in mind." The scarlet mask of embarrassment on Ford's face says it all.

I sag against the wall. "Oh, Ford. I am cold and tired and bruised and sad. You see this face? This is not my fun face. To be perfectly honest, sex is the last thing on my mind right now."

He pushes the hair off his forehead with one hand. "I'm kind of beat myself. It's just . . . This whole assignment's been something of a bust, and, well, they're sending me back to Virginia."

"Oh."

"They want me to tinker with the Biosensual formula. Funny thing is, I think I'm going to wind up working with Irina."

"I see."

"Do you? 'Cause I sure as hell don't." Ford rubs the back of his neck as if he'd like to unfasten his head from his shoulders. "One minute it's our case, the next some big hat from another department moseys in and tells us they're in charge. The implication being, of course, that we fucked things up." Ford meets my eyes. "So now we're not investigating Irina, we're paying her through the nose—excuse me, I mean, enlisting her help, and I guess the cash for her assistance is coming out of my bank account, 'cause I get the clear impression that I'm the guy with the 'kick me' sign on his back. You do realize that I'm not supposed to be telling you this?"

"I kind of figured."

Ford looks at me, waiting for something. A sign, I guess, some clue as to what to do next. I'm so not ready for this. I'm tired and cranky and a little numb and badly need the emptiness of my house to grieve for everything that's ending. But I also know that this man got inside my head for a little while, and a part of me is living in the hope that he'll come back for a visit. Or maybe even set up camp.

"Where's the dog?"

"My place."

I take a deep breath and try not to let it out as a sigh. "Tell you what. Why don't you go get him and bring him over here while I take a bath. Go get a video. We'll cuddle up, eat popcorn, and then you'll go home again. With Fardles."

Ford opens the door, and through his fatigue and pain, I can sense an undercurrent of satisfaction strong enough to carry me along. "What kind of video?"

I know that he's bound to bring back something like *Invasion of the Body Snatchers*. The truth is, I don't feel like opening myself up to some man's favorite films and music and vacation spots, only to find some ten years down the line that he's become a stranger.

I just don't have the energy or optimism to start over, especially when the chances are it'll end. Maybe well, maybe poorly, but still, it will probably end.

But I turn back to Ford and find myself saying, "Surprise me."

"Okay," he says, standing still for a moment on the threshold. I catch a flash of something in his eyes, the ghost of a thought not my own. "I will."

Bring your passion to life with
BIOSENSUAL!

Indulge in a world of sensual abandon with Biosensual lotion, bath beads, body mist and massage oil. Unleash your animal nature with a scent that awakens your most primitive desires.*

Chance to win a trip to New York City and a walk-on part in the popular daytime drama *Secrets!* with every purchase.

*There is no scientific proof that the active ingredient in Biosensual is an actual aphrodisiac.

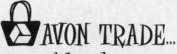 **AVON TRADE...**
because every great bag deserves a great book!